STAMPEDE!

A shot brought Smoke lunging to his feet, grabbing for his guns. He could hear the bawling of cattle and the thunderous roar of a stampede building. The camp filled with horses. He could just make out hooded men, all wearing long dusters, and all with guns in their hands. He could hear the cries of wounded men as his crew was being shot to pieces.

I should have placed more men on guard, Smoke thought. But there was no time left for thinking.

He jumped up behind a rider and hammered blows at the man, knocking him out of his saddle. Smoke fumbled for the reins and found them. Then something struck him on the side of the head and the last thing he remembered was grabbing hold of the saddle horn as the badly frightened animal took off in a panicked run into the black night.

<u>BOOK YOUR PLACE ON OUR WEBSITE</u> <u>AND MAKE THE</u> <u>READING CONNECTION!</u>

We've created a customized website just for our very special readers, where you can get the inside scoop on everything that's going on with Zebra, Pinnacle and Kensington books.

When you come online, you'll have the exciting opportunity to:

- View covers of upcoming books

- Read sample chapters

- Learn about our future publishing schedule (listed by publication month *and author*)

- Find out when your favorite authors will be visiting a city near you

- Search for and order backlist books from our online catalog

- Check out author bios and background information

- Send e-mail to your favorite authors

- Meet the Kensington staff online

- Join us in weekly chats with authors, readers and other guests

- Get writing guidelines

- AND MUCH MORE!

Visit our website at
http://www.pinnaclebooks.com

WILLIAM W. JOHNSTONE

COURAGE OF THE MOUNTAIN MAN

PINNACLE BOOKS
Kensington Publishing Corp.
http://www.pinnaclebooks.com

PINNACLE BOOKS are published by

Kensington Publishing Corp.
850 Third Avenue
New York, NY 10022

Copyright © 1992 by William W. Johnstone

All Kensington Titles, Imprints, and Distributed Lines are available at special quantity discounts for bulk purchases for sales promotions, premiums, fund-raising, and educational or institutional use. Special book excerpts or customized printings can also be created to fit specific needs. For details, write or phone the office of the Kensington special sales manager: Kensington Publishing Corp., 850 Third Avenue, New York, NY 10022, attn: Special Sales Department, Phone: 1-800-221-2647.

Pinnacle and the P logo Reg. U.S. Pat. & TM Off.

First Printing: April 1992
15 14 13 12 11 10 9

Printed in the United States of America

Necessity brings him here, not pleasure.
Dante

Those who'll play with cats must expect to be scratched.
Cervantes

Smoke Jensen

He drifted West with his pa, just a boy, right after the War Between the States ended. Hard work was all he'd ever known. After his ma died and his sister took off with a gambling fellow, Young Jensen had worked the hardscrabble farm in the hills and hollows of Missouri and just did manage to keep body and soul together. Pick up one rock and two more would take its place the next morning, seemed like. Then his pa came home.

They pulled out a week after the elder Jensen's return home. Heading west. Young Jensen had him a .36-caliber Navy Colt that Jesse James had given him after the boy had let some of the guerrilla troops of Bloody Bill Anderson rest and water their horses at the farm. Jesse had seemed a right nice person to Young Jensen.

Jesse had give him an extra cylinder for the pistol, too. Neighborly, that's what it was.

On the way West, an old mountain man fell in with the pair on the plains. Said his name was Preacher. Not thirty minutes after the introductions, a band of Indians looking for scalps hit the trio, and it was there that Young Jensen got the name hung on him that would stay with him forever. Although only a boy, Young Jensen fought a man's fight and killed his share of those who were trying to kill them.

7

A thin finger of smoke lifted from the barrel of the Navy .36 Young Jensen held in his hand. The old mountain man smiled and said, "Can't call you no boy now. You be a man. I think I'll call you Smoke."

One

Smoke Jensen stepped out of the café on the main street of Big Rock, Colorado. He leaned against an awning post and rolled a cigarette, lighting it just as Sheriff Monte Carson strolled up.

"Need to talk with you, Smoke," the sheriff said. "You like a beer?"

"No," the ruggedly handsome man with the cold eyes said with a smile. "But I'll watch you drink one."

The sheriff and the most feared gunhandler in all the West walked to the saloon, pushed open the batwings, and stepped inside. Monte ordered a beer and Smoke ordered coffee.

"I hear you're selling your stock, Smoke."

"Most of it. I'm going to raise horses, Monte. Oh, I'll keep a small herd. But nothing like we've had out on the Sugarloaf."

"You using the rails?"

"I wish, Monte. No. This will be a hard drive. All the way up to Montana. Into a big valley. Town's called Blackstown. Fellow up there name of T. J. Duggan wants the whole damn herd."

"The whole herd? Why?"

Smoke shrugged heavy muscular shoulders. "Beats me. He's an Eastern fellow. Said he was in a hurry to get into ranching. He's paying me good money, Monte. I couldn't turn down the offer."

"How about your hands once the drive is over?"

Smoke chuckled. "A few want to drift; you know cowboys. But I couldn't run most of them off with a shotgun. I'm going to be running a lot of horses, Monte. You know how I love the appaloosas. I'll be needing hands."

"When will you pull out?"

"Oh, about ten days, I think. Why? You want to come along and do some honest work for a change?"

"Hell, man! I'd love to. But no. We have trials set for all of next month. Smoke, you know you're going up into Clint Black's country."

"Clint Black doesn't bother me. I don't even know the man. All I know is he's a rancher who thinks he owns the whole damn Montana Territory."

"He's got some rough ol' boys ridin' for him, Smoke."

"I've run up against some rough ol' boys a time or two in my life, Monte." Smoke spoke the words softly. But there was lead and fire and gunsmoke behind them.

Clint Black better rein in his hands and his mouth when he meets up with Smoke Jensen, the sheriff thought. *If you aggravate him too much, Smoke will come after you lookin' like a demon out of Hell.*

Both men watched as three young riders came walking their horses slowly up the street. Both men noted that the riders sat on Texas saddles—without the wide skirt, the saddle horn was thicker and stronger for roping, and the stirrups were of the heavy-duty type. The brands were unfamiliar. All three cowboys wore their holsters tied down. One of the trio wore two guns.

"You know them," Smoke asked.

"Never saw them before this day. What do you think?"

"Wild and woolly and full of fleas, probably. Might even be on the prod, looking for trouble. They're young. Oldest one's not out of his early twenties, I'd say."

"This place does have a back door," Monte said with a wide smile. But there was a hopeful note in his voice. If the three young punchers wanted trouble, Smoke Jensen was the last man in the world they should brace. He didn't want trouble in Big Rock, and if it started, Smoke would not have initiated it. But there would be three dead rowdies on the barroom floor when the silence prevailed.

Smoke chuckled. "Then use it."

Sheriff Monte Carson laughed softly. "I was rather hoping you would."

Boots sounded heavily on the boardwalks and spurs jingled.

"Too late now."

The riders took off their hats and beat the trail dust from their clothing before stepping into the saloon. The one leading the pack slammed open the batwings, and that irritated Monte. He looked at Smoke. There was no change in his expression.

The trio ordered whiskey with a beer chaser. Their voices were too loud and too demanding.

"Huntin' trouble," Monte said softly.

"They came to the right place," Smoke replied in a soft voice.

"Hey!" one of the riders yelled. "What you two whisperin' about over yonder? You talkin' about us, maybe?"

Monte was sitting in a way that only presented one side of his torso to the bar. He shoved back his chair and stood up. His badge was now visible. He walked to the three young would-be gunhands and faced them.

"The name is Carson. Sheriff Monte Carson."

The trio stiffened. Monte Carson had been one of the West's premier gunfighters until he married and settled down in Big Rock. Everybody had heard of Monte Carson.

"If you boys are lookin' for a drink, some food, and a place to spend the night, you found it, right here in Big Rock. If you boys are lookin' for trouble, you found that. Right here and right now!"

One of Monte's deputies had seen the rowdies ride in. The back door of the saloon creaked. One of the young Texas toughs cut his eyes. The deputy stood behind them, a sawed-off double-barreled shotgun in his hands. He cocked both hammers. The slight sound was enormous in the now-quiet room.

"I'll take this punk here," Monte said, his temper rising. "Jimmy, you blow the guts out of two-gun over there by the bar . . ."

"And I'll take Tall Boy," Smoke said, pushing back his chair and standing up. It seemed like he never would get through standing up. Smoke Jensen was several inches over six feet, with the weight to go with it. Huge hands and wrists. Thickly muscled with massive shoulders and a barrel chest, he was lean at the hips, and his jeans bunched with powerful leg muscles. His hair was ash blond, worn short; his eyes were brown and cold. Smoke wore two guns, .44s, the left-hand gun worn high and butt forward, the right-hand gun low and tied down. He was snake-quick with either pistol. He carried a long-bladed Bowie knife behind his left-hand six-shooter. He could and did shave with it. Or fight with it, didn't make any difference to Smoke. "The name is Jensen. Smoke Jensen."

A sigh came from Tall Boy. Slowly he let his hands drift to the bar, where he placed them palms down. "Fightin' Monte Carson would be bad enough," he said. "A deputy with a Greener makes it worser. Add Smoke Jensen and a body'd be a damn pure idiot."

"Drink your drinks, get something to eat, and behave," Monte told them, his anger fading. He turned his back to them and started to the table and his unfinished beer.

"No, Jack!" Tall Boy yelled. "Don't do it."

Jack was grabbing for his gun. The sawed-off roared. The heavy charges nearly cut the Texas boy in two, flinging him against the wall and leaving a bloody smear as he slid down to stop butt-first on the floor. He died with his eyes wide open, staring into a terribly bleak eternity.

"I'm out of this!" the third rider screamed. "Jesus Christ, I'm clear out."

Folks came running, for gunfights were not a common thing in Big Rock, not with Monte Carson, Smoke Jensen, Pearlie, Johnny North, and half a dozen other heavy-duty gunslicks, who had turned into respectable citizens, only a breath away.

Dr. Colton Spalding stepped into the saloon. He needed only one look at the puncher. "Get the undertaker," he told the barkeep.

"Was that boy born a damn fool?" Monte asked, pointing to the dead would-be tough, "or did he have to work at it?"

"He . . . fancied hisself good with a gun," one of his shaken-up buddies said.

Monte shook his head in disgust and walked to the table. Smoke had sat down and was drinking his coffee.

"What do you think about it?" Monte asked.

"I think my coffee got cold," Smoke replied.

Sally, Smoke's wife, read the letters from her parents and their children, who were all in France attending school. One of their children was there for health reasons, being tended to by specialists. Smoke had picked up the letters in town and had not opened them, leaving that small pleasure for Sally.

"Any word on when they'll come back home?" Smoke asked.

"No. When do you leave?"

"Probably next week. I'd like to take you with me, honey. But a cattle drive is rough work."

"I'll be fine here," she assured him. "Just who is this Clint Black person?"

Smoke sipped his coffee for a moment. "A hard, unyielding tyrant of a man. I suspect that somebody sold this T. J. Duggan a bill of goods with this ranch he bought. Somebody wanted out of that country and found themselves a sucker. I don't even know the man and I feel sorry for him."

"Oh, my!" Sally said, but with a smile.

Her husband looked at her. "What's that all about?"

"I feel a quest coming on, oh man of La Mancha."

"Sally . . . !"

"I gave you the book to read."

13

He looked puzzled for a moment, then a wide grin cut his face and softened his eyes. "Oh, yeah. Don Quixote."

She gently corrected his pronunciation.

"Am I the Knight of the Woeful Figure?"

"Hardly," she said with a laugh. "But you do have this tendency to stand up for lost causes and the little person."

"You knew that when you married me, honey."

She stood up and walked to him, kissing him on the cheek. "And I love you all the more for it. Now stand up and put on an apron," she told the most feared gunfighter in all the West. "I'll wash, you dry."

"Yes, dear."

Smoke Jensen had not sought out the reputation of gunfighter. Most of the known ones hadn't. For several years after he and Sally were married, he had changed his name and lived quietly. Then outlaws come to town and he was forced to once more strap on his guns to protect hearth and home and kith and kin. He never went back to his false name. He was Smoke Jensen, a man of peace if allowed, a warrior when he had to be. Back in '72, when he was just out of his teens, Smoke Jensen tracked down the men who had raped and killed his wife, Nicole, and had brutally murdered their baby son, Arthur. He cornered them in a raw silver-mining town in the Uncompahgre. Writers of dime novels wrote that there were fifty gunhands in the town, and balladeers sang that Smoke Jensen killed a hundred or more desperados. In a play later written about him, with Smoke portrayed in New York City by a dandy who had never been west of Philadelphia, Smoke was acted out to have killed five hundred men on that fateful day. In reality, Smoke faced fourteen men that day. Smoke rode away, wounded a half a dozen times. The miners buried fourteen gunhands.

A month later, his wounds nearly healed, Smoke went after the men who had killed his brother and his father years back. He found them in Idaho. When he rode away, he left a burning town and the streets littered with dead.

It was there that Smoke met Sally.

No one really knew how many murderers, outlaws, rapists, and other assorted human slime had fallen under the guns of Smoke Jensen. Smoke himself didn't know. And he didn't worry about it. But the figure was staggeringly high.

Around Big Rock, Smoke was known as a man who loved kids and dogs and horses, who sang solos in church every now and then, and would pitch in with a barn or house-raising. He would climb a tree to rescue a cat, take in stray dogs and make sure they had good homes or keep them himself. There were at least twenty running around the fenced-in acres where the house stood on the Sugarloaf. He would help a stranger in need and had completely outfitted — at his own expense — numerous settlers who had lost everything in their march West.

But crowd him, insult his wife, make a hostile move against an innocent — as Sally had pointed out in the kitchen, even an innocent he didn't know — hurt one of his dogs or horses, and Smoke Jensen would hunt that man down, call him out, and either beat him half to death with those huge fists, or kill him.

There is an old Western expression that men would use to test another man's courage. It reads, "I ain't never seen none of your graveyards."

Nobody ever said that to Smoke Jensen.

On this drive north to Montana Territory, Smoke had hired eight boys who were out of school for the summer. One sixteen-year-old, four fifteen-year-olds, and three fourteen-year-olds. They were young, but they were good hands. Willie, Jake, Bobby, Rabbit, Louie, Dan, Sonny, and Guy. In addition to his regular hands, Smoke had hired on four more men who had drifted through. He wired their former employers — the telegraph was making life a lot easier in the West — and received replies that the men were good hands who would give a day's work for a day's pay. That would give him seventeen men for the drive. It wasn't enough, for the herd was very large, but he could pick up other hands along the way.

The drive would be hard work for the boys, and it would also be an adventure for them.

Smoke was kind of looking forward to it himself.

Two

On the morning of the pullout, the boys from the neighboring farms and ranches were so excited they could hardly contain themselves. Not only were they going on a real cattle drive, clear up into Montana Territory, but they were in the company of Smoke Jensen. How much better could it get?

The boys knew they would be close to the drag most of the time, herding the remuda on either the right or left flank of the cattle, but that was all right. It was a very responsible job, and they knew it.

Smoke had figured it close as far as manpower was concerned. Some trail bosses figure one cowboy for every 400 cows. Smoke figured one cowboy for every 250 cows. They would be pushing slightly over 3,500 head, not all belonging to Smoke. A half a dozen other ranchers had put a number of their cattle up for sale as well. The price Duggan was paying was more than fair, so why not throw in with Smoke?

The remuda was made up of more than a hundred horses, so the boys would have their young hands full.

Just before pullout, Smoke found two more punchers drifting through and hired them. They were down at the heels and looked like they needed a good meal just to stay alive one more day. But their horses were in good shape and they had honest eyes and easy grins. Their hands were so callused from handling cattle and ropes, Smoke knew they couldn't be outlaws.

The cook was a sour-faced old coot with never a kind

word for anybody. But he was the best trail cook in five counties and could be counted on to have coffee ready anytime the men wanted it. While they were in camp, that is.

"Damn bunch of snot-nosed boys gonna eat us out of grub 'fore we get fifty miles," he had groused. "This many men, we're gonna need another wagon and I got to have me a helper, too. That's that, or I ain't goin'."

"Will I do, Denver?" Sally asked, stepping up.

"A *female?*" Denver shouted. "Hell, no!"

"She's a durn sight better cook than you, you old goat," one of Smoke's regular hands told him.

Denver threw his hat on the ground. "That's a tooken bet, boy!"

"Now wait just a minute," Smoke said. "I run this outfit. I say who goes along, and Sally is *not* coming along on this cattle drive."

The hands all gathered around, grinning like a bunch of fools. None of them would have missed this for a month's wages and a little speckled pup.

She marched up to him. She wore men's britches and the men all admired that sight too. But there wasn't a man among them — including the new hands — who wouldn't stomp any man who said anything about Sally's shape. Outside of their own bunch, that is, and that would be said very respectfully.

"I see, Mr. Jensen," Sally said, her head just about reaching the center of Smoke's chest. "It wasn't too dangerous for me to ride all over Hell's creation a few months back with a rifle in my hand, getting you out of a bad situation . . ."

"Now, Sally," Smoke said.

"Oh, no. That was quite all right for me to do that . . ."

Smoke sighed.

"Why, there ain't no way this little bit of thing could keep up with me," Denver stuck his mouth into the situation. "And what if we run into quarrelsome Injuns? I never seen a woman who could shoot worth a damn."

"I really wish you hadn't said that," Smoke muttered.

Sally jerked one of Smoke's .44s from leather and put all

five rounds into the knot on a log some fifty feet away. She handed the pistol back to Smoke.

Denver chewed his tobacco for a moment. "What do you know about a chuck wagon, little lady?"

"I wish you hadn't asked that, either," Smoke muttered, reloading his .44.

"I know how to doctor cuts, drive a wagon, prepare three hot," she smiled, "and *tasty* meals a day. And I know to point the tongue of the wagon toward the north star every night."

Denver chewed, spat, and then grinned. "You and me, little lady, are gonna get along just fine."

"I didn't say she was coming along," Smoke protested.

"I reckon you didn't, boss. But I can see that you ain't the only one who wears pants around here neither."

The drive was delayed for one day while Sally got ready to go and made arrangements for this, that, and the other thing, as females are wont to do before a journey. Just as dawn was cracking the sky, the drovers hi-hoed the herd and started them moving north. One of the boys would take turns driving Miss Sally's wagon, which was not a chore for any of them. Miss Sally was beautiful and she smelled good, too.

Only bad thing was all the hands, men and boys, knew that Miss Sally had laid in a goodly number of bars of soap—like about five *cases*. And that meant that every time they stopped, if there was water handy, everybody was going to take a bath. Whether they needed it or not. And the boys were looking forward to doing a whole lot of cussing on this trip. That was out too. Well, they all could gather in a bunch and cuss quiet, they reckoned.

After the second day out, the lead cows were established and the herd moved along. "Keep them out of the dew in the morning," Smoke reminded the men. Dew tended to soften the cattle hooves.

They would average ten to twelve miles a day. The chuck

19

wagons were new, both bought from the Studebaker Brothers Manufacturing Company. Sally had seen to it that the coffee beans were Arbuckles, which always had a stick of peppermint packed in each one-pound bag. Cowboys had been known to come to blows — and sometimes guns — over who got the peppermint. Sally straightened out that problem easily by buying a huge box of peppermint candy before leaving. Everybody got a peppermint occasionally. Even Smoke, if he behaved.

Sally and Denver worked well together, and the meals, although simple, were tasty and with Sally along, varied. Smoke picked up the Western Trail just outside of Cheyenne and headed due north. They would stay on that trail until they got into Montana Territory. Once they crossed the Powder in Montana, Smoke would cut north and west, heading for the mountains and the town of Blackton. That final leg would be the real test, for the drovers would be pushing the huge herd over no established trail.

"Are we going to see wild Indians, Mr. Smoke?" young Rabbit asked.

Smoke looked at the boy across the flames of the fire. He'd been just about his age when he killed his first man, back on the plains of Kansas. He smiled at Rabbit. "I'm sure we will, Rabbit. But it's unlikely they'll be hostile ones. More than likely they'll be begging for food. The route I've mapped out will keep us off of any reservation land. But not by many miles."

Later, when the crew had bedded down, Smoke was having a cup of coffee with Denver. "You know Clint Black, Smoke?" the cook asked.

"Not personally. Only by reputation."

"He's a bad one. Tried to hire me one time, right after the war, when he first come out here. I wouldn't work for him."

Smoke sipped his coffee and waited, knowing there was more.

"He runs the biggest cattle operation in the territory. Hundreds of thousands of acres. He started the town of Blacktown. It's grown so much now that he don't control it no more. But he does swing a mighty big loop when it comes to town matters. In my opinion, this Duggan feller's a damn fool for goin' up agin someone as powerful as Black."

"Surely Black is not the only rancher in the county."

"Oh, no. 'Course he ain't. But the others is just hangin' on. Black controls the best water, the best graze, the best everything. This is a story that's been played out a thousand times in the West, Smoke. But . . . this Duggan feller just might hold the joker in the deck."

"How do you mean?"

"Several rivers and some fair-sized cricks run through that part of the country. Black is big, but he ain't so big that all the water, or all the best graze is on his holdin's. You say Duggan's brand is the Double D?"

"That's right."

"More than one Duggan, then."

"Unless his name is Don Duggan."

Denver smiled. "Dumb Duggan is more like it."

"What's Black's brand?"

"The Circle 45. And brother, his hands don't hesitate to back up that brand with lead."

"If he leaves me alone, I'll certainly leave him alone."

"This many cattle comin' into a part of the country Black thinks he's the lord and master of? No, he'll stick his nose in to see what's goin' on. And if he thinks he can get away with it, he'll take this herd."

"No law in that part of the territory?"

Denver snorted. "The sheriff is Clint's brother."

Smoke delayed the start of the drive the next morning. He sat alone, drinking coffee and giving some serious thought to sending the boys back home. Sally came over and sat down beside him, on the ground.

"What's the matter, honey?"

Smoke laid it out for her. He never kept anything from her and was going to ask her opinion anyway.

"Well, the boys would be awfully disappointed. Do you

21

really think this Black person would harm a boy?"

"From what I've heard about him, I think he's probably capable of doing just about anything. But it's hard for me to believe that a man who would do that could make it as big as he has here in the West. You know how Western people feel about kids. But all that means is he's either never done something like that before, or didn't get caught. Maybe Denver is stretching the truth a bit. I don't know. I do know that I've got a contract to deliver this herd and I'm going to push it through. Come on, let's go meet with the crew."

Smoke laid it out for them all. He knew what the reaction of the men would be and Shorty put it into words.

Shorty spat on the ground and hitched up his gunbelt. "Sounds like this ol' boy is meaner than a snake, Boss. But I've killed a lot of snakes in my time. As far as him hurtin' these youngsters, I can't see him doin' that. Western folks just wouldn't stand for it. No matter how big and powerful he is, if he ever done something like that, a lynch mob would string him up real quick."

The other men nodded their heads in agreement. Even Denver agreed with the majority. " 'Specially if the boys wasn't totin' no iron," the old cook said.

Smoke looked at the boys. "Any of you packing guns?"

They shuffled their booted feet and exchanged sheepish glances that silently spoke volumes.

"Get your saddlebags and bedrolls and spread them out right here in front of me," Smoke told them.

Every boy had a pistol tucked away. Smoke took the guns and gave them to Denver. "Tuck them away." Smoke looked hard at the youngsters. "Boys, you know that out here, if you strap on a gun, that makes you a man on the spot. Now if we're attacked, you certainly have the right to defend yourself. Your guns won't be locked away. They're handy if you need them. I'm going to squat down by the fire and have another cup of coffee. All of you talk this out and come up with some sort of decision. You let me know what it is."

Smoke chewed on a biscuit and drank a cup of hot, strong coffee while he waited. Sally stayed with the hands.

Smoke's drive foreman, Nate, broke off from the group and came over, squatting down and pouring a cup of coffee. "Boss, me and Miss Sally voted against these boys goin' on. I think this drive is shapin' up like trouble. But the others, they voted to go on. I reckon it's up to you."

Smoke shook his head. "No. If the majority voted to go on, that's it. Finish your coffee and let's put some miles behind us."

There are those who paint a cattle drive as romantic and exciting. A cattle drive is just plain work. Hot, hard, dirty, dusty, muddy, often dangerous work. If it wasn't too dry it was too wet. If it wasn't too hot it was too cold. Mosquitoes could drive both man and beast half crazy. Rivers and creeks could be no more than a trickle or flooding over their banks. Water holes might be no more than caked mud. There wasn't a damn thing romantic about it.

People have been led to believe that the man who rode at the head of the drive was the point man. Not true. That was the trail boss. The chuck wagon was to the left of the trail boss. The point men — always two — rode behind the trail boss, on the left and right of the cattle. Behind the point men rode the drovers in the swing position. Behind them were the cowboys on the flank. The remuda was just behind and outside of the left flank, with the wranglers. In the rear were the drovers who made up the drag. It was the job of the trail boss to scout ahead for water and pasture. The other cowboys rotated positions. How often that occurred sometimes depended on the disposition of the trail boss, but usually it was left up to the cowboys to equally share the good and bad positions found on any drive.

No sooner had the herd entered Wyoming than one of the point men shouted, pointing to the west. A dozen riders were coming up, trotting their horses. The riders didn't look a bit friendly.

Three

Smoke rode out to meet them, putting some distance between himself and the herd. If there was to be shooting, he didn't want the herd stampeded. The riders pulled up and sat looking at Smoke. They were all pretty well set up, so they probably weren't rustlers. But they all appeared sullen and Smoke didn't take to them at all.

"We're from the cattlemen's association," one finally said, after Smoke refused to be stared down. His tone indicated that was a big deal to him. Didn't impress Smoke at all.

"Congratulations. Do you want applause?"

"Oh, we got us a real smart-mouth here, Walt," another said.

Walt pointed a finger at Smoke. "You best button your lip, mister."

"I wasn't born with a button on it," Smoke told him. "Now state your business and get out of my way. I've got cattle to drive."

Nate and Shorty had left the herd, to ride up alongside the boss. While neither one was a gunslinger, they could both shuck a Colt or Remington out of leather mighty quick and they were crack shots.

"By God!" another member of the association said. "I'll not stand for talk like that. We're here to inspect your herd and you best just stand aside."

"Inspect my herd for what?" Smoke asked, his right

hand resting on his thigh, close to the butt of his .44.

"Been a lot of rustlin' goin' on," Walt said. "You're a stranger here, so we take a look at your cattle, whether you like it or not."

"I don't care if you inspect my herd. But you'll do it while they're moving. Now get out of the way."

"Just who in the hell do you think you are, buddy?" another asked, belligerence in his tone.

"Smoke Jensen."

Those among them with any sense at all made certain their hands were in plain sight and they made no quick moves. But there is always one. . . .

"That don't spell jack-crap to me," a burly, unshaven man said. "I never believed nine-tenths of them stories 'bout you no way."

"That is your option," Smoke told him. He glanced at Shorty. "Get the herd moving. If these gentlemen want to inspect it, that's fine with me. But they'll do it on the move."

"Right, boss." Shorty wheeled his horse, took off his hat, and waved it in the air. "Head them out!" he shouted.

"You gonna sit there and let this two-bit fancy-dan gunhawk get away with this, Walt?" the loudmouth asked.

"Shut up, Baylis," a man whispered hoarsely.

Smoke lifted the reins and walked his horse into the group, stopping by the side of Baylis. He smiled at the man. Baylis not only didn't believe in shaving every day, he didn't bathe much either. "What's your problem?" Smoke asked him. "Other than having to smell your own stink, that is."

"Baylis," Walt said. "Close your mouth and keep it closed. I recognize the gentlemen now."

"Jensen," Baylis said, "I think I'll just get off this horse and whup your butt."

"Oh, I don't think so." Smoke pulled his hat brim lower and then sucker-punched the man. He busted Baylis smack in the mouth; the blow knocked the man out of the

25

saddle. Baylis sprawled on the hoof-churned ground, his mouth a bloody mess.

Smoke backed his horse out of the group, stopping between Nate and Shorty. "If you gentlemen wish to ride along and inspect the herd, feel free to do so. We'll be stopping for lunch in about an hour. You're welcome to eat with us. And that includes the fool on the ground."

Several of the men tried to hide their smiles.

"That's very kind of you, Mr. Jensen," Walt said. "We'll just ride along for a time and then take you up on your most generous offer of a meal."

Smoke nodded and he and Shorty and Nate rejoined the herd. Walt looked down at Baylis, who was hanging onto a stirrup, trying to get up. "Baylis, I always suspicioned that your mamma raised at least one fool. Now I know I was right."

Over lunch, which was the thick rich stew sometimes called Sonofabitch Stew, with sourdough bread to sop in it, dried apple pie for dessert, and all the coffee anybody could drink, Smoke asked Walt about Clint Black.

"I never met the man, Smoke. But I know about him. Runs the biggest spread in all of Montana Territory. The Circle 45. Has maybe . . . depending on the time of year . . . anywhere from fifty to a hundred men on the payroll. You're not taking these cattle to him, are you?"

"No. To a man named Duggan. Runs the Double D spread."

"I never heard of him."

"I think he's new out here. He bought my whole herd and about a thousand from neighboring ranches. Said he wanted to get into the cattle business fast. I've never met him. Everything was handled through lawyers."

"Gettin' to be a man can't break wind without checking first with a lawyer," Walt grumbled.

Smoke grinned at him. He shared the same opinion of

most lawyers. "Speaking of sons of bitches, have some more stew, Walt."

Walt laughed and a new friendship was bonded.

Baylis glared at Smoke and hatred was fanned.

Walt gave Smoke a handwritten note and with it said, "You'll have no trouble in Wyoming. Just show anyone who stops you that note and they'll wave you right on through and help you with the drive for a time."

The men shook hands all the way around. All but Baylis. He rode out alone right after lunch. Nobody missed him until he couldn't be found and a drover told them he saw him ridin' out toward the northwest.

"I hope he keeps on riding," Walt said. "Baylis is a troublemaker. Runs a little rawhide spread not far from here. There is a mean streak in the man that I never could cotton to. Shame too, 'cause he came from good stock. I knew both his parents 'fore they died."

"How's he live?" Smoke asked. "That was a good horse and a fancy rig."

"Lot of us have wondered that," another association member told Smoke. "I ain't sayin' he's crooked, but it wouldn't surprise me to find out he was."

"Maybe he's headin' back to Montana," yet another suggested. "He worked up there for years. Say! I think he worked for the Circle 45, come to think of it."

The herd pushed on and for a time they had nothing but beautiful weather. The boys were turning into good hands, and it surprised everybody to see how closely they watched the remuda and how well they took to accepting responsibility.

The days began to blend together as they pushed north. The herd was stopped several times by cattlemen association members, and by curious ranchers, but the letter Walt had given Smoke quickly brought smiles and offers of meals and a chance to take a real bath in a tub, something Sally jumped at.

"I've heard about you for years, Smoke," a rancher said, over a fine meal of fried chicken and potatoes and gravy. "I figured you'd be a much older man."

"I got started young," Smoke said with a smile.

"Oh?"

"After my pa was killed, an old mountain man name of Preacher took me in . . ."

"Why, say! Preacher's famous. He took the first wagon train over the Oregon Trail, didn't he?"

"Something like that. Preacher was the first to do a lot of things out here. My teenage years were spent in the company of old mountain men. I got a pretty good education."

The rancher's kids, ranging in age from about twelve to twenty, sat at the long table, eyes bright with excitement. Smoke Jensen, the gunfighter who'd killed about a zillion bad hombres was really here and eating fried chicken just like everybody else.

"And you and Sally have been married . . . how long?" a teenage girl asked.

"Well," Smoke said. "Ah . . ."

"You'd better get it right," Sally warned and everybody laughed.

"We've been married, ah . . . ten years," Smoke said.

"That's close," Sally said.

"Your first wife was . . ." The boy closed his mouth at a hard glance from his father.

"It's all right," Smoke said. "Her name was Nicole. We were married, sort of. Had a bent nail for a wedding ring. We had a son. Named him Arthur, that was Preacher's name. Outlaws came one day while I was gone. They killed the baby and then raped and killed Nicole. I tracked them down and called them out in a mining town."

"How many of them were there, Mr. Smoke?" a girl asked.

28

"Fourteen."

"Jesus," the rancher whispered.

"Did you get them all, Smoke?" the oldest boy asked.

"I got them all."

"How old were you, Smoke?" the rancher's wife asked in a soft voice.

"I think I was twenty-one. I'm not real sure how old I am," ma'am.

The father put a stop to it. "No more questions."

The young kids were off to bed; the women went to the parlor — much to Sally's disgust — while the rancher, his oldest son, and Smoke, went into the den for whiskey and cigars. Smoke waved off the cigar and rolled a cigarette.

"What do you know about a man named Clint Black?" Smoke asked.

The rancher's eyebrows lifted as he was lighting his cigar. When he had the tip glowing just right, he said, "He's a bad one, Smoke. I'd say he's probably in his mid-to-late forties. Ruthless and dangerous and powerful. He took country that was untamed and built an empire out of it. He's big and strong as a bull. And there is no backup in him. It's his way, or no way at all."

"Nobody is right but him."

"That's it. Anybody gets in his way, he just rides right over them."

"Would he hurt a boy? Those boys I have with me, for instance?"

"Oh . . . I wouldn't think so. But with a man like that, hell, you never know. I know he's run off nesters, but I never heard of him or his men ever harming a child. Hell, I ran off nesters, 'til I got tired of it and learned to live with them."

"You know anything at all about T. J. Duggan and the Double D ranch?"

The rancher shook his head. "Can't say as I've ever heard of him or his brand. T. J. Duggan. Don't ring a bell with me."

The herd slowly put the miles behind them. They crossed rivers, pulled cattle out of quicksand and fought the heat and ate the dust and endured the loneliness of the trail, with the older men remembering how it was years back, when there were no towns along the way. When there was nothing except an empty, seemingly never-ending vastness and then screaming Indians that came out of nowhere.

It was bad now, but it was worse back then.

About fifty miles after crossing the North Platte, they hit a vast grassland, and the cattle slowly ate their way across, regaining the few pounds lost on the way north.

Holding the herd outside of a small town in northern Wyoming, Smoke and several other riders accompanied the wagon in for supplies.

It wasn't much of a town, even by Western standards. A large general store, a blacksmith, a saloon. The stage stopped twice a week. The town had sprung up out of nowhere, had lasted a few years, now was dying. Another couple of years and it would join the many other towns that failed in the West.

Not too many miles to the west, there was another settlement called Donkey Town, although some were trying to get its name changed to Rocky Pile.

While the supplies were being loaded, Smoke walked the short distance to the saloon. If there was any news worth hearing, he would learn of it at the saloon. There were half a dozen horses at the hitchrail and two wagons in the street. Smoke pushed open the batwings and the buzz of conversation slowed, then stopped as he ordered a beer and leaned against the bar.

He was used to that. Nearly everyone in the rural west carried a gun; few carried two guns; almost no one wore his guns the way Smoke wore his. It branded him. Smoke moved to the shadows at the far end of the bar. He hadn't had time to lift the mug to his lips when the batwings flew open and two young men stomped in.

"Hell of a herd outside of town," one said. "And, boy, you ought to see the cook. She's a looker, let me tell you."

"Wears men's britches," the second one said. "Rob here like to have fell off his horse starin'."

"Got a bunch of snot-nosed kids wranglin'," Rob said. "Might be fun to go out there and hoo-rah 'em some. What'd you say, Carl?"

"Kids?" a man questioned. He sat at a table with three other men. "What kind of a damn fool outfit hires kids as drovers?"

The pair obviously had not seen any hands except the boys at the remuda. Smoke sipped his beer and waited and listened. Talk was one thing, but hoo-rahing the herd was quite another.

The batwings were shoved open and a young man rushed in, his face flushed. "You heard the news?" The words rushed out of his mouth. "That herd outside of town belongs to Smoke Jensen!"

"You're crazy!" Carl told him. "Who told you that?"

"One of them kids at the remuda."

"Aw, he's just sayin' that so's no one will bother 'em. Smoke Jensen ain't got no herd. I don't even think there is such a person noways. I think all that's made-up stuff."

Rob hitched at his gun belt. "Oh, he's a real person, all right. My brother seen him a couple of years ago. Backed him down, too, my brother did. Jensen ain't much. I'd like to see Jensen in action. I think I'm faster."

"Your brother's got a fat mouth," a cowboy spoke from a table. "Smoke Jensen ain't never backed down from no one. And leave them boys out yonder alone. Nobody but a tinhorn would hoo-rah a herd."

"If my brother was here, you'd not be sayin' them words," Rob yelled.

"Go get him," the cowboy said. "I'll say it to his face. As far as you bein' better than Smoke Jensen . . . you're a fool. You best take them pearl-handled six shooters off before somebody snatches 'em offen you and shoves 'em

31

down your throat. Or shoves 'em up another part of your a-natomy."

"You think you're big enough to do it!" Rob screamed.

"Yeah," the cowboy said. "I sure do."

"How have you been, Al?" Smoke broke into the conversation.

The cowboy smiled. "Pretty good. I wondered if you recognized me."

"Stay out of this!" Rob yelled at Smoke.

Smoke ignored him. "I heard you were working up this way. Heard you had your own spread."

"Sure do. Got married and all that. How's things down on the Sugarloaf?"

"Couldn't be better."

"Keep your mouth shut!" Rob yelled at the tall man in the shadows. "When I want you to butt into my affairs, I'll let you know. You hear me?"

"Al Jacobs will eat your lunch, boy," Smoke told him. "He's a bad man to tangle with. Me and Al go way back. He used to work for me down in Colorado."

"I don't give a damn where he used to work and I don't give a damn about you. Now why don't you just shut up and mind your own business. That two-bit rawhider insulted my brother and in-sulted me. Stay out of things that don't concern you 'fore I call you out too."

Al laughed at that. "The kid's sure got his dander up, don't he?"

"Hey, don't you call me no kid, you son of a bitch!" Rob yelled.

The saloon became very quiet. Call a cowboy a flea-bitten, no-count, worthless saddle bum, and he'll probably laugh at you. Besmirch a cowboy's mother's name, and in all probability he'll kill you.

Al slowly rose from his chair, his hand hovering over the butt of his .45.

"Back off, Rob," Smoke said quietly. "Back off and apologize to Al. That remark was uncalled for."

Carl decided it was time for him to stick his mouth into the tense situation. "Hey, mister! Who the hell asked you to butt in? You a friend of Al?"

"That's right," Smoke said, still standing in the shadows.

"Then you get your butt out here and face me."

"Now boys," the barkeep said. "I just mopped this floor."

"Shut up!" Carl told him. He stared into the gloom where Smoke stood. "You! Get your butt out here."

Sonny, one of the boys who had come into town for some licorice, stood at the batwings. "We're all loaded and ready to go, Mr. Smoke," he called.

The saloon became as quiet as a grave.

Four

"Go on back to the herd, Sonny," Smoke told him. "I'll be along presently."

The boy had sized up the situation instantly. "Yes, sir!" Sonny hit the air.

"Jesus God Amighty," one of the seated men breathed.

Smoke stepped out of the shadows. He didn't have to wonder if he'd slipped the hammer thongs from his .44s. That was done by reflex as soon as his boots touched ground out of the stirrups. "This does not have to be," he told Rob and Carl. "Rob, you insulted a man and you owe him an apology. Carl, from now on, you'd best think before you challenge a man."

"You can go right straight to Hell," Carl said, his words thick, almost slurred.

"Don't do this, Carl." The barkeep said his words softly. "Don't do it, son."

"Shut up!" Carl told him. "I'll be famous. I'll be the man who killed Smoke Jensen."

"No, you won't," one of the card-playing men called. "You'll just be dead."

"We'll pull together, Smoke," Al said. "If it comes to that."

"All right," Smoke replied, his eyes riveted on Carl. "It won't be any disgrace for you to just walk out of here, boys."

34

"I ain't no boy!" Rob screamed. "I'm a man grown."

"Then act like one!" Smoke snapped at him. "Men admit their mistakes and grow more mature each time they do. Boys let their mouths get them into trouble and then let pride get them killed. A man is dead a long time. Think about that."

"I think he's yeller," Carl said, a mean smile moving his lips. "The big shot Smoke Jensen is takin' water."

"Yeah," Rob said, his eyes lighting up. "Both of 'em are pure-dee yeller-bellies."

"It's no use, Smoke," Al said. "You and me, we've seen this played out ten dozen times."

"I'm afraid you're right," Smoke admitted.

"Damn, they're gonna do it," a man said, as chairs were pushed back and the tables emptied with men moving about, hoping to get out of the way of any stray bullets.

Smoke felt a sadness take him. The young man was obviously scared, but his stupid pride was crawling all over him, refusing to allow him to back down.

The young man jerked his iron. He was pitifully slow.

Smoke put two rounds into Carl's gun hand. The first hit his gun and tore it from his hand, the second round smashed into the hand, breaking it. Al's draw had been smooth and his aim true. Rob stood holding a bloody shoulder.

"I just don't want to kill no more, Smoke," the gunfighter turned rancher said. "Not unless I just have to do it. You know what I mean?"

"Oh, yes. I sure do."

"You ruined my hand!" Carl sobbed. "It's all busted up."

"My shoulder's broken," Rob moaned.

"But you're both alive," the barkeep said, after picking himself up off the floor. "Now get the hell over to the barber shop so's Ed can patch you both up. Go on,

35

now, move. You're leakin' blood all over the floor."

Sobbing and stumbling, the two young men whose gunfighting days had just begun and ended staggered to the batwings and into the street.

Smoke and Al holstered their guns. Al smiled. "Good to see you again, Smoke."

"Same here, Al. You take care."

"Will do." The man walked out of the saloon and mounted up, riding away without even so much as a glance over his shoulder.

Smoke held up his empty mug. "Want to fill this up?"

"Oh, yes, sir!" the barkeep said. "It's on the house, Mr. Jensen. Yessiree, bob. On the house."

Smoke took his drink to a table by the window and sat down. "What about this brother of Rob's?" Smoke tossed the question out.

"Oh, I reckon he'll catch up with the herd and call you out, all right," a man said. "He ain't got no more sense than Rob. But he is a mite faster, I'll warn you of that. But I don't think you're in any mortal danger," he added drily.

"I already know that."

"They call him Rocky," another said.

Smoke was thoughtful for a moment. "He live far from here?"

" 'Bout three miles out of town."

"I don't want my herd stampeded or any of my hands hit by stray bullets. Go get him and let's straighten this mess out right now."

A man stood up. "I'll do that, Mr. Jensen. Yes, sir, I sure will."

The barkeep opened his mouth.

"I don't wish any further conversation," Smoke spoke the words softly.

"Right," the barkeep said. "Mouth is hereby closed."

It didn't take long for Rocky to ride in and swing

down from the saddle in front of the barber shop. Two guns and all. Smoke knew by the way he walked the man wasn't in any mood to talk. The man who had fetched him got him a beer and returned to his table.

"He says he's gonna kill you, Smoke."

"No, I don't think so."

"Well, here he comes," another stated.

Smoke waited about four feet inside the batwings. He had slipped on leather gloves.

Boots thudded on the old boards. "Jensen! You better make your peace with the Lord. 'Cause I'm shore gonna kill you for what you done to my brother."

Rocky slammed open the batwings and charged inside. Smoke hit him flush in the mouth. Rocky's boots went out from under him and he sailed right back out into the street, landing on his butt. The dust flew.

Smoke stepped out and kicked the gun from Rocky's hand. He reached down and slapped the man hard, twice across the face, addling him, and then jerked out his other Colt and tossed it into a horse trough. Then he hauled Rocky up and proceeded to beat the snot out of him.

Rocky didn't get a chance to land a single punch. All he did was receive them, and he received a goodly number of them, divided about equally between ribs and face.

When Smoke finally let the would-be gunslinger fall, he was pretty sure that Rocky's jaw was broken in at least two places and he had numerous broken ribs. Rocky would not be riding for a long time.

Smoke swung up into the saddle and faced the crowd of men and women. "Give him a message from me. Tell him I gave him his life. This time only. Explain to him that Carl and Rob crowded Al and me. Not the other way around. Try to get it through Rocky's head that if I ever see him again, and he's wearing a gun, I fully intend to kill him. On the spot." He turned his horse and rode out of town.

"I do like a feller who knows his mind and speaks it," a man said. "And Jensen can sure enough speak it plain. Well, come on. Let's drag Rocky over to Ed's. Most excitement we've had in this town in ten years."

At the herd, Sally walked to her husband's side. "Any trouble in town?"

"Not to speak of. Saw Al Jacobs and we had a beer together. He's ranching and married now. I forgot to ask if he had any kids. He looked real good."

Sally looked at the blood splattered on Smoke's shirt. "It must have been a lively conversation. Get out of that shirt so I can soak it before the blood sets. What in the world did you two talk about?"

Smoke stripped off his shirt and handed it to her, then rummaged around in his bedroll for a fresh shirt. "We saved some lives there in the town. Al and me, we put two young fellows back on the right road. You might say we read to them from the scriptures."

She patted his arm. "I'm sure it was quite a sermon. Do we stay here for the night?"

"I think it would be best if we moved on for a few more miles. No point in wasting good weather."

Sally put hazel eyes on her husband. "Someday you must tell me about your impromptu Bible reading."

"Oh, I will. When we get a few more miles up the road."

They experienced no more trouble as the herd moved slowly north. The drovers pushed them into Montana, and after three days drive they turned the herd west. Now the real test began, for they were on no known trail. That meant that Smoke stayed busy all day, seeking a right of way for the herd and being careful not to damage the property of other ranchers and farmers. And the drovers had to work twice as hard in order to keep the herd together and not pick up anyone else's cows.

Hands from other ranches willingly pitched in to help. They did it for many reasons, including the chance to pick up news and to taste some of Sally's cooking, for the word had spread before them.

Many of them also wanted the chance to size up Smoke Jensen. The majority of the hands and ranchers who met him quickly found themselves liking the man, for they found in him a man who worked just as hard as his hands and who told it the way he saw it, pulling no punches. That was the Western way.

And the story of the shoot-out back in that little Wyoming town, and the fistfight that followed had already spread, to be told and retold around the campfires of the West.

The boys in the drive got their wish, and they met some Indians. They were not hostile and appeared to be starving. But there was no way they were going to beg. They had been defeated on the battlefields, and now were not much of a threat to anyone. But beg they would not. Smoke could see that. He could also see hungry children and he couldn't stand that. Smoke gave them ten of his own cattle and wished them well.

"What kind of Injuns were those, Mr. Smoke?" Young Guy asked.

"Cheyenne. Proud people."

"They didn't look like very much to me."

"Some of the fiercest warriors that ever lived," Smoke told the boy. "Back when I was not much older than you, I lived with them part of one winter. Me and old Preacher. Indians are good people . . . in their own way. Their ways are just not like ours, that's all."

Smoke cut north for several days, to avoid the Indian reservations, then again pointed the herd west. They had one hell of the time crossing the Yellowstone, almost

39

losing a hand when his horse panicked and floundered. They saved the hand, but the horse was swept downstream and the cowboy lost horse, saddle, saddlebags, and Winchester.

Then they hit days of hot, dry weather before they reached the Sweet Grass River. The cattle almost stampeded when they smelled the water. One old mossyhorn bull who had joined the herd a few days back charged a horse and gored it so badly the horse had to be shot. When the horse fell, Harris was pinned under the saddle. The bull took out his mad on Harris before Smoke could kill it. Harris was buried beside the trail. He wasn't the first to have been killed on a cattle drive, and certainly would not be the last.

Smoke made a short talk after the body was lowered and covered, saying a few good things about Harris, and Denver read words from the Bible. Some of the boys had a hard time keeping back the tears.

When Sally sang "What A Friend We Have In Jesus," several of the boys and more than one of the men could no longer contain themselves and even old Denver had to horn his nose a couple of times. The whole affair just about did Smoke in, too, and he was glad to be back in the saddle and moving. It wasn't the first lonely grave he'd helped dig.

Smoke led them south of the Crazy Mountains and then led them north and west across the Sixteenmile River, keeping the Big Belt Mountains to the north. Smoke told his people they could visit Helena after the herd was delivered and have a rip-roarin' good time. Right now, the herd needed to be delivered.

Mountains towered all around them as Smoke wound the herd through valleys lush with summer vegetation. These were not yet the towering peaks that lay farther north, but they were respectable mountains just the same.

Smoke halted the herd in a long, wide, beautiful valley and told his people to let them graze. "This is where Duggan said he'd meet us," he told his crew. "So make camp and relax. We're a couple of days early." He smiled. "Give or take a week or so."

"This is puzzling," Sally told her husband, snuggled next to him that night, and the nights were cool. "Why didn't this Duggan want the herd taken straight to his range?"

"I don't know. Unless he doesn't want Clint Black to know about it, just yet."

"That must be it."

The next morning, Nate came fogging his horse into camp. "Two women comin', boss. Ridin' sidesaddle an' all. They some duded up, too. Funniest lookin' hats I ever did see."

"Two *women?*" Smoke asked. "Here?"

"There they come, boss. See for yourself."

The women were twins, and identical twins at that. They were elegantly dressed, in the very latest Eastern riding habits. Their hats were huge things, with what looked to Smoke like mosquito netting tied under their chins. They walked their horses over to a natural rise and stepped daintily from the saddle, handing the reins to a dumbstruck young Rabbit, who was bug-eyed staring at the pair.

"Which one of you is Mr. Jensen?" one twin asked.

"Right here, ma'am." Smoke walked toward them and took off his hat. "And you two would be. . . ?"

"I am Toni and this is my sister, Jeanne. Duggan."

Smoke got it then. T. J. Duggan. "You have got to be kidding!"

"Quite the contrary, Mr. Jensen. We own the Double D ranch."

Everybody gathered around, staring.

"Ah . . . this is my wife, Sally," Smoke finally

41

managed to say.

"Pleased, I'm sure," the other twin said, and then dismissed Sally silently.

"Of the New Hampshire Reynolds," Smoke said, before Sally could step forward and bust one of these ladies right in the chops.

"Oh, my!" the other twin said. "I didn't realize. Of course! We've read about you, Sally. How wonderful to find some degree of breeding out here in this . . ." She looked around. ". . . bastion of coarseness and vulgarity."

"What the hell did she say?" Denver whispered to Shorty.

"Don't git me to lyin'," Shorty told him. "But I don't think it was no compliment."

"That's what I think, too."

"Where are your hands, Miss Duggan?" Smoke asked.

"I beg your pardon?"

"Your hands? No. I don't mean them. Not *your* hands. Your crew? Your cowboys?"

"Oh, we don't have any yet."

"You . . . don't have any? Well, how in the he . . . heck are you going to handle these cattle without a crew?"

"Oh, we'll leave that up to you," Toni said brightly. "I mean, that's what you do, isn't it?"

"On my own ranch, yes. I don't hire out to other people."

"Well, I'm certain we can work something out," Jeanne said. "Come now, time's wasting. Let's don't dawdle. We have quite a distance to go."

"Wait a minute!" Smoke said, exasperation in his voice. "Where is your ranch?"

"Twelve miles, that way," Toni said, pointing. "We camped in the timber last night. We'll pick up our equipment on the way back. We're quite expert in the woods, you know."

"No, I didn't know," Smoke said. "Camped in the woods," he muttered. "Experts, no less. All right," he said. "Get the cattle ready for the trail."

Sally was laughing at his expression. "Don't dawdle now, honey."

Smoke was muttering low curses as he mounted up.

"Did we do something wrong?" Jeanne asked Sally. "We've been out here from Boston for several months and we seem to, well, anger all the people we've come in contact with."

Sally climbed up on the wagon seat and took the reins. "I wonder why?" she said drily.

Five

The ladies' camp was equipped like an African safari. Smoke and the other hands had never seen so much junk in their lives.

"What's that thing?" Rabbit asked, pointing to a canvas tent at the edge of the camp area. "It ain't even got no top to it."

"Don't ask me," Smoke said.

"One side is for bathing and the other side is a toilet," Sally informed them.

"Do tell?" Rabbit muttered.

"We're not going to make the ranch by nightfall," Smoke told the twins. "We'll be lucky to make two miles in this country. Best thing we can do is camp here for the night and leave early in the morning. You really have no one at the ranch?"

"Well, we have a cook and a nice young Spanish boy who takes care of the horses and does the lawn work," Jeanne replied. "We just can't get anyone else to work for us. We're obviously doing something wrong but no one will tell us what it is."

"You're just new out here," Smoke told them, putting on his diplomat's hat and lying through his teeth. "Takes Western folks a while to size a person up." He wanted to tell the twins that if they'd stop looking down their blue-blood noses at everybody, things might ease up a mite.

44

"Oh!" Toni said. "Well. I have an idea. We'll give a party and that will break the ice. What is it called out here? A whigdig?"

"A shindig, ma'am," Smoke corrected.

"Yes! That's it. I don't suppose there are any violinists close by?"

"I rather doubt it," Smoke said.

"Oh, well. My sister and I will entertain. We're very accomplished musicians."

"Wonderful," Smoke said.

"Yes. Jeanne is a flutist and I was trained as a classical pianist."

"Ought to be a real entertaining evening," Smoke said.

"Oh, quite! Are you familiar with Chopin?"

Smoke shook his head. He was getting a bad case of indigestion.

"Do you know the closest place where we might order caviar, Mr. Jensen?"

"No, ma'am," Smoke said wearily. "I sure don't."

"You see," Toni said during supper. "After our parents were killed, my sister and I came into quite a sizable inheritance. We have funds in other businesses, of course, but we felt it would be exciting to own a ranch."

"Right," Smoke said. "Have you met your neighbor yet, a Clint Black?"

"He came to call. He found something hysterically amusing. He laughed the entire time he visited. I found him quite boorish, to be truthful."

"What's boorish?" Ben whispered to Duke.

"Hell, I don't know. But I bet it ain't real nice."

"Yes," Jeanne said. "Mr. Black is a rather nice-looking man, in a rugged sort of way. But he's terribly coarse. His table manners were an abomination. We fixed cucumber sandwiches for him and he said he wouldn't feed those to his horse."

"You have to understand," Sally said, "that Western fare is simple, but filling and wholesome. Most out here grew up on beef and beans."

From the expression on her face, that cuisine didn't meet her approval. At all.

"Just where is the town of Blackstown?" Smoke asked.

"About twenty-five miles west of our location," Toni said. "A rather quaint little town."

The way she said it gave Smoke the idea that Blackstown appealed to her about as much as sticking her big toe into a fresh pile of cow droppings.

"Did Clint Black say anything, well, threatening to either of you?" Smoke asked the twins.

They exchanged glances. Toni replied. "Not . . . directly, Mr. Jensen. But we both feel there were some thinly veiled threats."

"Tell me about them."

"Well, he is an unmarried man and women are scarce out here. He made some rather crude advances at Jeanne, and then when she rebuffed him, he directed his attentions toward me. I told him that I was not interested. He said I'd come begging before all this was over. I asked what in the world he meant by that. He just laughed and walked away."

Jeanne said, "Then I noticed that we were being watched and followed constantly. When we tried to hire people to work on our ranch, they would just shake their heads, mumble something and walk off. It's obvious that Mister Black had ordered us boycotted, for some reason. We are able to shop in the town, for many of the merchants there don't care for the man or his high-handed tactics. Mister Black's brother, Harris, a thug if I ever saw one, is the Sheriff, and his deputies are just as bad as he is, if not worse. All in all, it is not a pleasant situation."

"Who sold you this ranch?"

"It wasn't sold directly to us," Jeanne said. "Our attorneys are always looking for places to make our monies work, and when this property came on the market, they bought the ranch. However, they had no idea that we would personally come out here to run it." She looked directly at Smoke. "You think that we are ill-suited to do so and that we were wrong to come out here, don't you, Mr. Jensen?"

"Smoke. My name is Smoke. And in answer to your question, yes, I do think you're out of place here. Clint Black is a dangerous, ruthless, and power-hungry man. From what I was able to learn about him, he's about as easy to get along with as a rattlesnake."

The twins smiled, Toni saying, "Our attorneys said much the same about you, Mr. Jensen."

Smoke chuckled. "Have your attorneys ever been west of the Mississippi?"

"Heavens no!" Jeanne said. "But everyone they communicated with said you were a bad man."

Sally laughed. "Out here, Jeanne, the phrase 'a bad man' doesn't hold the same connotation as back East. It doesn't mean that person is evil, or not to be trusted, or anything like that. It means that person is a bad man to crowd or try to harm. It might mean he's a dangerous man in a fight. My husband is known as a bad man because he has the name of gunfighter."

"We saw the play," Toni said.

"That's too bad," Smoke told her. "I'm told it's terrible."

"And we've read the books," Jeanne said.

"They're even worse," Smoke replied.

"I must admit," Toni said, "that you are a rather, ah, imposing figure of a man. Have you really gunned down five thousand men?"

Smoke laughed aloud. "If I had done that, when would I have had the time to get married, build a home, father children, and run a ranch? I'm afraid the stories about me are highly exaggerated." He stood up and tossed out the dregs of his coffee cup. "I'm going to make a turn around the herd. It's getting late. We'd all best get ready to hit the sack."

"He's only gunned down about a thousand men," Sally said, with a mischievous glint in her eyes.

Smoke sighed.

"Oh, my!" the twins gasped.

A shot brought Smoke lunging to his feet, grabbing for his guns. He could hear the bawling of cattle and the thunderous roar of a stampede building. He jammed his feet into his boots and slung his gun belt around his waist just as the camp filled with horses. He could just make out hooded men, all wearing long dusters, and all with guns in their hands. A horse hit him and knocked him sprawling.

"Sally!" he called. "Run for the timber. Run, honey."

He struggled to get to his feet. A bullet tore into his shoulder and staggered him. He could hear the cries of wounded men as his crew was being shot to pieces. He was again knocked spinning by a running horse. He grabbed ahold of a rider's leg and jerked him out of the saddle, smashing him in the face with a big fist. A bullet nicked his head and he fell to the ground calling out Sally's name. Through the painful fog in his brain, he could hear the screaming of men and women and boys and the roar of a full-blown stampede. Clint Black! he thought. I should have placed more men on guard. I should have guessed he'd have the twins followed.

Then there was no more time left for thinking. Smoke had to stay alive. He had to find Sally. He had to fight.

He jumped up behind a rider and hammered blows at the man, knocking him out of the saddle. In the saddle, Smoke fumbled for the reins and found them. The night was so black he could not see five feet in any direction. Something struck him on the head and the last thing he remembered was grabbing hold of the saddle horn as the badly frightened animal took off in a panicked run.

Warmth awakened him. He lay on the ground for several moments, not moving or opening his eyes. He listened. He could hear squirrels chattering and birds singing. A bee hummed past him. Without lifting his head, he opened his eyes. He was in the high country, he could tell that. But he didn't have the vaguest idea where in the high country. To make matters worse, he didn't know who he was.

He rolled over and pain tore through his left shoulder. Groaning, he sat up. His left shirtsleeve was bloody. Part of a large splinter was sticking out of his flesh. He remembered being shot, or thinking he'd been shot. He must have been hit with the stock of a rifle. The stock might have been broken and it ripped apart when whoever it was hit him, driving the splinter into his shoulder. Gritting his teeth, he pulled the long piece of wood out of his shoulder. He looked at it and threw it away. He gingerly felt his head. It hurt. There were two lumps on his noggin and dried blood.

"Sally!" he said aloud, his voice a croak. He cleared his throat as the events of the night before came crashing back to him.

He looked up at the sun. About ten o'clock. He felt sudden panic try to overtake his emotions. He pushed panic aside and regained control. He pushed himself to his boots and almost fell, reaching out to grab a small tree for support. He leaned against the tree for a moment. Damn, but he was weak.

The camp had been attacked—he tried to sort out the jumble in his aching head. He remembered yelling for Sally to get away. He recalled the shooting and the hooded riders. He suddenly and vividly remembered the screaming of the women, the yelling and moaning of his hands, and the stampeding herd.

And he was thirsty; God, what he wouldn't give for a long drink of cold water. Taking several deep breaths, he looked around him. He had absolutely no idea where he was. But at least now he knew who he was.

He inspected himself for further wounds and could find nothing except bruises from being knocked down several times by running horses. Maybe he'd been kicked too. He just couldn't remember. Smoke started carefully down the slope, for he was strangely weak. And that was a condition he was unaccustomed to.

He dropped his hands to his guns. They were in place. He felt for his knife. It was there. Obviously, the attack had come so quickly he had not had the time to pull his guns from leather.

He had to find Sally.

He fell twice on the way down the steep slope. He sat down and removed his spurs, sticking them in his back pocket. He found some berries and ate them and felt better. A few hundred yards later, he found a spring and bellied down on the ground and drank his fill. Smoke took off his bloody shirt and bathed his wounds. He found moss and placed that over the jagged rip in his shoulder, tying the moss secure with his kerchief. He drank again and could feel the strength returning to his powerful muscles and his head clearing.

A cold anger was filling his head. Smoke knew the sensation well. If Sally had been hurt, or killed—he knew he had to face that possibility—this countryside was going to run red with blood. Any man who would order the killing of women and boys did not deserve to live, and Clint Black had made one very large mistake. He had let Smoke Jensen live.

In a clearing, Smoke got his bearings. He picked out landmarks he had seen coming in and now knew his approximate location. He started toward the last camp they had made, figuring it was about five miles away.

He found a body but the rampaging cattle had trampled it beyond recognition. Then he found a boot and recognized it as belonging to one of the new hands. Eton. Smoke stuck a stick in the ground to mark the spot and walked on. He would be back to bury the remains.

He found Willie next. He knew it was the fifteen-year-old because of his overalls. He preferred them over jeans. Using another stick, he marked the spot and walked on, sadness mixed with the coldest anger he had ever experienced washing over him with every step.

Duke lay on the ground facedown. He had been shot a dozen times. In the back. Rabbit was next. Someone had roped and dragged him.

"Fourteen years old," Smoke muttered. "Fourteen years old."

He walked on. He could smell the wood smoke now.

The raiders had probably torched the wagons. And probably piled on as many bodies as they could find.

Shorty had made a stand of it behind some rocks. But it didn't do him much good. He was riddled with bullet holes. Smoke took his rifle and all his cartridges. Davy had taken a round right through the head. Smoke took his leather waistcoat and slipped it on. He found Johnson and took his hat and gloves. A horse nickered close by and Smoke turned. The foreman's horse walked slowly toward him. Nate had managed to get saddled up. Smoke had no way of knowing the foreman's fate—but he could guess.

He pulled the saddle off the horse and rubbed him down with dry grass, talking to the animal, calming it. He smoothed out the saddle blanket, saddled up, and swung into the leather. Nate's Winchester was in the boot, so Smoke rode with Shorty's rifle across the saddle horn. He only rode a few hundred yards before he found his foreman. Nate and Little Ben had stood and fought it out to the end. Smoke took their weapons and ammunition and the canteen that one of them had grabbed.

"Goddamnit!" he cursed. "I'll see you in Hell, Black. I'll personally send you there."

He looked around him. "Where are you, Sally?"

The wind sighed and gave no answers.

"But, Jeanne . . . ?" Toni said.

"If she's alive we'll find her," Sally assured the woman. "Right now we've got to stay low and quiet. The raiders are still beating the bushes for us. Now stay calm. We'll get out of this."

"Your husband . . . ?" Toni whispered.

"My husband is a hard man to kill. Now listen to

52

me, Toni. These words are going to sound unfeeling to you. But I know how Smoke thinks. Smoke can take care of himself. If he's alive. And I've got to face that. Right now, he would want me to concentrate on survival. That's what we've got to do. We're no good to anybody dead. Come the night, I've got to strip some pants off of a dead hand and get you in them and out of that stupid-looking riding habit."

"Men's pants!"

"Yes, damnit, men's pants. That thing you're wearing would hang up on every twig and branch. We've got to be able to move quickly and silently. Have you ever fired a gun?"

"Heavens no!"

"This valley we're in. How long is it?"

"I . . . don't know. But it's very long and winding. Miles. And Sally? There aren't that many ways in and out."

"I was afraid of that. They chose the ambush site well. We're boxed in and you can bet they've got the passes covered. So we're better off staying right here for the time being. Well, I've got a rifle and my pistol, and my cartridge belt is full. Right now, we need blankets and food and water. Horses would be nice, but I think we're probably better off on foot. Now, Toni, you stay right here. Don't you move one inch from this spot. Do you understand me?"

"Don't leave me, Sally!"

"I've got to. I've got to get supplies. If I don't, we'll die. Don't move from here, Toni. For God's sake, *don't move.*"

"I promise I won't. I swear it, Sally."

"I won't be gone long. Perhaps an hour. If I'm lucky, less than that. You stay low and quiet." She smiled at the woman. "You're tougher than you think, Toni. We all are when the going gets rough." She patted her arm and slipped into the brush. Away from Toni, she paused to compose herself. She was scared, but she couldn't let Toni see that.

"Smoke, honey," she muttered. "Where are you?"

Six

Sally found Jake's body. The boy had been gut-shot and had dragged himself off in the bushes to die.

"Dear merciful God," Sally murmured. "Fifteen years old." She tugged the boy's jeans off and started to cover him up, then thought better of it. That would be a sign that she sure wouldn't want the raiders to find. "Sorry, Jake. You were a good hand."

Unlike Smoke, she had caught a glimpse of the brand on the horses of the raiders. The Circle 45. And one had seen her looking at the brand just a second before she leaped into the darkness of the bushes, dragging Toni with her. So they had to kill her. They couldn't afford to let her live and be a witness against them.

Circling, Sally found the body of one of the new men. Forrest. She took his gun and gun belt and hat and left him as she had found him. She made her way cautiously to the campsite and studied it for several moments before slipping up to the smoldering ruins of the wagons. All the bodies had been dragged away. She could see that sign. She grabbed up two blankets, a full canteen, a tarp, a knife still in its sheath, and sack of canned foods. She was disappearing into the brush just as Smoke injuned his way up to the ruins.

Smoke had found no more bodies, and like Sally he read the sign where the bodies had been dragged off. He squatted, only his eyes moving, picking out the scattered articles he wanted. He moved very quickly, scooping up a blanket—there was a ground sheet and blanket tied behind the saddle of his horse—a side of bacon that was half buried in the dust, a battered coffee pot and a sack of Arbuckles, another canteen and a loaf of bread that had been only slightly scorched by the fire. Then he was gone.

"You made a big mistake, Mr. Black," he muttered, swinging into the saddle. "You left me alive."

"Now listen up," Bobby told the young cowboys. "We're afoot, we ain't got no weapons, and we're in big trouble." He looked at Louie, Dan, Sonny, and Guy. "And yeah, I'm just as scared as you are. But Mr. Smoke made me ramrod of the remuda crew, so I'm givin' the orders. You take them. Understood?"

The quartet of very scared boys nodded their heads.

"We're in a pretty good place here. This blowdown ain't gonna let no horses through, and there ain't no cowboy gonna do nothin' much that he can't do from the saddle. So we stay right here. There's water to drink from that crick over yonder, and we all got a little poke of food. It ain't much. But it's got to do. We can't talk above a whisper. We can't move around. Just remember this, we seen them brands. Circle 45. So that means them thugs got to kill us all. If we keep our heads, maybe they'll give up after a time thinkin' they got us all. It's the best I can do, boys."

Denver eased his old bones into a more comfortable position in the rocks where he lay about a mile from the ambush site. He wasn't hurt bad, just bruised all to hell and gone. He'd managed to grab some gear just as that damn horse hit him and knocked the crap out of him. He had a canteen of water, some biscuits, and a rifle. And he was alive.

Harvey and Jeff, Smoke's regular hands, lay in a thicket and tried to blend in with the earth. Jeff had a bullet in his leg and Harvey's left arm was busted. But they were alive.

Tim was the only one of the new hands to make it out alive. But he was weaponless, except for the sheath knife he carried in his boot. He'd seen those dirty bastards shoot down and ride down his friends with no mercy. One thing Tim knew for a dead-bang fact was that he was going to find those responsible and make them pay a terrible price. He'd prayed to God to give him the wherewithal to do just that.

Jeanne lay behind a log and listened to the men search for her. She cringed when she heard the things they said they were going to do with her and to her when they found her. She clutched a butcher knife in her right hand. Maybe they would do those terrible things. But she'd make one of them pay a fearful price before the others got to her. Then she listened to them ride off and the silence that followed was just about as terrifying. Jeanne did not think she had ever been this frightened. She rose from her hiding place and had not walked a hundred yards before discovering the body of one of Smoke's men. She stifled a scream and knelt down by the body, making up her mind to do what she felt she must.

She tugged off his boots and forced herself to pull off his jeans and shirt. Always keeping a wary and watchful eye, Jeanne undressed and then dressed in jeans and men's shirt. The cowboy's holster was empty. She looked around frantically for his gun. No gun; she couldn't find it.

Now she felt she had a chance of staying alive. If she could just get her fear under control.

Smoke picketed his horse near water and sat down to think matters through. Several times he'd come very close to being spotted on horseback, so he decided to stay on foot until he had scouted the valley through and arrived at a plan of action.

Clint Black had no choice but to kill them all. He could not leave a one of them alive. Keeping that in mind, Smoke had ridden back to the bodies he'd found and pulled out the marking stake. That was a sign of a survivor that he just couldn't leave behind. Then, only a short time afterwards, from where he sat on the ridges, he had watched Circle 45 riders return to the bodies and drag them off. There was to be a mass grave somewhere to the south of the ambush site.

He and Nate had scouted out the long valley and found only a few passes. Clint had planned his ambush well. But how did he know a herd was coming? How could he have known? Toni and Jeanne's attorneys were Boston-based, and the twins had assured Smoke they had told no one local about the herd. A puzzle.

Smoke tensed at the sound of a steel-shod hoof striking stone. He quickly shifted locations, moving into brush at the edge of the small clearing. His big hand closed around a rock about the size of an apple. His smile was hard, for Smoke had always been pretty good at chunking stones.

A Circle 45 rider, his dark duster tied behind the saddle, walked his horse slowly into the clearing. He gave the area a close once-over and then turned his horse, putting his back to Smoke. Smoke rose up, took aim, and flung the stone. The rock smacked into the rider's head and knocked him slap out of the saddle. He hit the ground and did not move. His horse trotted off a few yards and stopped.

Smoke moved from his hiding place and walked slowly toward the seemingly lifeless form. He walked slowly so he would not alarm the horse. He wanted that canteen, rifle, and rope. And he might have a bait of food in the saddlebags.

The rider's skull was busted open. He was alive, but just barely. Smoke looked down at the man and felt no pity, no remorse. Nothing. The man had chosen his way of life. To hell with him.

Smoke took the man's gun belt and then dragged the raider into some bushes and dumped him. He pulled the saddle off the horse and picketed it with his own. The saddlebags contained a sack of cartridges, some dirty socks, and two biscuits and bacon wrapped in paper. Smoke ate those, drank some water, and felt better. He then wrapped the dead man's weapons in a ground sheet and carefully hid them under a rotting log. If he found any of his own people alive, the chances were they would need weapons.

With a grim expression on his face, Smoke picked up his rifle and started walking. He was going hunting.

Toni had not moved. But she was so relieved to see Sally that she could not contain her tears. Wiping her eyes, she whispered, "They came so close I thought sure they would see me. I could hear them talking. They were saying vulgar, filthy things about what they would do to the women once they found us. I have never heard such disgusting things."

"They're not going to do anything to us," Sally assured her. "Put these jeans on while I go through the supplies I brought back. Go on, Toni, do it."

So they searched this area, Sally thought. *Good. Maybe they won't be back.*

But deep inside, she knew they would. And the search would be much more thorough this time, probably with men on foot. But she didn't share that with Toni.

Clint Black stood in the big family room of his house and glared at his foreman, Jud Howes. He got his temper back under control and took several deep breaths. "You're certain that none of the bodies found were those of women?"

"Positive, boss. We checked real close. All men and boys."

"And the bodies have been disposed of?"

"They'll never be found."

"What'd you do with them?"

"Put 'em in Jackson's Cave. Way back in there. I'll take dynamite up there later and seal the entrance."

"That's good. But be sure that you do that, Jud. The cattle?"

Jud shook his head. "They're scattered from one end of that valley to the other, boss. It'll take every hand we got a good two-three weeks to round them all up."

"We'll deal with that problem later. Just be sure that no one enters that area until we're done."

"Right, boss. I've got them covered."

"Get every hand we can spare in there. Search that area, find those damn people, and kill them."

"Right, boss. One thing puzzles me, though. Some of the guys we found didn't have no pants on."

"Probably didn't have time to pull them on, don't you imagine?"

"Yeah . . . we hit 'em hard and fast, for a fact."

"Get busy, Jud. Let's wrap this thing up and put it behind us."

Smoke rested the rest of that day and tended to his wounds and bruises. There was a bottle of horse liniment in the dead raider's saddlebags—the one with a busted head—and Smoke treated his bruises with that. He bathed his splinter wound and bound it with a strip of the dead man's shirt, once it had dried after Smoke washed it in the stream. One of the night herder's horses had found him, seeking human company, and Smoke found a pair of fresh socks and some .44 rounds in the saddlebags. As soon as the sun went down, Smoke went on the prod.

He had caught the smell of food cooking and decided he'd drop in for a bite . . . uninvited. He wanted a cup of coffee in the worst way.

And he wanted to spill some Circle 45 blood.

He put Sally as far out of his mind as he could. It wasn't a heartless act on his part, it was just practical.

He could hear the lowing of cattle from various parts of the valley, some faint, some no more than two hundred yards off. The cattle were probably scattered all to hell and gone. Smoke left the timber and fell in with a small bunch of cattle, slapping a few on the rump to get them moving in the direction he wanted to go. He got in the center of the bunch and crouched low.

When he drew close to the dot of flames from the campfire, he left the cattle and moved into the timber. He began huffing and coughing like a puma. The sound was so real it scared the cattle and they ran off a few hundred yards. Smoke used their noise to work close to the camp.

"Damn painter out yonder," a man said. "And close too."

"He won't come near the flames," another said. "Turn that bacon, Wilson. I'll give these beans a stir."

"You hope he don't come close," another said.

Smoke had pinpointed the raider's fires. The nearest one to his location was a good two miles away. Smoke moved in closer. Four men sat around the fire. A real stupid thing to do, for it destroyed their night vision. But that didn't make any difference, for in about thirty seconds, the only thing they'd be seeing was Hell.

He lifted his rifle and let it roar, working the action as fast as he could. When the roaring was only an echo, Smoke was running toward the fire and the food and the dead and dying bodies. He stripped the bodies of weapons and ammo.

One was still alive. "Damn your eyes!" he groaned.

Smoke, normally not a profane man, told the dying raider what he thought of men who would kill boys and women. The venom in his words shocked the man. Then, as the raider lay bleeding and dying by the fire, Smoke took two thick slices of bread, made a sandwich of the bacon and dug into the beans, then calmly poured himself a cup of coffee.

"You ain't human!" the raider managed to gasp the words.

Smoke threw back his head and howled like a great gray wolf, the howling echoing around the valley. Another wolf across the valley joined in the night's chorus as the raider lay on the ground, his eyes wide in astonishment.

Smoke huffed and coughed like a puma and then smiled at the man. But he was smiling at a dead man. Smoke dumped the weapons on a ground sheet, bundled it up, and taking the pot of beans and the bread, vanished into the night.

A mile away, Sally smiled. "That first call was no wolf," she told Toni. "That was Smoke. He's *alive!*"

Jud was the first to reach the death scene. He looked at the four men sprawled in their own blood and cussed.

"Jud," a Circle 45 hand said. "They was cookin' beans when I was over here."

"So what?"

"The pot's gone. Whoever done this took their guns and the bean pot."

"I think we're in trouble, Cleon. Big trouble. I don't think that body Fatso thought was Jensen was really him. I think Jensen's out yonder. I think that was Jensen howlin' like a lobo."

"He ain't but one man, Jud. And we got fifty men."

"Forty-six," Jud quietly corrected.

Seven

Harvey and Jeff had heard the gunshots and then the howling of a lobo wolf. They had looked at each other and smiled. They'd been with Smoke a long time, and they'd both heard him talk to the wolves and the pumas many times. They snuggled back into their hiding place. The raiders didn't know it, but they were in trouble.

Sally lay back on the ground sheet and smiled as she snuggled into her blanket. Her man was alive and on the prowl. The Circle 45 men had grabbed onto something they couldn't turn loose of. And they were about to find that out . . . in blood. Their own.

Smoke returned to his hidden camp and ate the beans, sopping out the juice with the bread. He wished he had another cup of coffee, but a man can't ask for everything.

Jud Howes was riding hard for the ranch. Clint had to be informed of this new development. With Jensen alive, that really put a fly in the ointment. Jud had heard about that crazy German fellow who'd chased Smoke all over the country—with a passel of hired gunslingers helping him—hunting Jensen like you would an animal. Smoke had turned the whole thing around and the hunters became the hunted in the deadliest game they'd ever found themselves in. Jensen won.

"Damn!" Jud said. "I wish that fool Baylis had stayed down in Wyoming and kept his mouth shut."

Denver eased his bruised body and smiled when he heard the wolf howling and the gunshots. He had him a hunch that Smoke Jensen was alive and well and on the prod. He just hoped that Miss Sally and those other two women were all right.

Smoke rolled up in his blankets and went to sleep. Tomorrow was going to be a busy day.

Just as gray was tinting the skies, Smoke took his rifle and eased down toward the valley floor. He'd picked out a good location the past afternoon and planned on really getting this war underway.

His anger and grief and sadness were buried deep within the man, the coals banked, kept hot and smoldering. Today was the day he was going to show Clint Black and his renegade hands that wars are not that easily won.

He just wished he knew whether Sally was alive or dead.

Harvey held the limb back with his good arm, but if that rider didn't come on, he was going to have to turn loose; his arm was trembling from the strain.

The Circle 45 hand looked around, was satisfied that this area was clean, and rode on. Harvey released the thick limb and the green, springy wood impacted with the raider's face. Harvey cringed as the sound of bones and teeth breaking came to him. The thick limb had caught the Circle 45 hand smack in the mouth, knocking him out of the saddle, knocking him unconscious, and smashing his face.

Harvey grabbed the reins and calmed the spooked horse. He limped over to the unconscious raider and ripped off his gunbelt, slinging it around his waist. He took the Winchester from the boot and removed the saddlebags and canteen. He turned around and almost messed his longhandles when he saw a man standing a few yards away. The Colt leaped into his hand and he almost killed a friend.

"Whoa, Harvey!" Tim said in a hoarse whisper. "For God's sake, man, don't shoot."

"Jesus, Tim. I'm sorry, boy." He holstered the Colt.

The men grinned and shook hands. "You alone?" Tim asked.

"Got Jeff with me. He's got a slug in his leg. But I don't think it's broke. Come on, help me tie this no-count in the saddle."

They took the raider's blanket and groundsheet, tied him belly across the saddle, and slapped the horse on the rump. The animal went bumping out of the timber and loping across the meadow.

"As many tracks as there is out yonder," Tim said, "they'll have a time tryin' to track that horse back to us. You got a good hole to hide in?"

"You bet. Come on."

Jeanne pulled back into a thicket as the search intensified. Once the searchers came so close she could have reached out and touched the leg of a horse. She was still badly frightened, but that fright had been tempered by anger and a strong resolve to survive. She knew nothing of guns, but if she could get her hands on a weapon, she would by God learn. What had happened and what was happening to her and the others was an outrage that she was not going to tolerate. She knew from listening to the raiders talk that her sister and Sally were alive. She knew that Smoke Jensen was alive and fighting back. She knew that some other cowboys had not been found. So that meant they had a chance of surviving this terrible act of . . . of what? She didn't know why Clint Black had done this. Could think of no logical reason.

She fought back tears.

Smoke sighted the rider in and the Winchester roared. It was a righteous hit, the slug knocking the Circle 45 hand from the saddle. The man did not move. Smoke bellied down and waited. It was not a long wait.

Three Circle 45 riders came pounding to the scene, which told Smoke they didn't have a whole lot of sense. Smoke emptied two of those saddles before the third one could lay on his horse's neck and get the hell gone from that place.

Smoke ran down the slope, ripped gunbelts from the three and gathered up the reins and ran back up the slope into the timber. He quickly roped the horses together, mounted up, and changed locations, moving about a mile before he once more left the saddle and got into position behind some rock, an earthen embankment behind him.

"Mr. Smoke?" the boy's voice came from behind him.

Smoke turned his head and looked up into the pale face of Bobby, peering over the lip of the embankment.

Smoke grinned at the boy. "You're pretty good, Bobby. Not many men could have injuned up on me."

"I didn't, sir," the lad admitted. "I was layin' up here watchin'. I got Louie, Dan, Sonny, and Guy hid out in a blowdown about five hundred yards from here."

"Good! Good! Take those guns I've got looped on the saddle horns and those canteens and food and bedrolls. Get back in there and stay put. Don't use those guns unless the night riders are right up on you and there is no way out. I know where you are, now, and I'll be back. We'll get out of this, Bobby. I promise you."

"Yes, sir, Mister Smoke. I'm gone."

"Get the men out of there," Clint told his foremen. "We're losing too many hands to that damn Jensen. He's turned into a savage. Get them all out and plug up the passes. Hell, we can keep them in there forever."

Jud wasn't too sure about that, but he wasn't running this show. He pulled out his pistol and fired the pre-arranged signal. From his hidden position, Smoke watched the hands stop, listen to the shots, then turn and ride toward the north end of the long valley.

"Your boss doesn't have much taste for the battle," he said aloud, then stood up. "Dirty, low-down, cowardly, ambushing son of a bitch!" he added.

Jeanne rose up to her knees just as the unshaven lout spotted her and opened his mouth to yell. She threw the butcher knife with all her strength, with no hope of doing any damage to the rider.

The knife turned slowly in the air and an astonished Jeanne watched as the blade buried itself in the rider's shoulder. He dropped his six-gun and yelled, the scream startling the horse. The animal took off like a lightning bolt, the rider holding on. Jeanne ran to the gun, picked it up, and cocked it. Holding it with both hands, she pointed it and pulled the trigger.

The slug just nicked the horse on the butt and he pitched his rider; the Circle 45 hand landed on his head, breaking his neck. Jeanne ran to the man; fighting back waves of nausea at the sight of the corpse, she jerked off the man's gun belt and ran back into the timber.

"Missy!" The call turned her around, bringing up the pistol.

Jeanne started weeping tears of joy at the sight of Denver, hobbling painfully toward her. "Oh, my God!" she cried.

"Hush, now, Missy," Denver soothed her. "We're all right. We made it. Them hands done been called back to the barn, so to speak. Smoke's been raisin' hob and hell with 'em. I think I know where he is. Come on."

"Let's go, boys," Smoke called from the saddle. "Let's see who is left alive. Ride single file, behind me and keep your eyes open."

Jeff, Harvey, and Tim hailed them from the timber and Smoke swung down and got Jeff into the saddle. They moved on toward the ambush site.

Sally had heard the signaling shots and watched as the riders gathered on the floor of the valley and pulled out. She walked back to Toni. "They're all leaving, Toni. Come on. Let's get back to the ambush site."

"Why?"

"Because that's where Smoke will expect to find me. Come on, Toni. We made it."

Smoke and Sally held on to each other for a long moment. Then they pulled back and smiled for a second. Sally sobered her smile.

"This is all that survived?" she asked, cutting her eyes.

"Yeah. We lost thirteen all told."

"The boys?"

"Willie, Jake, and Rabbit. They dragged Rabbit."

Denver cussed, low and long. For all his grousing, he liked the boys, and had let Rabbit swipe a cookie ever now and then when Rabbit thought he wasn't looking.

Smoke said, "The cattle trampled Eton. I recognized him by a boot. The herd got Willie. He was wearing overalls. Duke had been shot a dozen times, in the back."

Jeff and Harvey loaded their pistols up full and closed the loading gate. Tim continued pushing cartridges into his Winchester.

"Shorty made a stand of it, and he probably got lead in a few of them. Davy took a slug through the head. Johnson made a fight of it. Nate and Little Ben fought them to the end."

"I found Jake's body," Sally said somberly. "They shot him in the belly. He died hard."

"I found one of the men," Jeanne said. "I changed into his clothing. I'm sorry. I didn't know his name. Only his face."

"He'd be honored to have you wearin' his duds, ma'am," Tim said.

"We found several cases of food, boss," Denver said. "I reckon them raiders didn't do a good job of searchin'. And I dragged the big coffee pot out and we'll have some coffee directly."

"Good. You boys scrounge around and see what pots and pans you can come up with. Tim, ride over to that little bunch of cattle over there," he pointed, "and cut one out and butcher it. We'll have steaks, if nothing else. Sally, take a look at my shoulder and then we'll cut the slug out of Jeff's leg."

"Why?" Jeanne asked him, while Sally was cleaning out and redressing the splinter wound, and washing out the bullet groove in his scalp. She had never seen so many muscles on a man. The man's upper torso was huge. "Why did they attack us. Why?"

"To kill you, get the cattle, and then take possession of your ranch. By the time your Eastern attorneys got

70

wind of your deaths, and that might take months, and found their way out here, everything would be settled. False bill of sale, the whole bit."

"The man is *mad!*" Toni said.

"No. He's not crazy. He's just ruthless and greedy. Clint probably thinks he's got us trapped in here. But there are ways out he doesn't know of." Smoke smiled. "A cowboy will explore as long as he can do it sitting in leather," he spoke to the twins. "But walking for long distances is not something he's real fond of doing. They'll have the north and south ends guarded. They'll be guarding the trail that you ladies used coming in. And they'll have that notch over there on the other side guarded." He pointed across the valley. "But there are other ways in and out. We just have to find them."

"And you are confident that you will be able to do that?" Jeanne asked.

Smoke's smile was brief and savage. "I'm confident that I will find a way out this valley. I'm confident that I will get us out. And I am confident that I will kill the dirty son who ambushed us."

"Coffee's ready," Denver called.

"I found our saddles!" Guy called from the edge of the timber. "Them raiders wasn't gonna burn no good leather. They was gonna keep them for personal use. Includin' all our saddlebags."

"One more mistake Clint made," Smoke muttered.

"You damn fool!" Clint's brother raged at the man. "Don't you realize what you've done?"

Clint lazily lifted a hand and waved it off.

"No, Clint," the sheriff corrected. "You can't wave this off. The times and the ways may have changed somewhat in the West, but the treatment of women has

71

not. You even had four of your rowdies ride out when you told them of this ambush. Oh, I don't think they'll talk about it. They were loyal to the brand. But you've put something into motion that's like an avalanche. It can't be stopped; it's got to come crashing down and run its course."

"You worry too much," Clint said, pouring a fresh cup of coffee. Harris waved off the offer of coffee.

"Smoke Jensen! My God, man! Of all the herds to strike at, you picked one belonging to Smoke Jensen."

Clint looked at his brother. "You know him, Harris?"

"Not personal. But I saw him in action one time down in Colorado. The man is awesome. He's fearless. There ain't a nerve in his body. You can't beat him with guns. You can't beat him with fists . . ."

"I have never seen the man I couldn't stomp into the ground," Clint replied coldly.

"Don't try Smoke Jensen," his brother warned. Harris shook his head. "I thought we agreed the lawlessness was to end?"

"You goin' soft on me, brother?" Clint asked the question quietly.

"You know better. But times are changing and you're not changing with them. I say that in ten years we'll be a state. And with that comes a state police force and better law enforcement." He rose from his chair and paced the room. "I don't know how we can cover this up, Clint."

"We kill the rest of them in the valley," the rancher said. "It's simple."

Harris turned from the window to stare at his brother. "Women and boys, Clint? No. This ends now. You . . ."

Clint flew into a rage. He jumped from his chair and stalked across the large room to face his brother. "Goddamn you! Don't you be givin' no orders to *me*. I put you in office, I . . ."

"The *people* elected me, Clint," Harris corrected. "Yeah, yeah, you hung this badge on me years back. But then we held elections, and the *people* voted on who they wanted to be their sheriff. And they chose me. It's taken me ten years to weed the deputies loyal to you out of my department. But I did it. And now, you, by God, are going to listen to me. I'll cover for you just this one time. Then it's over. I'll not cover for you again."

Brothers stood toe to toe and eyeball to eyeball for a very long moment. Finally Clint grunted and winked. He walked back to his desk and sat down. "All right, Harris. Lay it out."

"I'm taking a posse out to the valley. This afternoon. All your rowdy hands had better be gone from the passes. Where were the bodies dumped?"

"I don't know what they done with them," Clint lied.

"I'll listen to the survivors' stories. I'll probably hear that the brand on the night riders' horses was Circle 45, since you gave me a report stating that a number of horses were stolen from you the other night. I'll apologize to the survivors. Smoke Jensen won't buy it. And he might come lookin' for you. I don't know. But if he calls you out, I won't interfere. The war is over, Clint. The lawlessness is over. I won't stand for it. I never liked your high-handed and roughriding ways. You're not the Almighty, no matter what you think. I've got a tarnish on my name just from being your brother. I'm going to clear my name, as best I can. Seeing you behind bars won't bring back the dead out there in that valley. Those . . . boys that came along for a summer's adventure. I don't see how you sleep at night. I can't undo what you and your men have done. But I can, by

God, see that it never happens again. And I mean it, Clint. I mean it. I don't want to have to lock you up. But I will. After this day, I've told the last lie for you. You and me, we're flesh and blood, Clint. But you took a wrong road. You and me, Clint, we took separate trails. And Clint? Don't ever think you're better with a gun than I am. I'll shoot your ears off if you ever drag iron against me."

Harris Black plopped his hat on his head and stalked out of the office. He slammed the door behind him.

Clint Black sat behind his desk, his mouth hanging open. He was very nearly in shock.

Eight

"Riders comin'!" Tim yelled from his lookout post. "Boss, I think it's the law."

"Is this Harris Black as bad as his brother?" Sally asked the twins.

"Some say yes, others say no," Jeanne said.

"He was elected by a clear majority of the people," Toni added.

The sheriff and four tough-looking deputies rode up to the ambush site and dismounted. They all took off their hats in deference to the ladies. They all stared briefly at the ladies dressed in men's clothing.

Sally accurately pegged the sheriff as a man torn between loyalties. A man in a mental quandary. His face was a study.

"Somebody tell me what happened," Harris said.

"That murderous brother of yours sent hooded night riders against us," Toni said. "They stampeded the herd and killed more than a dozen men and boys."

Harris sighed as his deputies exchanged glances, looks that were not lost on Smoke.

"If they were hooded, ma'am," Harris said. "How do you know they were from the Circle 45?"

"By the brands on the horses," Jeanne said.

Smoke and Sally were staying quiet.

"Clint Black reports horses stolen from him the other

night," Harris said. "That might account for it. And I said 'might.' "

Jeanne and Toni snorted quite unladylike.

Harris cut his eyes to Smoke. Lord, but the man looked awesome. He just stood there, big and tough and no backup in him. Harris knew there was no way he could stop the war that was about to start. He wasn't sure he wanted to. "I saw you once or twice. You'd be Smoke Jensen."

"That's right. And the hands that were murdered worked for me. Three of them young boys. It takes brave men to attack women and children. The boys, I'd like to add, were unarmed. I saw to that on the trail."

The sheriff rubbed a big hard hand across his face. That he was in mental pain was obvious to all.

"How did you hear about this, Sheriff?" Sally asked.

"My brother told me," the sheriff replied truthfully.

Smoke sensed that the man had carefully rehearsed this in his mind on the ride out.

"And you intend to do what about it?" Toni asked.

"See that it never happens again. And if it does, it'll be only over my dead body. Now, these deputies will stay out here with you to see to your safety." He tried a smile. "You feed 'em right and they'll probably help you round up your stock and get it over to the Double D. Your place is all right, Miss Toni, Miss Jeanne. I checked on that comin' out."

"Thank you, Sheriff," Jeanne said. "I just may have to revise my opinion of you."

Harris nodded his head. He chose not to reply to that.

Smoke said, "Start rounding up the cattle, boys. Dan and Guy, you'll come with me into town at first light. We'll rent a wagon to haul back supplies."

"The supplies will be paid for, Mr. Jensen," Harris

said. "I've seen to that. Whatever you need, you just pick up and lay on the counter at Hanlon's Emporium. Leather goods and clothing and guns and so forth is waiting for you at shops all over town. There are rooms at no cost for you at the hotel." He didn't tell them his brother was picking up the tab for everything. His brother didn't know it yet.

Smoke and Sheriff Harris Black were left together for a few moments. "You real fond of your brother, Sheriff?" Smoke asked.

"I wonder now if I ever even liked him." He cut his eyes to the man some called the last mountain man. "Why do you ask?"

"Because it's real easy to prove that your brother sent his hands to ambush us."

"He lost some," Harris spoke the words very softly.

"Yeah. And I got them laid real neat, all in a row, about a half a mile from where we're standing."

"Why are you telling me this?"

"So you can take a probably much-needed vacation."

Harris stood silent for a few seconds. "I don't think I like that idea."

"Sheriff," Smoke spoke low, "I can have twenty-five or so of the randiest old gunfighters the West has ever known in here in a week. I can travel about fifty miles from where we're standing and round up just about that many old mountain men—they raised me, Sheriff. Or helped to. You don't think those men would like to go out of this life in a blaze of glory? Think again. My neighbor down in Colorado is Johnny North. The sheriff is Monte Carson. One of my best friends in this world is Louis Longmont. I'm friends with the Mexican gunfighters, Carbone and Martine. Cotton Pickens is a friend of mine. Do you want me to continue with this list, Sheriff?"

"It won't be necessary," Sheriff Black said, some stiffness to his words. He got Smoke's message, very loud and clear.

"What I'm going to do, Sheriff, is this: I'm going into the horse-breeding business. So I think I'll just stick around this part of the country, looking at horses. And while I'm here, I'll just act as the foreman of the Double D. I'll do the hiring. After I send a few telegrams for hands. Hands, Sheriff. Hands. Not gunfighters. Just good steady cowboys who ride for the brand. You know the type, don't you?"

Oh, yes, Harris Black knew the type. Men born with the bark on. Men who were not gunfighters, but who could and would damn sure use a rifle or pistol. Men who rode for the brand and God help anyone who tried to rustle cattle from that brand or who bad-mouthed the owner of that brand. Peaceful men for the most part, men who would give you two day's work for a day's pay. Men who would eat dust, ride through torrential rain or blizzards, work from can to can't, all for thirty or forty a month and grub. The American cowboy. And his brother didn't have a man on his place who could shine a cowboy's boots.

"I figure there are probably two hundred head of cattle, maybe more than that, that were injured so badly in the stampede they'll die or have to be destroyed. I expect your brother to replace every one of them. And make sure that a half a dozen of them are bulls."

The sheriff looked at Smoke for a moment, then shrugged his shoulders philosophically.

"Your brother have many gunslicks on his payroll?"

"Most of them are gunhands. Or fancy themselves as such. I got out of that business before the name stuck to me."

Smoke smiled. "Yeah, I know, Sandy."

Harris cut his eyes and smiled. "I wondered if you'd recognize me. I was hoping you wouldn't."

"It's safe with me. Gunslicks and cattle aren't a good mix. What's your brother doing about branding and roping and night-herding and such?"

"He sold off most of his herd."

"And had plans to seize this one."

Harris's eyes tightened just a bit before he spoke. "Your words, not mine."

"Your eyes gave you away."

"I'm hoping my brother will pull in his horns and get straightened out."

"Too late."

"Why?"

"Because I'm going to kill him, that's why."

The blunt statement from Smoke had shocked Harris. He was still thinking about it as he rode back to town. Blood was thick, yes, but on the practical side of it, he could not be angry with Jensen for going after his brother. His brother had plotted the coldblooded murders of over a dozen men and boys, and had planned on killing three women.

That was inexcusable and unforgivable in a country where even a careless remark to a lady or a slight jostling of a woman on the street could culminate in a killing.

It had been the matter-of-fact and careless way Smoke had stated his intentions that had shocked Harris. He had spoken the words with no more emotion than if he had said he was going to kill a rattlesnake.

Well, the thought came to him, his brother could be compared to a rattlesnake, he supposed.

He was still ruminating on the subject when he swung down in front of his office. His one remaining deputy in town was sitting on the bench on the board-walk.

"Jensen gonna come hell for leather, Sheriff?" the deputy asked.

"No," Harris said, sitting down. "But he is going to kill my brother. He told me so."

The deputy took his time rolling a cigarette. He lit it and said, "That's something that's past due."

Harris looked at the man. He could not even work up a slight anger at the words. Not anymore. He knew how true they were. But it did hurt just a little. His baby brother.

He had been in another part of the west when Clint came into this area, and Harris still had never found out where and how his brother had started his empire. Probably with stolen cattle . . . and killings.

Harris had accepted the badge he now wore because he felt his brother was an honorable man. It didn't take him long to see how wrong he was. But still he stuck it out while the town and the country grew, turning his back on his brother's schemes and cheating and the night-riding of his men. Finally Harris had told him, "No more. No more burning out of farmers and small ranchers. It's over."

And surprisingly, it had stopped. But by then, Clint had grown so wealthy and powerful and land-rich that he could afford to stop it.

Now this . . . disgrace.

He stood up from the bench. "Pitiful sight out there, Harry. Make a man's blood run cold. And Jensen killed about a dozen of Clint's men. Had them all stretched out neat and in a row for me to see. No question that Clint was behind it. Then he looked at me with those

80

cold rattlesnake eyes and told me flat out he was going to kill my brother."

"And you said . . .?"

"Nothing. I just walked off. I never met a man like Jensen before. And you can believe I've known some damn salty ol' boys in my time. I've covered up a lot for Clint over the years, but nothing like this. I've never covered up murder. That I know of. He's got all his hands ready to testify that no one left the ranch the night of the raid. And Clint's gonna say that he fired them dead hands a week before the raid. It would be Jensen and them's word against forty or more hands. No court would convict any of them. I don't know what to do, Harry."

"You want a suggestion?"

"I'm open."

"Back off. Don't get in Jensen's way. It's a hard thing to have to swallow, but your brother is no good. Now he's tangled with a man who don't have no backup in him and who's got the wherewithal to stand tough. Don't get caught up in the middle of this."

Harris shook his head. "I'm a poor excuse for a lawman, Harry."

"That's not true," the deputy said sharply. "We've got a good department. Judges have complimented you on your performance. There is a legal word for what you ought to do in this, but I can't think of it right off. It means stay the hell out of it, or get someone else in here to handle it, or something like that."

"I do that, it just proves that I'm not capable of sheriffin' this county. But I think, Harry, there comes a time when the law's got to back off and let men settle their own affairs. There ain't no law against men callin' each other out. Not yet anyways. If that happens, it happens. Tomorrow is gonna be an interestin' day, I'm thinking."

The townspeople gathered on the boardwalks as the line of horses came walking slowly up the street. The bodies of the Circle 45 night riders were tied belly down across the saddles. It was not a pleasant sight and the smell was more than slightly worse. Smoke stopped the grisly parade in the center of town and dumped the bodies in the dust of the street.

The foreman of the Circle 45, Jud Howes, was standing under the awning in front of a saloon. Several of his men stood with him.

"Oh, hell," Harry whispered.

"Yeah," Harris replied. "Me, too."

Smoke stood by the pile of bodies and said to the crowds that lined the streets, "I'm Smoke Jensen. These dead men are, or were, Circle 45 riders. They attacked our camp a couple of nights ago. They killed ten of my men and murdered three young boys. They tried to kill the Duggan twins and my wife. Dispose of the bodies in any manner you see fit."

Smoke turned, spotted the horses wearing the Circle 45 brand, and lifted his eyes to the men in front of the saloon. They were fine animals and the saddles were top quality.

"Who rides these horses?" Smoke called.

"Me and these boys here," Jud said. He was thinking that this just might be his last day on earth.

"Write me out a bill of sale for them. All of them. Including the saddles and the rifles and the ropes."

"Do . . . what?" Jud asked.

"A lot of our stock was killed, run off, or maimed in that ambush the other night. I'm claiming these horses as part of the replacement. Now either write out a bill of sale, or drag iron. Either way. It doesn't make a damn to me."

"We can take him, Jud," a hand called Ron said. "Let's do it."

"Shut up," Jud whispered. "You know what Clint said. All right, Jensen," he raised his voice. "We didn't have nothin' to do with that raid. But if you think these horses will help make up for your loss, you're welcome to them."

"I'll be damned!" Ron said. "I paid Clint a hundred and fifty dollars for that roan. That ain't no rough string horse. That's mine! And you can go to hell, Jensen."

Smoke shot him. His draw was so smooth and quick it was not possible for the human eye to follow. The slug took Ron in the center of the chest and he was dead before he hit the boardwalk. His hand had not even closed around the butt of his .45.

"Good God!" Harry whispered.

"And I thought I was fast," Harris said.

"Your play," Smoke said to Jud. He had slipped his .44 back into leather.

"I said you could have them horses, Jensen," Jud replied, his voice husky from shock. He had never seen anyone draw a gun that fast. "Soon as I can find pen and paper, I'll write out a bill of sale."

"That's good. And you boys are gonna walk back to the Circle 45."

"We gonna do what?" a hand named Cleon asked.

"I said you're going to walk back. Because no one in this town is going to sell or loan you a horse. Now write out that bill of sale and start hoofin' it. Now!"

A shopkeeper came up with a tablet and a pen and ink. With a smile, he handed them to Jud. The smile infuriated Jud, but he wisely said nothing about it.

Smoke couldn't hang around forever. Their day would come. He wrote out the bill of sale, waved the paper dry, and held it out to Smoke.

Smoke stepped forward, took it, inspected it, and then said, "Start walking."

"What about Ron?" Jud asked, pointing to the dead night-rider.

"He'll be taken care of," Smoke told him. "And your boss will receive the bill for the burying. Now unbuckle your gun belts and let them fall. We lost guns in the raid, too. Do it and then move out."

The astonished and mostly amused townspeople watched as the Circle 45 men dropped their gun belts and slowly stepped off the boardwalk and began the long trek back to their range. There would be several gunslicks soaking their blistered feet that night.

The undertaker strolled up and began measuring Ron for a box.

Smoke turned to face the sheriff. "You said something about wagons to haul the supplies back?"

"Down at the livery," Harris replied. "You do have a way of getting your point across, Smoke."

"Yeah, I do, don't I?"

Nine

Smoke walked into Hanlon's Emporium where the boys, Dan and Guy were waiting for him. A nervous Hanlon was behind the counter.

"That was some shooting there, Mr. Jensen," Hanlon said. "Yes, sir. That's something I can tell my grandchildren about, for sure. Anything in the store you want, sir, you and your hands just lay it out here on the counter and it's all taken care of. Yes, siree."

Smoke had taken all the raiders' guns, so they were high on guns and ammo and low and out of everything else. It didn't take long to fill the bed of the wagon.

"Charge it all to my brother's account, Hanlon." Sheriff Black spoke from the door.

"Yes, sir, Sheriff. I'll certainly do that."

Harris walked in and got him several crackers from the barrel and cut off a wedge. He looked at Smoke and held out the crackers and cheese.

"Yeah," Smoke said. "And the boys too." He smiled. "Since your brother is buying."

Harris laughed and cut two enormous slices for the boys and a smaller slice for Smoke. "Pickles in that barrel, boys," he said. "Help yourselves."

Smoke had noticed two hands lounging out front. "You know those fellows, Sheriff?"

"Oh, yeah. That's Ted and Stony. Good punchers and

they ride for the brand. They're out of work."

"They can be trusted?"

"They hate my brother," Harris said simply.

"That's good enough for me." Smoke walked to the door, digging in his pocket for folding money. "You boys looking for work?" he asked the pair.

"You bet we are, Mr. Jensen. I'm Stony and this terrible-lookin' feller with the mop of red hair is Ted."

Smoke handed them each fifty dollars. Their eyes widened. "That's a bonus just for going to work for me and after I'm gone, sticking with the Duggan twins at the Double D. Can you use those guns you're wearing?"

"We can hit what we're shootin' at, Mr. Jensen," Ted said. "But we ain't gunhands."

"That's fine. You got horses?"

They both looked embarrassed and Smoke knew they were down on their luck. They were young, probably in their mid-twenties, but fate had dealt them a hard hand. "We had to hock our saddles just to eat, Mr. Jensen. And we ain't done that in two days."

"Get yourselves some cheese and crackers and a pickle. Cut off a wedge for the trail while you're at it. Clint Black is paying for this treat."

A wicked glint sprang into the eyes of both young punchers at that news.

"Then go down to the livery and rope out what you think you can ride. After that, ride escort for these boys and drive those horses with the 45 brand back to the valley." He handed them the bill of sale. "Pull the rig of that puncher I just shot off his horse and one of you use that. There are plenty of other rigs over across the street."

"Why don't we just ride the 45 horses?" Ted suggested.

Smoke had anticipated that. He shrugged massive

shoulders. "You can if you want. But there might be trouble in the days ahead."

They both smiled. "I 'spect there will be," Stony said. "But we'll face that when the time comes."

"Fine. Get yourselves something to munch on."

Sally, Toni, and Jeanne had handed him a shopping list . . . for new jeans and men's work shirts. If they ever rode into town decked out like that they'd scandalize the territory—and they probably would ride in just like that. Do it for pure spite.

The wagon was going to be groaning and squeaking when it pulled out.

"You're not riding back with the wagon?" Harris asked.

"No."

"You're crowding, Smoke. You know that?"

"I sure do."

"What if my brother comes riding hell for leather into town with about forty hands while you're here?"

"Be a hell of a fight."

"You'd fight forty men!"

"If they pushed me to it."

Exasperated, the sheriff stalked away, muttering to himself. Smoke watched him go, smiled, and then stepped across the street to the saloon. As soon as he entered, men, women, and small boys and girls crowded the boardwalk, peeping through the windows of the saloon. Actually, he planned on leaving shortly after the wagon. He just liked to needle Harris Black. Basically, Smoke felt the man was a decent sort. He just had a bastard for a brother, that's all. And blood was thicker than water. Smoke thought it best to bear that in mind.

He drank a beer and left, walking up to the doctor's office. He'd dug the slug out of Jeff's leg, and there was no sign of any infection, and he'd set Harvey's arm—the man refused to come in and see the doctor. Said he didn't trust them. Smoke wanted some medical supplies just in case. While he was there, he had the doctor look at his shoulder. It was healing nicely and nearly all of the soreness was gone.

The doctor insisted upon checking Smoke's head where the bullet had grazed him. He looked disgusted when he found the slight wound was nearly healed.

"You have amazing recuperative powers, Mr. Jensen."

Smoke gathered up his medical supplies and was walking back to his horse when he heard the thunder of hooves. He stowed the supplies in the wagon and stepped up onto the boardwalk in front of the emporium.

"His Majesty, himself," Stony said, rolling a cigarette. "Lord of the county and all you can see. Clint Black and some of his gunslicks."

"I can't stand to see a man abuse a horse that way," Smoke said. "No need in it. Any man who'd deliberately abuse an animal is a no-good."

"Clint likes to shoot dogs," Ted said. "Just for the hell of it. I had me a little mutt when I worked for him. He killed it. I hate that son of a bitch."

Harris Black and his deputy suddenly appeared, walking up the boardwalk, both of them carrying sawed-off shotguns. Takes a mighty foolish man to go up against a sawed-off, and the sheriff knew it.

Clint Black jerked and fought the reins and came to a dusty halt facing the men on the boardwalk. His own riders left and right of him.

Smoke fanned the dust. "You always this inconsiderate of other people, Black?" he asked.

Clint ignored that. "I found my men hoofing it back to the ranch. You're Jensen, aren't you?"

"Yeah, Black, I'm Jensen. And yeah, I took your

hands' horses. Got a clear title to them. And yeah, I put lead in some loudmouth named Ron."

"That's it!" Harris said, cocking both hammers to the shotgun. "There will be no trouble in this town. Damn you, Clint. I sent a note for you to stay clear of Blackstown. I know you can read, 'cause mother taught us."

"Me? You order *me* to stay clear. I built this town, damn you. I brought the people in. I brought the stage in. I *own* the bank."

"Oh, that's something else that slipped my mind, Sheriff. You met my wife, Sally? Well, she is a woman of considerable wealth. Comes from a long line of bankers. And the Duggan twins, you know, I'm sure, are quite wealthy. So we decided, last evening, that this town needs another bank. That empty building right over there will do nicely, I'm thinking. I've got to send a wire off and start making arrangements." Actually, nothing of the kind had been discussed. But it would be discussed at length that night. And Smoke knew Sally would jump at it and in all likelihood, so would the Duggan twins.

Clint looked like he was working himself up into a good case of apoplexy. His eyes were bugging out and his face was turning red.

"Why are your ears red?" Smoke asked him.

"My ears are not red!" Clint yelled.

"Oh, yes, they are," Smoke said. "Don't you think the man's ears are red, boys?"

"Sure are," Stony said. "Look like two little jugs of beets." He stared. "Well, maybe not so little."

"Red as can be," Ted said. "Looks plumb funny to me."

"Both of you saddle bums shut up. Another bank!" Clint yelled. He sputtered for a moment. "You can't do that."

89

"Who is going to stop me?" Smoke asked in a calm tone of voice. "You?"

"Back off, Clint," Harris said in a warning tone. "If another bank wants to come in, there is nothing you can do about it. Is that understood?"

The citizens of the town had gathered left and right of the confrontation. Those in front and back of the volatile situation had cleared out, getting away from the line of fire. Stony and Ted stood left and right of Smoke, the three of them facing Clint and his dozen or so rowdies.

"How's the feet of your de-horsed boys?" Smoke asked the rancher, smiling as he spoke.

"Don't worry about it," Clint replied, regaining what composure he had left him, which was very little when he didn't get his way in any given situation. "I hear you're accusin' me of raidin' your camp. I didn't have a thing to do with that, Jensen. And if you say I did, you're a damn liar."

"I say you did, Black," Smoke told the man and everybody else who was close enough to hear. "I say you gave the orders to kill men, women, and kids. And that makes you snake-low and dirty. You don't have the nerve to do your own fighting. You're a coward, Black. Step out of that saddle and fight me. Right here and now."

The sheriff walked between the men. He put his back to Smoke and faced his brother. "Take your men and get out of town, Clint. Right now. Leave now or I'll put you in jail."

"On what charge?" Clint asked. He wanted to leave, wanted desperately to leave. But how to do that without losing face in front of the townspeople and his men? Clint was many things, but a fool was not one of them. After getting a good look at Jensen, Clint, for the first time since he was a boy, had experienced fear. And he hated himself for it.

"Refusing to obey the orders of a peace officer," his brother told him. "Now take your men and leave. Jensen, you do the same. And do it right now."

"All right," Smoke said. He looked at Clint. "Some other time, Black. Let's go, boys."

With his brother and his men heading in one direction, Smoke and his hands going in another, Harris eased the hammers down on his sawed-off and his deputy relaxed.

"All you did was put it off for another time," the deputy said. "It's bound to come."

"Yeah, I know," Harris said. "But I got it out of town." He stepped back, leaned the shotgun against the building, and rolled a cigarette. "My brother was scared this day," he remarked, lighting up. "I saw fear on his face."

"Hell, who wouldn't be scared?" The deputy bit off a chew from a plug. "Jensen would have been killed, for sure, but he would have emptied eight or ten saddles before he went down. A man that size can take a lot of lead."

"What bothers me is that a scared man will do desperate things, Harry. My brother took water this day. I gave him a way out, but he still took water. He was shamed this day, and he'll not forget it. He was always a vain and a vengeful person."

"Well . . . like you say, we got it out of town."

Riding back to the valley of death, Smoke asked the new hands, "You boys know of other men who might like a job?"

"I know of a few," Stony said. "And I 'magine Ted

91

knows of several." Ted nodded his head.

"OK. You two veer off now and find them. I'm offering top wages and the best food you ever put in your mouth." He dug in his pocket and handed Stony a wad of bills.

Stony looked at the money and whistled. "How do you know we won't just take that money and clear out, Smoke? That's two years pay for most hands."

Smoke grinned. "I'm a good judge of character, Stony. See you boys later on."

The new hands headed off, leaving Smoke and the boys and the heavily laden wagon. "Ol' Waymore hates Clint Black," Stony said. "He'd jump at this chance."

"You bet," Ted agreed. "And I was thinkin' 'bout Rich and Malvern."

"They'll do to ride the river with. How about Paul and Cletus?"

"Suits me. Say, I just remembered something. Jud accused Joe Owens of stealin' that time. Pistol-whipped him."

"Yeah. And Joe never stole nothin' in his life. His shack ain't a mile from here."

"I think we got the makin's of a pretty good crew and don't none of 'em live more'un a half hour away. We could be back in time for supper."

"Let's go round 'em up, then. I'm hungry!"

Ten

Stony and Ted showed up at the camp in the valley just at sundown. They brought with them the most disreputable-looking bunch of men Toni and Jeanne had ever seen. Sally had lived nearly all her adult life in the West, and she knew that appearances could be very deceiving out here. She suspected these new men were top hands who, for whatever reason, had been blackballed for employment in this area by Clint Black. Turned out she was right.

"We just didn't cotton to takin' orders from the likes of Clint Black and Jud Howes and that pack of gunslingers they got workin' out on the Circle 45," Waymore said, accepting a plate of food.

"They's other smaller ranches scattered all over this country," Cletus added. "But Clint's got them buffaloed. Didn't none of them dare hire us. We don't hold no grudges against them for it. Man has his entire life put into a small spread, well, he can't stand up to a rich and mean person that has forty or fifty gunslicks on the payroll. Or men who fancy themselves slick with a short gun."

"Mighty good grub," Malvern said. "Best I think I ever eat."

"When was the last time you did eat, Mr. Malvern?" Toni asked.

"Just Malvern, ma'am. Mal for short. Oh, I been

eatin' regular. Seems as how one of Mr. High and Mighty Clint Black's cows wandered over to my place and fell down. Broke its leg and I had to put the poor thing out of its misery. It was the Christian thing to do. I can't stand to see no animal suffer. And it seemed right foolish of me to just let all that meat go to waste. So I butchered it and ate some and smoked and jerked the rest. Then, lo and behold, about a week later, durned if *another* one of Mr. Black's cows didn't come over to my place and fall down. Right in the same spot. Poor thing broke its leg. Well, I had to end its sufferin', so I shot it, too. This has been going on for about six months. Now, since Mr. Big Shot Black has forbid me from ever settin' foot on his land, there just wasn't no way I could get word to him about his cows. It's really put me in a state of confusion." He shook his head. "And I do try to do right by my fellow man, ma'am."

Toni looked at him for a moment, then slowly smiled. "You, Mr. Malvern, tell big whackers."

"Occasional, I do, Miss Toni," Mal said with a grin. "Occasional, deed I do."

The next week went by in a blur of work, with everybody who was able pitching in and rounding up cattle and stampeded horses. Smoke would work until noon and then go off exploring. The bodies of his men had to have been dumped somewhere, and he was determined to find that location.

On the afternoon of the seventh day, he found a boot. Smoke swung down from the saddle and knelt down by the ripped boot. he ran his hand over the dead leaves that were all around it.

Dead leaves? In the middle of summer? He swept

them away and looked at the clear impressions of hooves. Leading his horse, he began following the trail of dead leaves that led upward. Someone had gathered up great handfuls of leaves and scattered them over the tracks. He climbed on. Now he could clearly see the tracks of horses and something else, too: a clear path where bodies had been dragged up this way.

It had gotten back to Smoke that Clint had been saying Smoke had made the attack up. That there were no bodies, so how could have an attack ever taken place?

Smoke began carefully looking around him as he moved along the ridge. Here the trail was harder to follow because of the rocks. Then the smell of death reached him.

He picketed his horse on a small stand of grass and walked on, the smell growing stronger. He could see the mouth of the cave now, and he walked to it. The smell was very nearly overpowering. He picked up a dry branch and tied twigs to the end of it, using some dead vines and then lighting the brand. It would only burn for two or three minutes, but that would be time aplenty.

He stepped into the mouth of the cave and almost lost his lunch. He struggled to keep it down. Smoke walked into the foul semigloom. He did not have to walk far. The first body he found was that of fourteen-year-old Rabbit. Then he saw the others, all piled like garbage. He walked back out into the sweet air. He was sweating and mad clear through. He stood for a moment, composing himself, and then rode back down to the valley, stopping the first hand he found.

"Cletus, ride for town and fetch the sheriff. Tell him I've found the bodies of my men . . . and boys."

It was late afternoon when the sheriff arrived, and growing dark when Smoke pointed out the cave. "I hope you have a strong stomach," Smoke told him. "You're going to need it."

The sheriff and two of his deputies lit torches and stepped inside. Harry came out much quicker than he entered, kneeling by the side of the mouth of the cave and puking.

Harris Black came out. He was badly shaken by what he'd just seen. He leaned against a tree and struggled to regain his composure. Smoke walked over to stand by the man. All work had stopped and everyone was gathered around the cave, as close as they could get without being overpowered by the terrible smell.

"I'll bring Doc Garrett out with me in the morning," Sheriff Black finally said. He refused to meet Smoke's steady gaze. "I want him to see this and write up a report. This is the worst thing I have ever seen. Horrible."

"Maybe this will shut your brother's mouth," Smoke spoke the words harshly.

Harris said nothing.

"You know he's responsible for this, don't you, Sheriff?"

Harris remained silent.

"How long are you going to keep covering for him, Sheriff. How long?"

Harris wiped his sweaty face with a handkerchief, wiped the sweat band of his hat, and plopped it back on his head. "I won't stand for vigilante action, Smoke."

"Oh, I wouldn't dream of that, Sheriff. Your brother has already cornered the market."

* * *

When Dr. Garrett emerged from the cave, he was pale and badly shaken. He had to sit down on the ground for a moment before he could speak. He finally took a shuddering breath and looked up at Smoke and the sheriff.

"I've ordered canvas to be sent out from town. I'll ask for volunteers to help place the bodies on a tarp and wrap them. Once they are out in the light, I will inspect each body more carefully. Then I would suggest they be buried close by. Perhaps on that flat right over there." He pointed. "Their names could be chiseled on the face of that huge rock, or perhaps on the face of the mountain itself. That's up to you." He shook his head. "The bodies are in a terrible state of decomposition. Thirteen men and boys, trampled and shot. My God, it's hideous. It's . . . unthinkable. The man behind this must be mad. Mad, I tell you!"

Sheriff Black opened his mouth to speak, then thought better of it. He turned and walked away.

Dr. Garrett looked up at Smoke. "You're going to start a war over this, aren't you, Mr. Jensen."

Smoke shook his head. "The war has already begun, Doctor. And I didn't start it."

"The families of the men and boys?"

"I've wired them. Services have already been held down home."

"I don't know what else to say or do, Mr. Jensen."

"Time for talk is over. As for what you can do. you can stock up on medical supplies. I think you're going to be treating a lot of gunshot wounds."

Smoke left the rounding up of the cattle in the hands of his men. He kissed Sally and saddled up the next morning. No one spoke to him. No one had to. Nearly everyone in the camp knew what he was going to do. His face was hard and uncompromising as he swung up into the saddle. He pointed his horse toward town and rode off without a look back.

"What is he going to do, Sally?" Jeanne asked.

"He's going to make war," she replied, busying herself washing dishes.

"By *himself?*" Toni asked.

"Smoke Jensen is a one man army, missy," Denver said, drying a plate. "He's tooken on meaner odds than this. 'Sides, this is real personal for him. He feels responsible for what happened to them men; 'specially the boys."

"But if it's anyone's fault, it's ours," Jeanne said.

"No, it ain't neither," Denver said. "And don't you be thinkin' that."

"Denver is right," Sally said. "You had no way of knowing something like this would happen. Neither did we. Only Clint Black and his men had knowledge of it. The responsibility for it lies squarely on their shoulders. I think Sheriff Black is covering for his brother, but I don't believe he knew about the ambush—until after it happened."

"You don't appear worried about your husband," Toni said, looking at Sally.

"Oh, I'm plenty worried about him. But he has to do what he has to do, that's all. I would have been shocked had he not. He's waited a week for the law to do something. The law has done nothing. Now Smoke will see to the administering of justice. The Western way."

There was something about the way he sat his horse, something about his bearing, that cleared the streets of

Blackstown the instant he rode in. Smoke stabled his horse and checked his guns. He had seen horses at the hitchrail in front of the saloon; horses that wore the Circle 45 brand. He walked slowly up the boardwalk. Sheriff Black stepped out of his office, blocking Smoke's way.

"Goin' somewhere, Smoke?"

"To the saloon for a drink. You have some objections to my doing that, Sheriff?"

"Damnit, Jensen. You know there are Circle 45 hands over there."

"It's a free country."

"You know what I mean."

"The services for the dead will be at sundown this evening, Sheriff. You plan to attend?"

"Which dead?" the sheriff asked sourly. "The dead found in the cave or the men you're about to kill?"

Smoke stood and stared at the man. Finally he said, "I waited for the law to act. The law did nothing. You know your brother ordered that ambush. And you know that all the Circle 45 hands either took part in it or had direct knowledge of it. Now you either stand aside, or you help me kill dangerous rabid animals. You really don't want to get in my way, Sandy," he called him by the name the sheriff used back when he was a gunfighter. "The choice is yours to make."

Sheriff Black knew he was not as fast as Jensen. And he also knew that Smoke was right. He was sworn to uphold the law and protect decent, law-abiding citizens, but the words "decent and law-abiding," he knew, did not include his brother or the men working for his brother. The sheriff sighed. "Go stomp on your snakes, Jensen." He turned and walked back into his office, closing the door behind him.

Smoke walked on up the street, then cut across to the

other side, approaching the saloon from the one side that butted up against another building. He pushed open the batwings and stepped inside. Four men sat at a table, drinking beer and playing cards. Everybody else had vacated the saloon at the news of Smoke Jensen riding into town.

Only the barkeep was left, and he was so scared he looked like he was going to pass out any moment.

Smoke put his hand on a chair back and said, "You boys dumb enough to ride a Circle 45 horse?"

The card players sat quietly, their hands on the table. They knew better than to have them by their sides when Jensen walked in, for he was on the prod. "We're ridin' 'em, yeah," one hand said.

"Did you steal them or are you on Clint Black's payroll?"

"We ride for the Circle 45," another said. "And we been ridin' for Clint for a long time."

"Is that a fact?"

"That's a fact, Jensen."

Smoke cut his eyes to the barkeep. "Is there a dentist in this town, friend?"

"Why . . . ah, yeah. There is. Right over the undertaker's place. You got a toothache, Mr. Jensen?"

"No. But this dirty, back-shooting, murderous ambusher here does."

The hand just had time to turn around and say, "Who are you callin' a . . . ?"

Smoke hit him in the face with the hickory chair. Blood and teeth and snot flew. The chair splintered. Holding the back rail of the busted chair, Smoke hit another hand smack in the mouth, then bounced the hickory off the noggin of a third. The fourth jumped up clawing for his six-gun. Smoke hit him right between the eyes with the hickory club and the

100

Circle 45 rider went down like a sack of potatoes.

Smoke grabbed the first one he'd hit and tossed him through the big window. The hand smashed through the hitchrail and landed in the dirt, out cold with several broken ribs. Smoke backhanded another and sent him sprawling, then the third 45 hand staggered to his feet and Smoke sent him sailing out the batwings. Smoke hit another five times in the side, the blows sounding like swinging a sledge hammer against a side of raw beef. Ribs cracked under the blows and the man fell to the floor, moaning in pain.

The one Smoke backhanded came to his feet, his face bloody and ugly and one hand closing around the butt of his Colt. Smoke stepped forward and clubbed the man with one huge fist. Then he grabbed the man's gun arm and broke it by slamming it against the bar. The would-be gunhandler screamed and passed out.

Smoke dragged them outside and threw them in the dirt. Sheriff Black and his deputies stood on the other side of the wide main street and did not interfere. Smoke dunked one in the horse trough several times and got him on his feet. His nose was spread all over his face and his lips were pulped.

"I'll say this one time, mister," Smoke told the man. "You and rest of this trash here ride out of this part of Montana. Go back to the ranch, pack your kit, and ride out—today. If I see you again, I'll kill you where you stand and I won't give you one second's warning. Do you understand all that?"

"Yes, sir," the man mumbled through ruined lips.

"Ride!"

Smoke released the man and the cowboy almost fell down. He managed to get his friends on their feet and on their horses. They left town without looking back.

Smoke went back into the saloon and tossed money

on the bar. "That will pay for the busted window and the chair. Give me a beer."

Smoke was sitting down sipping his brew when the sheriff walked in and over to the table. He sat down and stared at Smoke for a moment.

"You do understand that you just whipped four pretty tough ol' boys?"

"So?"

Harris shook his head. "You think they'll really haul their ashes?"

"They'll either pull out or be buried here. I meant what I said."

"I could wire the territorial governor and have him send the state militia in."

"Go ahead."

"That wouldn't stop you, would it?"

"No."

"You're really going to kill my brother, aren't you?"

"First I'm going to bring him to his knees."

"That will never happen."

Smoke's smile was close to a death's-head. His words were very softly spoken. "You want to bet?"

Eleven

Clint Black sat in the study of his fine home and pondered his future. At the moment, it did not appear to be very bright. He had seen the four punchers come riding in, all beat up to hell and back, and watched as Jud paid them off and they left, that day, taking their broken ribs and busted arms and tore up faces and hauling their ashes out of the country. It had not set well with his other hands.

That Jensen had whipped four pretty rough ol' boys in a fight shocked the rancher. He'd whipped two men at a time more than once. But *four* men! Nobody whips four men at a time. But Smoke Jensen had done it, and then, according to what Clint had heard from spies in town, Jensen just calmly sat down and had him a beer with the sheriff.

He had made a mistake by attacking the camp site. He admitted that. He was sorry he'd done it. He was genuinely sorry about it. But he wasn't sorry enough about it to admit to it in any court of law. Clint certainly was sorry, but not for the right reasons.

So some forty-dollar-a-month cowhands and some snot-nosed kids had been killed. Well, big deal. Clint could buy people like that all day long. They were nothing. Nobodies.

He didn't know what to do. He couldn't admit his

part in the attack. At worst he'd be hanged, at best he'd be run out of the country. And now Jensen had made his brags that he was going to put Clint Black on his knees. Well, that had been tried before. Clint was still standing tall while the men who'd tried to bring him down were rotting in the grave.

And Jensen moved fast. Already carpenters were banging away inside and outside the new First United Bank of Blackstown. And Clint had heard rumblings that most of his depositors were going to pull out once the new bank opened. He sighed heavily. That wouldn't hurt him; the bank was solvent. It was losing face that bothered Clint. Worse than that, it was a slap in the face.

All in all, Clint concluded, Smoke Jensen was becoming a royal pain in the butt.

"What happened to the man who owned this spread?" Smoke asked.

The herd had been rounded up and moved to Double D land. Clint had yet to replace those cattle that had been lost; indeed, nothing had been heard from the man or any of his hands and it was a week past the fight in the saloon.

"Rustlers," Stony told him. "Ever' time he'd get his herd built up, night riders would come in and wipe him out. He finally gave up and sold out. But not to Clint, and that really galled Black. Boss? Have you given any thought to grabbin' one of the Circle 45 bunch and makin' him talk?"

"Torture, Stony? No. For a lot of reasons. It boils down to it'd be his word against forty others. It wouldn't even come to court. I've got all summer. We'll just keep whittling away at Clint. Nipping at his heels and being a splinter in his butt that he can't get to. It'll get to him. He'll eventually lose his temper and make that one big mistake."

"And then, boss?"

"And then he'll face me."

Stony looked at Smoke and felt a chill crawl around in his belly. He knew then for an ironclad fact that his boss had placed a death sentence on Clint Black and meant to carry it out. And Smoke Jensen didn't give a tinker's damn what the law might have to say about it. Jensen was going to angle Clint into a position where he had no back-out room, and then Smoke was going to force-feed him lead.

But first he was going to break Clint Black, slowly and steadily.

Stony shifted his eyes for another look at Smoke Jensen. He had ridden back to the camp after the saloon fight and had not said one word about it. Only after a hand had ridden into town for some tobacco had the word come back. Jensen had walked into the saloon, tossed down the gloves and proceeded to stomp the snot out of four men. Stony hid a smile. Things were sure going to be interesting this summer. Real interesting. And he sure was glad he had stuck around.

Lucas, one of Sheriff Black's deputies, noticed the men ride slowly into town. Six of them. They wore long dusters and rode fine horses. Horses way too costly for the average cowhand to ever afford. Then his half-rolled cigarette was forgotten as he recognized the man on the big, high-steppin' bay. Yukon Golden. He stepped to the office door.

"Harris," he said softly. "I think your brother's done gone and hired himself some real gunslingers. That's Yukon Golden in that bunch reinin' in by the hotel."

With a curse, Harris shoved back from the paperwork at his desk and grabbed his hat. He stepped out onto the boardwalk for a look.

"Bronco Ford," Harris said, eyeballing the six men as they dismounted and stood on the boardwalk in front of the hotel. "He's a bad one."

"You know them yahoos, Harris?"

"I know them all, Lucas. That short stumpy one is Austin Charles. He's hell on wheels with a gun. That's Red Hyde next to him. That long tall drink of water is Slim King. The big one in the bunch is Carson. They call him Grub 'cause he eats all the time. When he's not hiring out his gun to kill people."

"We got trouble."

"Oh, they won't mess with any of us. But they'll sure try Smoke Jensen. The man who kills Smoke Jensen can name his price after that."

"That sorry-lookin' bunch is that fast?"

"They're professional gunhandlers, Lucas. It's how they make their living. Damn my brother. Damn his eyes. He's declared war and he doesn't know what he's begun."

"Harris?"

"Huh?"

"Smoke Jensen's ridin' in."

Harris cut his eyes. "Oh, hell!" he said.

Smoke walked his horse over to the hitchrail and swung down. He had seen the six men lounging in front of the hotel, and his eyes had picked up on the strange brands. He knew the men for what they were. They had the mark on them just as plainly as the brands on their horses.

Smoke stepped up on the boardwalk and nodded at the sheriff and his deputy.

"Trouble over yonder, Smoke," Harris said.

"I see them. Did your brother hire them?"

"I don't know, Smoke. He no longer speaks to me.

But I'd say it would be a safe bet that he sent for those men."

"Then they'll be more coming in," Smoke said. "Men like those over there smell blood money. They've got the damndest pipeline I have ever known. Word gets around like lightning. Your brother's made up his mind."

"To do what?" Harris asked. "Defend his own land? Goddamnit, it's his, Jensen. He settled it and proved it up years ago. You came in here and laid down your challenge. What the hell do you expect him to do?"

"You defending him now, Harris?"

"No. No, I'm not. He did wrong and I know it. But even if I went to a judge and signed a deposition that my brother told me he planned the raid, it's doubtful that the judge would let it be entered as evidence. Yes, Jensen, damn you, yes. My brother admitted to me that he ordered the raid. But it comes down to my word against his. I can't show any solid proof that Clint engineered the ambush. That's the way it stands now."

"I see. Well, you ask what I expected of your brother, now let me ask what you expect of me?"

"Take your wife and what hands you have left and go back to Colorado."

"And let murderers go unpunished?"

"It's not up to you, Jensen!" Harris flared at him. "That's my job, and the judges and the lawyers and the juries. You don't want justice, Jensen. You want revenge. Just like when the Slater gang attacked Big Rock and shot up the place. How many of them did you kill, Jensen?"

"All of them."

"Just tracked them down, one by one, and killed them?"

"We faced each other, Black. You know me that well."

"Suppose . . . suppose I could guarantee you that my

brother would never harm another person? That I would personally see to that. That he would fire his gunhands—his whole crew—hire nothing but cowboys, and stick with ranching his property. If I could convince him to do that, would you leave?"

Smoke took that time to roll a cigarette and light it. He took a draw and said, "Yes. Yes, I would. When he comes to me and faces me and tells me that personally. When he swears to me that the Double D, and all the other ranches in this area will be left alone and I see his hands leave and new men come in, cowboys, I'll leave. You have my word."

"Fine. I think I can get him to agree to that. You meet me here at my office, first thing in the morning."

"I'll be here."

"You've got to be out of your mind," Clint told him. "You want me to apologize to Jensen and crawl around on my belly like a whipped dog? You go to hell, Harris. You just go straight back to town and take your stupid suggestions with you. Just go to hell, Big Brother. And stay out of my affairs."

"You break the law, Clint, you're going to jail. That's a promise."

"You'll never put me behind bars, Harris," his brother warned. "Don't ever try to do that."

"If the time comes, I won't try to do it, Clint. I'll just do it. Clint, think about this offer. Think on it, man. It means peace. Clint, my God, you're a wealthy man. You have all the money you could ever spend. You've got a fine home, great holdings of land. You've got it made! Jensen is willing to ride out and put this . . . tragedy behind him."

Clint shook his head and laughed at his brother. "Sure, Harris. But only after I grovel in the dirt like a bum begging for a handout. No way."

Harris opened his mouth to plead with his brother. Clint's hard words closed it.

"I don't want to hear any more of your sniveling. No more of it, Sheriff Black." He slurred the "sheriff." "Not another word. Leave me alone about it and stay out of my affairs. Now get out of my house, Harris. And don't come back. You hear me? Don't come back!"

"You're a fool, Clint. You're a fool. I don't care how many gunslicks you hire, you're not going to win this fight with Jensen. He'll kill you. He'll break you, humiliate you, and then he'll kill you."

"Get out!" Clint screamed, half rising from his chair. "Get out of my house, goddamn you. Get out, I say!"

Harris picked up his hat and started for the door. He turned around and looked at his brother. "Goodbye, Clint. I used to think that mother and father would be proud of you. They wouldn't be. Ma would have prayed nightly for you, and Dad would have slapped you down to the ground for what you've become. You're a common thief, a treacherous schemer, a cheat, and now a murderer. You're a disgrace to our parents' good names. I'm glad they're dead so they don't have to see this."

"Why . . . you hypocrite!" Clint sputtered the words. "You were nothin' but a goddamn paid gunfighter for years. I dragged you out of the gutter and made you what you are."

"I was never in the gutter, Clint. And yes, I hired my gun. But I never shot a man who wasn't facing me with a Colt in his hand or in his holster. And I never bushwhacked or drew first. Like Jensen, I never had to. And I never harmed a child, or a woman, or killed anyone's pet dog or cat or horse for meanness. Like you've done more than once."

"I don't need a damn sermon from you!"

"I was proud to come be the law in Blackstown, Clint. Chest-swellin' proud. My little brother had made it big. I was so proud of you. I just didn't know at the time how you made it. Then I finally pieced it all together and found out it was by lying and cheating and stealing and . . ." He swallowed hard. "I reckon by murder too. But you kept me out of that. 'Cause you knew I wouldn't stand for it. You dragged my name down in the filth with you, Clint. But I stood by and let you do it. 'Cause we're brothers, I reckon. But this tears it, brother. This is the end of it."

"Who the hell needs some broken-down old gunhawk?" Clint sneered the words at his brother. "You're nothin'. *Nothin'!* You got nothin'. I got it all. Money, the finest wines and whiskeys, all the women I want any time I want them. Hell, you don't even own a decent pair of boots! I got a dozen pair in my bedroom. The finest made. You got nothin', Harris. Holes in your socks, probably."

Harris put his hat on his head and smiled. "You know, Clint, you were almost right about one thing. Only it wasn't the gutter I was in, it was the sewer. A stinking, slimy sewer. And I climbed in it when I went to work for you. But I climbed out, Clint. You're still wallowing around in the filth. You stink of it."

He jerked open the door and left the great room, slamming the door behind him.

Twelve

Smoke took one look at Sheriff Black's face and knew he had failed in his mission to convince his brother to pull in his horns. He said as much as he poured a cup of coffee.

"So I guess the next move is up to you, Smoke," Harris said.

Smoke sugared his coffee and sat down in front of the desk. "I am sorry that you failed, Harris."

"I believe that, Smoke. You could have killed those hands in the saloon. But you were content to hang a pretty fair country butt-whippin' on them and let them go. That tells me a lot about you." He stood up and hottened his own cup of coffee. "One of my men spotted a couple more gunslicks this morning. They avoided town and headed for the Circle 45. It looks like trouble is coming and there is nothing I can do about it."

"I'm going to call your brother out, Harris," Smoke said.

"Yeah. I figured you were. But you're going to wait until he comes to town and make him take water. I told him last night that he couldn't win this fight. That you would humiliate him. He didn't believe me."

"Will he fight?"

"No," Harris said without hesitation. "He's a vain

111

strutting rooster, but he's not a fool. He's not going to pull on you. It would surprise me if he even came to town wearing his gun. I know my brother, Smoke. I don't think he brought — is bringing — those hired guns in here to kill you. I think he's bringing them in to protect himself. From you. He's going to try to wait you out."

"He's got a long wait."

A deputy stuck his head into the office. "Here comes your brother, Harris. And he's got a lot of men with him. Includin' them new-hired gunhandlers."

Harris cut his eyes to Smoke. He knew the man had ridden in alone. The expression on Smoke's face had not changed. Harris didn't think Jensen had one ounce of fear in him.

"They're goin' into the saloon," the deputy reported.

Smoke sipped his coffee.

Harris stared at him for a moment. "Well, damnit, man! What are you going to do?"

Smoke set his coffee cup on the desk and rose from the chair. He smiled at the sheriff. "Why . . . go pay my respects to your brother, of course." He turned and walked out of the office.

"Damn!" The word exploded out of the sheriff's mouth. He rose quickly and took a sawed-off shotgun from the rack, calling for his deputies. "Everybody get a Greener and load it up. I'm not going to have trouble in this town."

Smoke pushed open the batwings and stepped inside the beery-smelling saloon. As Harris had predicted, Clint was not wearing a gun. But those men surrounding him had plenty of six-guns belted around their waists. Smoke unbuckled and untied and hung his guns on a peg of the hatrack. Clint watched him, puzzlement in his eyes. The gunhands exchanged glances, not understanding what was going on.

"Is that a fresh pot of coffee I smell?" Smoke asked the barkeep.

112

"Yes, sir, Mr. Jensen. Just boiled it."

"I'll have a cup with a little sugar in it, please. Down there at the end of the bar."

"Yes, sir."

Smoke paused at Clint's side. "Morning, Clint. Fine day, isn't it?"

Clint grunted and turned his back to Smoke.

"What's the matter, Clint?" Smoke asked. "Didn't you sleep well last night?"

The owner of the Circle 45 turned to face Smoke. "What the hell's that supposed to mean?"

Harris and his deputies had entered the bar, spreading out, all of them with sawed off shotguns in their hands.

"Why . . . I'm just concerned about your health, that's all," Smoke told the man. "You seem a little out of sorts this morning. Maybe you need a good dose of salts."

"Why don't you just mind your own damn business?" Clint replied. "And don't you worry about my health. It's none of your business."

"My, my. How touchy we are." Smoke walked to the end of the bar and picked up his coffee cup and took a sip.

Clint and his hands all ordered either beer or whiskey.

"Alcohol this early in the morning is not good for a body," Smoke chided them all. "I read that in a medical advisor."

"Who the hell cares what you read?" Clint told him, anger in his words. "If I want a drink in the morning, I'll have a drink in the morning." He knocked back his shotglass of whiskey and shuddered as the booze hit his stomach.

"Oh, by all means, go ahead." Smoke sat his coffee cup on the bar. "A man never knows when it might be his last one."

Clint cut his eyes. "What the hell does that mean?"

Smoke shrugged. "Oh, you know how it is out here, Clint. A man's horse might throw him, a snake might

113

bite him, some Indian might leave the reservation looking for a scalp. Lots of things could happen. Have another drink."

"I don't want another drink!"

"Your option." Smoke sipped his coffee. "Mighty good coffee, barkeep. Mighty good. Coffee, now, that's good for a man. Sharpens the senses. Whiskey, now, it fills a man with false confidence. Makes him do foolish things. You're wise not to have but one drink, Clint."

"Gimme another damn drink!" Clint snarled at the nervous barkeep.

"Two whiskeys, now, that probably won't hurt a thing," Smoke said. "Man takes more than two, though, 'specially this early in the day, he's asking for trouble."

"Will you shut up?" Clint yelled.

"I'm not talking to you, Clint," Smoke told him. "I was speaking to the barkeep."

"Well, I'm tired of hearin' your mouth rattle."

"Free country. Of course, if you feel like you're a big enough man to shut me up, come on."

"That's it!" Harris said, moving toward the men. "I'll have no trouble in this town."

"Damnit, Harris, I come in town for a drink and some conversation," Clint said. "I don't have to listen to someone pop off at the mouth."

"Neither one of us is armed, Sheriff," Smoke said. "What trouble could we cause?"

Dr. Garrett had quietly entered the saloon, taking a seat at a far table.

"Of course now," Smoke took it further, "I see all these gunslingers are totin' two guns, at least. Yukon there, I know he carries a .41 derringer in his boot. Slim King's got a knife hung down his back. And a man doesn't ever want to turn his back to Red Hyde, he's a back-shooter . . ."

"By God," Red stepped away from the bar. "You can't call me no back-shooter, Jensen. Git a gun."

114

"I said no trouble!" Harris said. "You, Red, get out of town."

"Me!" Red hollered. "I ain't done nothin'."

A deputy lifted his sawed off, those cavernous muzzles pointed right at Red's stomach.

"All right, all right!" Red said, sweat suddenly beading up on his face. "I'm goin'. But you, Jensen . . . you and me will meet up sometime, and we'll settle this."

"We can settle it now," Smoke said. "With fists. But you won't do that, will you, Red? No. You won't. You're yellow without those guns of yours."

"Smoke . . ." Harris warned.

"That's you, Red. A damn coward."

"You dirty . . ." Red cussed him.

Smoke laughed at him. "Come on, Red. Show everybody how bad you are without those guns. You're afraid to take them off, aren't you, Red. Because you know when you do, the whole roomful of people will see you for what you are: a dirty back-shooting coward!"

Red grabbed for his guns. Deputy Harry Simpson's Greener roared, the buckshot taking Red in the side and almost cutting the man in two. The force of the impacting buckshot lifted Red off his boots and slung him against the bar, splattering bits of Red all over the front of the long bar.

Sheriff Black looked at Smoke while some of the gunhands coughed and struggled to keep down their breakfast at the sight of what was left of Red. "Very neatly done, Smoke," the sheriff complimented him. "Very neat, indeed."

Smoke lifted his cup in a mock salute and finished the coffee.

"What are you talking about?" Clint said.

"How about you, Clint?" Smoke asked from the end of the bar. "Do you have the guts to fight me?"

"That's all for this day, Smoke," Harris warned. "No more of this. I'm ordering you from this town, and you'd better heed that order."

"Fine," Smoke said. "I'm a law-abiding man, Sheriff." He paused by Clint and whispered, "You're about six feet, three inches tall, aren't you?"

"Yeah. What of it?"

"I just didn't know that crap would stack that high, that's all."

Jud grabbed his boss and spun him around before he could take a swing. "Don't do it, Clint. That's what he wants. Can't you see that?"

Smoke stood smiling at Clint. Then he arrogantly tipped his hat at the man and walked out of the saloon, lifting his gunbelt from the peg on his way out.

"Somebody pick up Red and tote him to the undertakers," Jud ordered.

"What are we gonna use?" Fatso Ross asked. "A shovel?"

Clint Black sat in his study, in a leather chair by the fireplace, drinking shot after shot of whiskey. Drinking it neat and chasing it with water. He had thanked Jud for stopping him that morning back in the saloon. Clint was under no illusions about who would have been the victor in that fight. Smoke Jensen would have killed him with his fists, or at least crippled him. He could see it in Smoke's eyes. A cold killing fury.

He poured another glass of whiskey. It was one of those times when the alcohol had no effect on him. He reached for a cigar then pulled his hand back. He didn't want another cigar and really didn't want the whiskey he'd just poured. He threw glass and contents into the fireplace. The small fire to chase away the evening's chill exploded harmlessly when the whiskey hit the flames.

He thought about Red and the supper he'd eaten turned sour in his stomach. Once he had gotten over his anger, he realized what his brother had meant that morning when he spoke to Smoke and said it was neatly done. Jensen had set that killing up as coldly as a striking rattler.

Clint sighed and rose to his feet. He walked to the window and looked out at the lamplit windows of the twin bunkhouses, set off to the side and slightly in front of the big house, a respectable distance away. He had more than fifty men at his command, hard men, good men with a gun, ruthless men who would kill man, woman, or child . . . and most had killed all three, at one time or another. He had more money than he could ever spend and vast holdings of land. And yet Clint felt a helpless sensation sweep over him. He didn't know what to do about Jensen. The man made him feel . . . well, *inadequate*.

Clint had expected Jensen to come charging in days ago, waging war. Instead, he was laying back and biding his time . . . but for what reason? What was his plan? The man had to have one. Clint just couldn't figure out what it might be.

Smoke and Sally were staying in one of the bedrooms of the ranch house on the Double D spread. It was a sturdy home, with half a dozen big comfortable rooms. The man who built it, or had it built, had looked to the future in his planning . . . but for him, it hadn't panned out well here.

Smoke was going to see to it that it did work out for the Duggan twins.

Lying in bed, with Sally snuggled close to her husband, she asked, "What is your plan, honey?"

"My plan? I don't really have one. I almost made Clint mad enough to fight me this morning, but the foreman apparently has more sense than his boss and grabbed him. I don't think Clint's not wearing a gun will last long, though. But I can't see him pulling on me. No

117

matter what I might say. But I will see him dead, Sally. Either by my hand or at the end of a rope. One way or the other."

"Do you trust Sheriff Black?"

"Up to a point. But that point is broadening. I think after he failed to convince his brother to back off and live in peace with his neighbors, Harris began to see him in a much different light. I get the impression that Harris is very disappointed in his brother."

"Disappointed enough to shoot him if it came to that?" Sally asked.

"I don't know, honey. I just don't know about that. I've known brother to shoot brother, and father to shoot son and the other way around. But I think for all his past, Harris Black is a good, decent man at the core. Could he kill his brother? I don't know. One thing I wish I did know: I wish I knew what Clint's next move was going to be."

Thirteen

Clint called his foreman over for breakfast at the main house. All the hands knew something was up, for anytime Jud was asked to eat with Clint, something big was in the works.

"When I came in here, Jud," Clint said, after shoveling food into his mouth, "I wasn't no more than a kid. Not yet twenty years old. There wasn't nothing in this part of the country exceptin' Indians and outlaws. Few nesters. I run the nesters off, fought the Indians, and killed the outlaws. This part of the territory is mine. Has been for years, and I intend to see that it remains that way."

The foreman ate slowly and said nothing. He listened.

"Tell the men they're going to start earning their money today," Clint told him. "I want Smoke Jensen dead."

Jud nodded his head and continued eating. The cook came in with a fresh pot of coffee, set it on the table, and quickly left the room. For a fact, Jud thought, things had sure changed in only a few weeks. Used to be that when a Circle 45 rider came to town, folks stepped lively in serving them. A person could smell the fear in them. All that had changed since Jensen arrived. The townspeople and even the damned farmers around the area were not properly respectful like they should be.

"Jensen's gone out of the cattle business for the most part," Clint said. "He's gonna raise horses. So he's got

119

time on his hands to hang around up here and meddle in everybody's business. Well, I'm tired of him meddlin' in mine. Can't count on Harris anymore. But that don't make any difference. He never really was included in any major plannin'. Next thing we know, he'll have got religion and be goin' to church. The new hands arrive?"

Jud nodded his head. "Eight of them. We still got empty bunks we could fill. Problem is, Clint, there ain't nothin' for them to do. They're just hangin' around the bunkhouse loafin' and drawin' their pay."

"Weldon and Tex come in?"

"Late yesterday."

"We start crowdin' the Double D hands. Push 'em into a fight. But make sure our boys got lots of witnesses. Leave the women alone."

"How about them snot-nosed kids Jensen brung up with him?"

"They're drawin' a man's pay and sittin' a saddle. If they get in the way, too bad. After breakfast, send the boys out in groups of five and six." Clint raised his head and smiled at his foreman. "Tell them to get into trouble."

Raul, the young Mexican who took care of the house and the lawn at the Double D had taken the wagon into town for supplies early that morning. When he wasn't back by midafternoon, the twins got worried.

"Raul does not drink," Toni told Smoke. "And he is very dependable. He's stood by us through the worst. I'm afraid something has happened to him."

"I'll ride in and check on him."

Smoke found the wagon a few miles from the ranch. It was overturned and the supplies scattered. The harnesses had been cut and the horses were gone. A few minutes later he found Raul. The young man had been badly beaten and then dragged. He was alive, but just barely. Smoke emptied a pistol into the air, knowing that would bring the Double D hands at a gallop.

Waymore and Cletus were the first to arrive. "Get to the ranch and get a buckboard, Cletus. Waymore, you get Stony and Ted and start tracking the raiders. Ride with your rifles in hand."

Smoke got his canteen and bathed the young man's badly battered face. Raul opened his eyes. "Lie still, you're bad hurt, Raul."

"Fatso was in the bunch, Mr. Smoke," Raul whispered. "So was Art Long. They beat me and dragged me."

"Don't talk anymore. We'll get you into town to the doctor. You'll be all right. Just lie still for now."

Everybody came fogging down the road with the buckboard. The bed had been filled with hay and Raul was lifted as gently as possible and placed on the softness.

"Get him to town," Smoke told Jeff, who was driving the wagon. He looked at the boys who'd come on the drive north. "You boys are now in charge of the house and the grounds, including the barn and corral. You are not to leave the grounds unless I say so. Is that clear?"

They nodded their heads.

"Get back up to the ranch and see to things. And stay in sight of the house. I'll tan your butts if you disobey me. Get moving."

The boys gone, Smoke looked at Denver. "Look after them, Denver."

"Will do, boss." The old cook swung into the saddle and headed back to the ranch.

"No riding, Sally," Smoke told her. "You keep on teaching the twins how to shoot a rifle and stay close to the house and go armed at all times. Load up all the guns, especially the shotguns, and place them in every room and on the front and back porches. The war has started."

Smoke waited on the boardwalk in front of Dr. Garrett's office and small clinic. He turned as Sheriff Black quietly closed the door and stepped out.

"Doc says he'll probably make it. But he's busted up

121

pretty good. I got his statement, for all the good it'll do."

"The Circle 45 hands will alibi for each other." It was not put as a question.

"You know it. Raul is well-liked in town. He was polite and would do anything in the world for people. He came in with some sheepmen. My brother ran the sheep off, killed a lot of them, and probably had a hand in killing the sheepmen. Raul stayed around doing odd jobs. When the Duggan twins came in, he went to work for them . . . in direct defiance of Clint's orders. I warned Raul to go armed. But he didn't like guns. Goddamnit!" Harris summed up his feelings in one word.

Smoke said nothing.

Harris hitched at his gun belt. "I'm going out to my brother's place. But don't expect any arrests."

"I know you'll do all that you can, Harris. And I'm not being sarcastic. I mean that."

The sheriff nodded his head and walked toward the stable. "Try to keep your guns in leather," he called over his shoulder.

Smoke didn't reply to that. He stood on the boardwalk until after the sheriff had ridden out, then crossed the street and took a chair in front of the hotel. He figured some of the Circle 45 rowdies would be riding into town shortly for a drink. He would be waiting.

It was not a long wait, and Smoke smiled when he saw the Wyoming man, Baylis, riding in with several of Clint's men. One of the deputies, Benny, stood across the street, watching Smoke and the Circle 45 men. The rest of the deputies were out tracking the men who attacked Raul. The Circle 45 men went into the saloon. Smoke stood up and headed for the saloon.

As he passed by the deputy, he paused and said, "I just heard there was some trouble out at that farm about three miles west of here. Maybe you'd best go check on that."

"Huh? I haven't heard about any trouble."

"I just told you."

The deputy got the message and nodded his head.

"That would be the Jefferson's place."

"Probably."

"It'll take the rest of the afternoon for me to do that."

"Pleasant ride though. See you."

"Ah . . . right, Mr. Jensen. See you."

Smoke walked over to the saloon and pushed open the batwings. A dozen locals were sitting at tables. The Circle 45 hands were lined up at the bar, Baylis among them. Smoke stepped to one side, away from the batwings, and put his back to a wall.

"Any of you trash seen Fatso and Art Long today?" Smoke called.

Baylis froze in the lifting of shot glass to mouth. He cut his eyes to Smoke. "You callin' me trash?"

"That's right, Baylis. And worse. You're the one who beat it up here from Wyoming to tell Clint about the herd. I can't say that you were in on the night attack, but you're just as guilty. You wanted to brace me back on the trail, Baylis. Still want to pull against me?"

Baylis lifted the shot glass and downed his drink. He thought for a moment, nodded his head, and turned, his hand by the butt of his gun. "Why not, Jensen? I think all that talk about you is bull anyway." Then he grabbed for his Colt.

Smoke's .44 roared and Baylis was leaning against the bar, his belly and chest leaking blood. The three Circle 45 hands jerked their guns and both of Smoke's hands were filled with .44s as he went to one knee and began thumbing and firing in one long continuous roll of deadly thunder.

A round blew Smoke's hat off his head and another slug came so close to his leg he could feel the heat. But Clint Black was four hands short.

Baylis was sitting on the barroom floor, his hands by his side and his dead eyes staring at eternity. Two other Circle 45 riders were dead and the fourth was not long for this world. He had taken two .44 slugs in the chest. Smoke walked to him, reloading as he went, and kicked his gun away. The man stared up at him.

"You played hell, Jensen," he gasped.

"I usually do, partner."

"I guess I took a wrong turn in life and just never got back on the right road."

"I reckon you did. But you can clean the slate some this day."

"How's that?"

"Did Clint Black order the attack on my herd?"

"Yeah. I won't lie for him no more. He ordered us to hit your camp and kill everyone there. Told us to bring them good-looking twins back to him. He wanted to have some fun with the gals before he got rid of them."

Dr. Garrett and Bigelow from the hotel had entered and were listening.

"Did you know about Raul being dragged and beaten today?"

"No. But Jud said Clint told him to have us start earnin' the fightin' wages we was gettin'. He put a bounty on your head, Jensen. Whichever one of us kills you gets five thousand dollars."

"Anything else you want to tell me?"

"Gettin' dark, Jensen. I think I'm goin'. Funny . . . but there ain't no pain. Yeah. Clint's done sent word all along the owlhoot trail for gunhands. I don't know how many's comin' in, but they'll be some, you can bet on that."

"What's your name?" Smoke asked, kneeling down beside the dying puncher turned gunslick.

"Doug. Doug Randel."

"I'll have that put on your marker."

" 'Preciate it. Maybe we'll get to ride down a better trail someday. I'd like that."

"Me, too, Doug."

Doug smiled, coughed up blood, and died.

Smoke looked around for his hat. He found it, stuck his finger through the bullet hole and shook his head. "Hat's not ten days old." He put it on and settled it. He looked at Dr. Garrett, who was inspecting the downed men for signs of life. He didn't find any and stood up with a sigh.

"A dead man's confession might hold up in court," the doctor said. "But I doubt it."

"We'll all testify that we heard it," one of the local men said. "If that'll help."

"Here comes Lucas," another local said, looking out the window. "Looks like his horse come up lame. Little Billy Thompson is tellin' him about the shootin', I reckon. Here he comes."

The deputy walked in, looked at the bodies by the bar, and cussed for a few seconds.

"Jensen didn't pull first," a local said. "But he shore laid him out neat, didn't he?"

"The sheriff ain't gonna like this," Lucas said. "All right, somebody tell me what happened."

Clint's joy at hearing about Raul was short-lived when one of his hands told him about the shooting in town. The hand took one look at Clint's face and immediately found an urge to be somewhere else . . . quickly.

"I put one of theirs out of action and Jensen kills four of mine," Clint muttered darkly. "I won't have any hands left at this rate."

His brother had been to see him and Clint told him he didn't know anything about Raul. Fatso and the others were working the range clear on the other side of his place and he'd swear to that in a court of law. And to get the hell off his property and stay off.

Clint had slammed the front door in his brother's face.

Furious, Harris Black wired a judge for advice. When the judge in the territorial capital of Helena ruled that the death bed confession of Doug Randel could not be used in a court of law, the people in the sparsely populated area around Blackstown braced themselves for war.

It was not long in coming. Less than twenty-four hours after the attack on Raul and the shooting in the saloon, a group of Circle 45 riders—after getting juiced up on whiskey—decided to have some fun and hoo-rah a local farmer. They rode their horses through the family's vegetable garden, shot the milk cows and the pigs, and trampled the chickens. The farmer grabbed a rifle and blew one rider out of the saddle. The Circle 45 riders shot him to bloody rags and as they were riding away, accidentally ran down one of the man's children, a six-year-old girl. She died in the back of the wagon long before the nearly hysterical mother could get her into town and to Doc Garrett's office.

So angry he was nearly trembling with rage, Harris Black rode out to confront his brother.

"It was a damn accident," Clint told him. "The punchers was just having some fun, that's all. The nester opened fire on them. What the hell was they supposed to do?"

"Fun!" Harris yelled at him. "Fun? A man and a little girl are dead. All because you think you're some sort of king around here and the law doesn't apply to you. I want the men responsible for this and I by God want them now, Clint."

"I paid them off and fired them."

"You're a damned liar, Clint."

Clint sucker-punched his brother, knocking him off the porch. The two brothers fought for a moment before Jud and half a dozen other men could pull them apart.

With hands holding both men, Clint yelled, "Get off my land, Harris. Get off and stay off. If you ever call me a liar again, I'll kill you!"

"I'll see you hang, Clint," Harris told him. "You're my brother, but you're no good. You're trash. You better toe the line from now on, Clint. Fire these no-count gunhands and walk light."

"Get him on his horse and out of my sight!" Clint screamed. "Right now."

In the saddle, Harris Black looked down at his younger brother. "You don't even realize what you've done, Clint. You're filled with such hate you don't know that I could arrest you for attacking me."

"You want to try it now?" Clint challenged, as more of his hands gathered around.

"I'm not a fool, brother. I might get lead in you and a couple of your men before I was shot out of the saddle, but it's just not worth it. You're not worth it."

"Get out while you still can, Harris," Clint warned him. "Before your big flappin' mouth gets you in trouble. And there isn't a damn thing you can do to me; I run this country. Not you. Don't get in my way, you might get hurt."

Harris lifted the reins. "Mother would want you buried proper, Clint. I'll see to that." Then he added, "You poor damn pitiful fool." He turned his horse and headed back to town.

Fourteen

Almost everyone who lived in the vicinity turned out for the funeral of the farmer and his daughter. Feelings were running very high and there was some talk of a hanging. Harris knew it was just talk and let it ride. But he knew that if more of this continued, the talk just might change to action. Just about an hour after the funeral, he watched it do just that.

An even dozen of Circle 45 riders came galloping into town, raising a cloud of dust and scattering people. A little dog was caught in the thundering hooves and was trampled. A small boy ran out and picked up the lifeless body of the pup.

"You dirty scum!" he screamed at the Circle 45 men. "Murderers. All of you. Patches didn't do none of you no harm. Why'd you run him down, you . . . crap?"

One of the rowdies walked to the boy and slapped him down into the dirt. The blow brought blood to the boy's lips. He lay in the dirt, sobbing, his arms wrapped around his dead pet.

"I'll kick your guts out, you little turd," the Circle 45 hand said menacingly.

The boy's father ran out of his store, a shotgun in his hands. He was just lifting the weapon to his shoulder when six-guns roared. The father fell back into the store, dead.

Suddenly, the street was filled with armed men and

women. The Circle 45 riders looked into the muzzles of six-guns, rifles, and shotguns.

Harris walked through the crowd of armed and angry citizens. "Put those pistols back in leather and get off those horses," he told the bunch. "If you want to stay alive."

The riders slowly complied.

"Doc," Harris called. "How many bullet holes in Mr. Wisdom?"

"Eight," the doctor called.

Harris pointed to the man who'd slapped the boy. "You're under arrest for assault and battery against a child." He turned and smiled at the 45 hands. "The rest of you are under arrest for murder."

"He was fixin' to kill Ned!" a hand yelled.

"After Ned threatened to do more harm to his son," Harris reminded the tough. "Not a court in the land would have convicted him. But they'll damn sure convict you boys."

The deputies had collected the guns from the Circle 45 riders.

"You boys know the way to the jail," Harris told them. "Now, move!"

Harris knelt down by the boy, who was still somewhat addled by the brutal blow from the tough. He helped the boy to his feet and handed the trampled little dog to a man standing near. "We'll see that your puppy gets a proper burial, lad. Now you go on over to your ma. She needs you right now."

Harris walked over to the tough who'd slapped the man and flattened him with one hard fist to the mouth. The Circle 45 hand lay in the dirt and kept his mouth shut. He could see cold killing fury in the sheriff's eyes.

"Goddamn filth!" Harris's words were spoken low and hard. "If I wasn't wearin' this badge I'd kick your face clear off your brainless head and let the hogs eat it."

The tough lay still in the dirt, blood leaking from his mouth. He knew that he'd get no more than a few days in jail and a fine for slapping the boy. He had not fired at the boy's father, and he could not be charged with murder. When he got out of jail, then he'd settle with Sheriff Harris Black.

Harris jerked the tough to his boots and threw him toward the jail. When he was slow getting to his feet, he felt the sheriff's big boot impact against his butt. He hollered and went sprawling face first into the dust. He crawled to his hands and knees and then came up cussing. He took a swing at Harris. Bad mistake.

Harris hit him five times. Blows so fast they seemed to come out of nowhere. The rowdy was slammed back against a hitchrail and Harris plowed in. Since the man's face was already ruined, Harris concentrated his big hard fists against the man's belly and sides. Ribs popped and the Circle 45 hand screamed in pain as the blows kept coming. When Harris was through, the rowdy fell to the dirt, his jaw broken, his nose flattened, his lips pulped and half a dozen ribs broken.

"Why?" he managed to gasp through his pain, looking up at the still enraged Harris Black.

"I like kids and dogs," Harris told him.

Clint Black and hands rode into town the next morning. He had sense enough to come in unarmed. He left his horse at the livery and he and half a dozen of his men walked to the sheriff's office. They walked in a sweat, all of them knowing at least fifty or more guns were trained on them from doorways and windows all along the main street.

At the sheriff's office, they were met with sawed-off shotgun-carrying deputies. More sweat.

"Keep your gunslicks out on the boardwalk," Harris told his brother. "And you don't sit down. You're not going to be here that long. State your business and then get the hell gone."

"Bail for my hands," Clint said.

"No bail for murderers." He held up a telegram.

"Judge's orders. That all you got to say?"

"You won't get a conviction from the people around here," Clint boasted. "And you know it. I'll hire the best lawyer in the state and beat it."

"Trial is not going to be here," Harris told him. "It'll be held in Helena. Hire your lawyer and go to hell with him. Anything else?"

"You want a war, Harris?"

"Is that a threat? You want to join your no-count hands behind bars for threatening a peace officer?"

Smoke sat on a bench outside the jail. He smiled at the Circle 45 riders.

They did not see any humor in their situation.

"You mind if me and my boys have a drink in town?" Clint asked.

"Don't cause any trouble. The townspeople will shoot you to ribbons. They've had it with you, Clint. They won't stand for any more crap from you or your hired guns. You can try to buy a drink. But I doubt if the barkeep will serve you."

"Can I see my men?"

"After I search you."

That infuriated the rancher. He drew back from the desk and straightened up, his face flushed with rage. "You tin-star piece of crap. Who in the hell do you think you're talking to?"

"A thug," Harris replied. "One that needs to be back there behind bars. And I'm going to put you there, Clint. Believe that."

Clint balled his hands into big fists. He struggled to keep control. He took several deep breaths and calmed himself. "Are my men being fed?"

"You know they are. Three meals a day. Now if there is nothing else, I'm busy with paperwork."

"You're . . . *dismissing* me?"

"That's right, Clint. Good choice of words. I am indeed dismissing you. Oh, it might be a nice gesture on your part to go see the widow Wisdom. Since it was your men who

131

killed her husband."

"Go to hell!" Clint spun around and stalked out of the office. He pulled up short at the sight of Smoke, sitting on a bench smiling at him. "You!"

"Just me," Smoke said. "You were expecting maybe the President of the United States? I mean, with you being such an important person and all, it wouldn't surprise me."

Clint stared at Smoke for a moment. He knew he'd been insulted and cut down, but he couldn't think of a proper response.

Smoke lifted a big hand and waggled his fingers at the rancher. "Run along, now, Clint. Bye-bye."

"Run along? I don't take orders from you, you sorry . . ." He started cussing Smoke, screaming the obscenities. Several women across the street covered their ears and ran into the nearest store.

Harris jerked open the door and stepped out. "Shut up, Clint! I said shut up!" he hollered.

Wild-eyed with fury, Clint turned on his brother, his fists balled.

"Don't even think about doing that," Harris warned him. "Calm down and ride out of here. That's right, Clint. I'm ordering you from town. Right now."

Clint cut his eyes to Smoke. Smoke smiled, lifted his hand, and waggled his fingers at the rancher. "Like I said, bye-bye."

Clint reached down and grabbed Smoke by the front of his shirt and hauled him to his boots. Bad mistake.

Smoke popped him on the side of the jaw with two short punches, left and right, that jarred Clint down to his toenails. He released the grip on the shirt and Smoke popped him again, this time right in the mouth. Clint's head jerked back and blood sprayed from his lips.

He screamed in fury and waded in, swinging with both fists. Smoke sidestepped and ducked and swung one foot, catching Clint on the ankle and sending the man tumbling to the boardwalk. Smoke backed up. "You better stop it

132

now, Harris," he warned. "Because if he gets up, it'll be the last time he does it in this life."

"Grab him, boys!" Harris yelled to the men gathered around.

They all piled on, deputies and Circle 45 riders. Deputies and punchers were flung around like rag dolls as the enraged Clint Black struggled to get to his feet. Smoke had backed up further, his fists up and ready to go.

"I'll kill you, Jensen!" Clint screamed, as the big man was once more ridden down to the boards by a pile of men. "You're a dead man."

"All I did was say bye-bye," Smoke told a gathering of women across the narrow alleyway.

"Disgusting," one woman said.

"He's an animal," another said.

"Is there anything wrong with saying bye-bye?" Smoke asked the ladies.

Clint was cussing to the high heavens and throwing men off as fast as they could pile on the fist-throwing rancher.

"Oh, hell," Harris said, as he reached behind him and pulled a leather-bound cosh from his back pocket. He shifted a couple of times, for a better angle, then rapped his brother on the noggin.

Clint's eyes rolled back in his head and he stopped his thrashing and cussing.

"Jesus," one of the Circle 45 men said, holding a bandanna to a busted lip. "He's strong as a bull."

"Tie him across a saddle and get him out of town and by God, I mean right now!" Harris ordered. "Move!" he hollered.

Clint was tossed belly-down across a saddle, tied securely, and the horse led out of town.

Harris looked at Smoke for a few seconds, then walked back into his office. Smoke went across the street to buy a new shirt. Clint had torn the whole front out of the one he was wearing. But it was worth ten shirts just to get a couple of good licks in on the man.

That night, several holes were blown out of the back of the jail and all the Circle 45 hands except the one charged with assault and battery escaped. He was lying on his bunk, hands behind his head, and smiling when Harris and his deputies arrived.

"What can I say, Sheriff?" he asked. "I ain't no criminal. No point in me runnin'."

Harris opened the cell door. "Get out. Your horse is at the livery. Be kind of stupid leaving you in here with that hole in the wall behind you."

"Now what?" a deputy asked.

"They're out on the Circle 45 range. You can bet my brother had fresh horses stashed every few miles along the way. He got this idea from me," Harris said ruefully. "Twenty years ago I busted some friends of mine out of jail down in Kansas. They weren't in there for murder, just for barroom fighting. Clint took a page from out of my past in doing this. He'll think it funny. We'll ride out come first light. I'll get flyers made up at the print shop and get them posted out across the territory. Come on, let's get this mess cleaned up."

That morning, Smoke did something he felt he should have done as soon as they cleared the ambush valley. He brought the teenage boys into town and sent them home on the stage. Three went one day and the remaining two the next day. He wanted them out of harm's way.

He walked down to Garrett's office and checked on Raul. The young man was looking and feeling better and the doctor said he could be taken back to the ranch in a couple of days. After talking with Raul for a moment, Smoke walked over to the jail and looked at the holes blown into the rear of the jail building. Benny was the only deputy left in town. Harris and the others had ridden out to Circle 45 range.

"How mad was Harris?" he asked the deputy.

"Not too bad. Not as upset as I thought he'd be."

"The sheriff knows this situation is coming to a head and he's feeling his way slow," Smoke said. "I don't blame him. He's taking his life in his hands just by riding out to his brother's place."

"Oh, they might tie up in a fistfight," the deputy said. "But when it comes to killing, I think Clint will walk up to the line and then back off on that. Look at all he's got to lose if he pulls a gun on Harris. If he just keeps that temper of his in check maybe this thing can be smoothed down."

"If I'd leave the country, you mean?"

"Something like that." The deputy wasn't going to push the issue too hard.

"And if you were me?"

Benny met the cold steady gaze from Smoke. Without giving much away, he said, "A man's got to do what he's got to do, I reckon."

Fifteen

"They're up in the high country, staying out of sight," Harris said to Smoke the next afternoon. "Clint was actually civil to me yesterday. But he couldn't keep from smiling. He feels pretty good about what he did." He stared at Smoke for a moment. "You look like a man who just ate a sour apple. What's your problem?"

"I feel responsible for that merchant getting killed the other day."

"That's nonsense. You didn't start this war, my brother did. No one in this town blames you. Hell, if you did anything, you stuck some steel into a lot of backbones around here. No, Smoke. No. In one way, my life would be a lot simpler if you'd leave, but that would just make my brother even more cockier. I am glad you got those boys out of this mess."

"I should have done it days ago. I don't know why I waited so long."

Boots sounded on the boardwalk and the door was flung open. "Sheriff!" a man shouted. "Come quick."

Smoke and Harris stood on the boards and looked to the west. Plumes of dark smoke were spiraling into the sky.

"The Crawford farm," Harris said. "Clint's been trying to buy it for years. Good water and good graze. Crawford's told me that Clint's threatened him a time or two. Feel like taking a ride?"

"Let's go."

The farmer lay face down in his wife's flower bed. He'd been shot twice in the head. The woman and three girls stood under a huge old tree, sobbing. The house and barn were gone, burned to the ground. The cows, pigs, and horses were dead, all of them shot.

"In broad open daylight," Harris muttered.

"They were wearing hoods," the woman said, tears still streaming down her face, reddening her eyes. "And their horses were wearing brands that I'd never seen before."

Smoke dismounted and began inspecting the tracks left by the churning hooves. He found one horse with a nearly perfect Z somehow cut into the shoe. He waved Harris over and pointed it out.

"Let's look at the dead horses over there, just to be sure," Harris suggested.

The dead animals bore no such cut on any horseshoe.

Harris turned to his deputies. "Take off after them. But I've got a pretty good hunch where they're going. They probably get into the river and try to lose you that way. Then they'll come out on the gravel and probably go back in the river where it curves. Stay with them. Provision at the Bell spread."

"I'll ride back to town for a wagon," Smoke said. "Ma'am," he turned to the woman, "do you want to stay on this farm and work it?"

"No," she shook her head. "No. I want to leave this awful place."

"All right. When you get to town, go to the new bank and tell them who you are. I'll have everything set up. I'm buying your place. You just name your price."

Harris stared open-mouthed at Smoke. This would really anger his brother. Jensen was pushing and pushing hard. He closed his mouth before a fly could find it.

Smoke swung into the saddle. "See you, Harris." He headed into town.

"Was that Smoke Jensen, Sheriff?" the woman asked.

"Yes."

"He doesn't look at all like the stories depict him. What a nice young man."

Harris cut his eyes to the woman. "Believe me when I say there are those who do not share that opinion, Mrs. Crawford."

"Including your brother, Sheriff?"

"Especially my brother, Mrs. Crawford."

Smoke tossed the deed to the Crawford to Denver. "It's big enough to run a few head of cattle, some horses, and it has a whale of a garden there now. You said this run was going to be your last one. So happy retirement, Denver."

Sally smiled. Nothing that Smoke did surprised her any longer. If he liked a person, that person had a loyal friend for life. If he disliked a person, that person had better leave town on the first available horse, stage, or train.

Denver turned his head so those gathered around would not see the quick tears. He brushed them away and said, "You're a puzzlement, Smoke. I thank you."

"Well, you can't leave until we get this Clint Black situation put aside. You certainly don't want to stay over there by yourself. You'd end up like Crawford. Besides, there is no house or barn. When the time is right, the First United Bank will loan you the money to get started."

"Count on that," Sally said with a smile

"They killed the man right in front of his family," Toni said. "Horrible. Clint Black has certainly lost his mind!"

"Oh, he's mad, all right," Smoke said, after thanking

the cook for the cup of coffee she handed him. "But not in the way you think. He's crazy killing angry because for years he was the top fish in a small pond around here. He yelled frog and everybody jumped. Now the pond is a big lake and nobody is paying any attention to him. He's striking out at anybody he sees. He thinks everybody is his enemy, and he's just about right on that."

"And the sheriff seems powerless to act," Jeanne said.

"Harris is straight arrow, Jeanne," Smoke told her. "He wants everything done legal-like. All the Ts crossed and the Is dotted. He'd put him in jail in a heartbeat if he had some proof that would stand up in a court of law. But he doesn't have it."

"And not much chance of getting it," Denver said. He was still in mild shock upon learning he was now a landowner.

"Sadly true," Smoke agreed.

"So we're right back where we started," Toni said.

"Oh, no," Smoke told her. "You and your sister have the herd on Double D range, the people in the community have risen up against Clint Black and his men, the sheriff now sees his brother for what he really is, and I doubt that Clint's bank will last out the summer. A lot has been accomplished, I'd say."

"I just feel responsible for what's happened," Jeanne said. "All the tragedy."

"Don't," Smoke said. "Harris told me that before we came in, he'd heard rumblings of a citizens' group forming to fight Clint and the Circle 45 hands. The good people of the community had decided to make their stand. The fuse was already lit when Clint ordered the raid against us. Harris said, very reluctantly, that our coming in might just have prevented a lot more spilled blood of innocent people than has occurred since we arrived. I like to think so."

"What's next?" Denver asked.

Smoke shrugged his shoulders. "That's up to Clint, I reckon."

Jud walked slowly toward the big ranch house. He had to speak his piece to Clint, and he was not looking forward to it. What he had to say would not be said out of any compassion for his fellow man, for Jud was just as sorry and miserable and low-down a person as Clint and all the other Circle 45 hands. But the situation had reached the point where a man had to step back and do some thinking. It was down to survival now. The whole country was lined up solidly against the Circle 45. Once they left Circle 45 range, none of them had a friend within a hundred mile radius. It wouldn't be long before the whole kit and caboodle of them would be barred from town. Jud had seen that happen before. Back when he was a young hellion riding the owlhoot trail.

His head down, deep in thought, he was surprised to see Clint sitting on the front porch.

"We got to talk, boss," the foreman said, stepping up on the porch.

Clint waved the man to a chair. "You going to tell me to pull in my horns, Jud?"

"I'm sure gonna suggest it."

Jud hollered for the cook to bring them a pot of coffee and be damn quick about it. The cook might not like being hollered at, but there was precious little he could do about, since Jud knew he was wanted for murder back in Missouri. All in all, the Circle 45 riders, including Jud and Clint, made up just about the sorriest gathering of humanity anywhere west of the Mississippi.

Coffee poured, Clint sipped in silence for several minutes. He sat the mug down and said, "What else were you going to tell me?"

"George Miller just come in from town. He said he was walkin' real light in there. It was some kind of scary. Everybody was carryin' guns. And he also said that Smoke Jensen bought the Crawford farm."

Clint hurled his coffee mug out into the yard and cussed. Then he yelled for the cook to bring him another cup. In a calmer voice, he said, "That five thousand dollar bounty on Jensen's head still stands, Jud."

"What good would it do, Clint? When an old elk turns to make his final stand against the wolves or a cougar or a fight for who's boss, he's made up his mind to stand or die. Same way with the people around here, now. The killin' would never stop. Two more hands rode out this mornin'. Clint, there ain't a real cowboy left on this place, 'ceptin' maybe you and me. You got thousands and thousands of acres with no cattle to speak of."

"You going to start attending church, Jud?" Clint asked sarcastically.

"Probably wouldn't hurt neither of us, although it's more 'un likely too late to do us any good. Clint, Smoke Jensen ain't even broke a sweat yet in this fight. You and me, now, we know all about the man. He's hell when he gets goin'. He'll do anything. Guns, dynamite, fire . . . you name it and Jensen will use it. He's a wild man when he gets riled up."

"He's just one man, Jud. Just one man. And I don't agree with you about the people around here. They kowtowed for years. They're yellow clear through. With Jensen out of the way, they'd slink back into their holes."

"There is one more thing: what about your brother?" Jud asked softly.

"I have no brother," Clint said. "He's turned his back to me and shown me his true colors. As far as I'm concerned, he's an enemy."

141

"You're going all the way with this, Clint?"

"Yes, I am. I don't have any choice in the matter. Do you see a choice for me?"

Jud looked at his boss for a moment, wondering if the man was kidding? But Clint's face was granite. Then he got it: Clint was talking honor. *Honor!* There wasn't a shred of honor between the two men. Both of them had cold-bloodedly murdered and stolen land and cattle and horses and God alone knew what else, and Clint was talking about *honor?*

Jud stood up. "All right, Clint. You know I'll stand with you all the way."

"I appreciate that, old friend. We'll whip Jensen. You just wait and see. We'll whip him."

When pigs fly, the foreman thought. But he kept that to himself.

On Stony's word, Smoke hired two more hands for the Double D. Two young, easy-to-grin men who had been working over in the Dakota Territory and had drifted back home when they learned that someone was fighting Clint Black.

"This here's Davy and Eli, Smoke," Stony said. "They ain't gunslingers, but they are good punchers. And they both hate Clint Black."

Smoke shook hands with the men and could feel the calluses on their hands. "What did Clint ever do to you boys?"

"Put my daddy out of the ranchin' business," Davy said. "I was just a kid. Clint and his no-count hands stole our cattle just after we rounded 'em up. Killed my brother and when ma heard that, she just collapsed. Died a couple of days later. Doc said it was a heart attack. Pa he went after Clint, but Jud Howes found him first and stomped him half to death. Pa died a few years after that. Lost the ranch and that stompin' broke his spirit. I was thirteen when I hit the road and startin' doin' a man's work. But I tell you this, Mr. Jensen . . ."

"Smoke. Just Smoke, Davy."

Davy grinned. "Fine, Smoke. What I was gonna say is this: if I ever get Clint or Jud in gunsights, it's my swore intention to kill 'em. I want you to know that up front."

"Neither one of them are worth hanging over, Davy," Smoke cautioned the young man. "Putting a rope around your own neck won't bring your ma and pa back. Don't worry, though, I feel sure you'll get your shot at one or both of those men. How about you, Eli?"

"Clint raped my sister," the young puncher said. "Took her like an animal, he did. This was years ago. I was no more than five or six years old. I seen him ridin' off from where he done it. Sis made me swear never to tell 'cause she knew Pa would go after him and Clint or his hands would kill Pa. When she learned she was with child, she killed herself rather than face the disgrace. It broke Ma's heart. Pa, he just was never the same. Clint, he come ridin' over big as brass, grinnin' like the cat who licked the cream, and told pa he was gonna buy him out. That day. Pa knew it was over. He took the money, piddlin' sum that it was, and we pulled out. Injuns hit us down on the Ruby. I had gone off into the woods to play and they never knew I was about. Church people took me in. I run off when I was eleven and never looked back. But I intend to kill Clint Black."

Smoke looked at the two young man. Clint Black had to be one of the sorriest excuses for a human being he had ever run up against. He had never met a man who didn't have any redeeming qualities — until now. "You boys toss your kit in the bunkhouse and get ready for supper. My wife's cooking tonight, so it's gonna be good."

"Mr. Jensen . . . ah, Smoke," Eli said. "Did your wife really strap on a pistol and take up a rifle and ride with you to help you out of a jam some months back?"

Smoke chuckled in the fading light of day. "She sure did. She was born back east to a wealthy family, but that lady can ride and shoot as good as any man. Better than most. It isn't wise to cross her. Bear that in mind."

The young cowboys solemnly nodded their heads. Davy asking, "Can she cook as good as she shoots?"

Smoke patted him on the back. "Better, Davy."

"Lord have mercy," Davy said. "Eli, I think we done found us a home."

Sixteen

That same night, while the townspeople slept, the new First United Bank of Blackstown was robbed and the whole back of the building blown out with dynamite. But Smoke had suspected something like that might happen and had brought in other workmen from back East to build a second safe in the ground under the building, accessible by a trap door which was covered by a rug. The Circle 45 hands made a clean getaway and beat it back to the ranch, taking a roundabout route.

When the Circle 45 hands ripped open the bank bags to count their loot, they found washers at the bottom of the sacks and stacks of worthless old Confederate money in place of greenbacks.

Clint was not amused.

"Burn all that crap," he ordered his men, pointing to the worthless money. "Save the washers, we might need them around the place. Two dollars worth of washers. Jesus!"

Yukon Golden, who had absolutely no reason at all to like Smoke Jensen, found the whole thing funny. Back in the bunkhouse, he said, "This deck is stacked, boys. I felt it when I first rode into town. This thing is windin' down to be a bloody mess, I'm thinkin'."

Bronco Ford cut hard eyes to the man. "You thinkin' about haulin' your ashes, Yukon?"

145

"No. I took the man's money, so I'll stay. But there ain't gonna be no good end to this. You mark my words."

"What do you mean?" Tex Mason asked.

"Well, I been hearin' talk that Clint has plans on treein' the town."

"There ain't nobody ever treed no Western town," Weldon Ball said. "And there ain't nobody ever gonna do it. That's a fool's game."

Grub Carson said, "I seen it tried a time or two. Man, them townspeople shot them ol' boys all to pieces. Most awfuliest thing I ever seen."

Slim King looked over at him. "Look what happened when Jesse James tried to rob that town over in Minnesota back a few years. They shore got their comeuppance there."

"I ain't attemptin' to tree no whole town," Austin Charles said, summing up the feelings of all the newly hired guns, " 'Cause it can't be done." He finished rolling a cigarette and added, "And I agree with Yukon. I think this deck is stacked against us. It's one thing goin' in an' runnin' out nester trash or shootin' sheepmen. Used to be no one give a damn about them. But times is changin'."

The men in the bunkhouse had all fallen silent, listening to Austin.

"I ain't sayin' our day has come and gone," Austin continued. "But it ain't gonna be too many more years 'fore jobs like this one will be hard to come by. And when that day comes, we're gonna have to start doin' more thinkin' and less shootin'."

"What do you mean?" a hand asked.

"Plannin' things out, is what I mean. This night ridin' hell for leather and shootin' everything that moves is damn near a thing of the past. As long as the jobs is like this one, stuck out here in the middle of nowhere, we can get away with it. Telegraph wires is everywhere. And I seen a machine that lets people talk to one another from miles away. It's scary."

"You ain't neither seen no machine like that!" a Circle 45 hand sneered at him.

Austin cut his eyes. "Don't be callin' me no liar, boy. I seen it. It's called a telephone. Lots of cities has them."

"I heard of 'em," Cleon said. "How do they work?"

"I don't know. Spooky, I say," Austin replied. "We're gettin' away from what I was talkin' about. Now let's face facts, boys: we ain't gonna whip Jensen with guns. Not unless we back-shoot him and that ain't my style. We got to use our heads in this."

"You ain't runnin' this show," Fatso Ross reminded him. "Clint is. I don't take orders from you; I take orders from Clint."

"For a fact," Austin said, taking no umbrage at the words. "For a fact."

Smoke rode into town early in the morning. Most of the businesses were not yet open. He had awakened with a feeling that this day would be eventful; that this day would mark the turning point in this high country war. And Smoke had long ago learned to play his hunches. He had left the ranch before dawn, and his stomach was telling him he had missed breakfast. His eyes were busy, moving from side to side, but he could see nothing to give cause for alarm. He stabled his horse and entered the cafe. He was the only customer. Smoke ordered breakfast and a pot of coffee. He watched as Doc Garrett walked slowly up the boardwalk and stepped into the cafe. The man looked weary.

"Mind if I join you, Mr. Jensen?" the doctor inquired.

"The name is Smoke. Please sit down, Doctor You look like you're about ready to fall down from exhaustion."

The man smiled. "Twins, Smoke. It was a hard delivery. But mother and babies are doing fine. No trouble last night from Clint?"

"No. But there will be today."

The doctor smiled as he poured himself a cup of coffee. "Can you predict the future, Smoke?"

"I play my hunches, Doctor. It's something I learned from mountain men. We're all born with that ability. You just have to work to develop it. It comes in very handy when danger is all around you."

"And what kind of trouble will be coming your way this day, Smoke?"

"Guns," he said softly. The sounds of hammering reached the cafe. The workmen were up early, repairing the rear of the new bank building.

The waitress took the doctor's order as more people entered the cafe, their faces still lumpy from sleep. They wanted no conversation until they'd had their coffee. They nodded at Smoke and the doctor, and the nods were returned.

The blacksmith came in and ordered a huge stack of flapjacks. "The sheriff and his deputies rode out early this morning," he told the waitress. "Seems like some fellers tried to rob the stage and they was headed this way. The news come in over the wires late last night."

"Set up," Smoke spoke very low. "Five will get you ten that one of Clint's men jumped the wires and sent that message to suck Harris and his deputies out of town."

"To attack this town?"

Smoke shook his head. "No. That would be very foolish. They're coming after me."

"You don't think they might attack the Double D?"

Again, Smoke shook his head. "No. That's coming. I'm certain of that. But not yet. Clint wants me out of this game first. And he wants people to see me go down. He thinks that will put the fear back in them. But he's wrong." He looked over at the smithy. "How far out of town did this attempted robbery take place?"

"Harris said they was goin' as far as Slater's Pass. That's a pretty fair piece out. I 'spect they'll be gone most of the day."

Smoke thanked him as the waitress put his plate in front of him and Smoke concentrated on eating his breakfast. The doctor did not attempt to engage him in conversation while eating. Eating was serious business for many a Western man. Soon the doctor was busy working on his own food.

"Well, bless Pete," a man said, looking up from his eggs. "Would you take a look at them two."

Smoke looked up and saw them. He silently cussed. He didn't know the two young men, but he was very familiar with the type. Young trouble-hunters out to make a reputation. They had heard he was in town, and here they came.

The smithy turned around, looked, and snorted. "Pearl-handled six-shooters, fancy rigs and boots. All decked out. Young toughs."

Smoke ate his breakfast, poured another cup of coffee, and waited. He watched as the trouble-hunters stepped up onto the boardwalk across the street and asked a man something. The citizen pointed to the cafe and Smoke sighed. It was down to minutes now.

"Am I missing something here?" Doc Garrett asked, looking at the expression on Smoke's face.

"A couple of young trouble-hunters heading this way. Probably looking for me."

The doctor turned and looked at them. "Not more

149

that twenty-one or two at the most."

"But they're wearing guns," Smoke told him. "Out here, Doc, when you strap on a gun, that makes you a man."

"How will you handle this?"

"That all depends on those two would-be gunslicks. Try to talk my way out of it if they'll let me."

The door opened and the young men swaggered in, trying to look tough. They managed to look pathetic. But Smoke had noticed they had taken the hammer thongs off their guns. The pair looked around the large room, their eyes settling on Smoke. Smoke was sipping his coffee and seemingly not paying any attention to them.

"You boys take a seat," the waitress called from the kitchen. "I'll be with you in a minute."

"Shake a leg there, baby," one of them called. "You got the Shawnee Kid and Hawk Evans in here."

Smoke shook his head in disgust.

"The only thing that's gonna be shakin' around here is your butts when I kick you out of here," the cook said, stepping out of the kitchen. "You watch your mouths around my wife, you hear me?"

"Shawnee," his partner said. "I think that feller's threatenin' us."

"Sounds like it, don't it? Maybe we ought to pin his ears back some?"

Smoke sat the coffee cup on the table.

"Oh, my!" Evans said. "But we got the world-famous Smoke Jensen in here, Shawnee. The cook might be a friend of his. Don't that scare you?"

"Why . . . I'm tremblin' in my boots just at the thought of Mr. Smoke Jensen. Tell you what, Hawk, maybe we ought to ride out to the Circle 45 and tell Clint Black that we'll take care of his little problem with Jensen. That is, if we can get Jensen away from

150

that coffee pot."

"If you boys have a problem," Smoke told them, finally turning his head to look at the pair, "I think it would be wise to carry it somewhere else. This is the wrong town to start trouble in."

"Because of you, Mr. Hotshot Gunfighter?" Hawk sneered at him.

"That's part of it," Smoke told him.

"What's the other part?" Shawnee asked.

"Actually there is more than one. They got the loneliest graveyard I have ever seen in any town. I'd hate to know I had to spend eternity on that hill."

"What's the other part?" Hawk asked.

"The cook has a double-barreled shotgun pointed right at your guts."

Both of their mouths dropped open and they jerked their heads toward the rear. Smoke left his chair like a striking snake and ran into the pair, knocking them sprawling. One jerked out a 45 and Smoke kicked it out of his hand. Whirling, he backhanded the other one just as he was crawling to his knees, the blow catching him on the side of the head and knocking him back to the floor. Smoke ripped the gun belts from them and hung them on a peg.

"Now stand up," he said in a very low and menacing voice. When they were slow in doing so, he shouted, "Stand up, damnit!"

They scrambled to their feet and faced him. Smoke stepped closer to the one called Shawnee. "Draw," he told him.

"Draw what?"

"Pretend you're drawing. Maybe this is the only way I can keep you alive and get you back home safely. Draw, damnit!"

Shawnee's elbow was just bending when Smoke's .44 leaped into the young man's face.

"Jesus Christ!" Evans said.

Sweat was pouring down Shawnee's face, even though the morning had dawned very cool for summer.

"You get the message, Shawnee?" Smoke asked.

"Yes . . . sir. I mean, *yes sir!*"

Smoke cut his eyes to Evans. "How about you?"

"Real plain, Mr. Jensen."

"Fine. Now you boys sit down and order you some breakfast. After you've eaten, ride back home, wherever home is, and forget about being gunfighters. The trails are long, the food is terrible, the company you keep is awful, the life expectancy is short, and the pay isn't worth a damn. Breakfast is on me, boys. Now sit down and eat."

"Yes, sir," they said in unison, and sat. Evans looked up at Jensen and smiled. "The cook ain't holdin' no shotgun, Mr. Jensen."

Smoke returned the smile. "I lied."

Smoke returned to his own table and the waitress brought him a fresh pot of coffee. She smiled and said in a whisper, "You could have killed them both and nobody would have blamed you."

"Ten years ago, I would have," Smoke told her.

"For a man of your size, you're devilishly quick, Smoke," the doctor said.

"It pays to be with the name I've got hung on me."

"Circle 45 riders coming in," a man called from a table by the window.

The doctor stared at Smoke. "I was planning on going home and getting a few hours sleep this morning."

"I think it's going to get busy around here this morning," Smoke said, shoving back his chair. "You'd better plan on an afternoon's nap."

Seventeen

Smoke walked outside while some of the cafe's patrons exited by the back door, heading for home to make sure their wives and kids stayed off the streets. Hawk Evans and the Shawnee Kid sat at their table and stared out the window. Both of them knew that from this point on, they would never again strap on a gun. Dr. Garrett looked at the two young men, staring wide-eyed at Smoke, then turned his chair around so he could see what was taking place in the street.

Smoke knew only one of the men who had ridden in, a two-bit gunhandler who went by the name of Earl Cobb. He knew none of the others. He watched as they reined in and swung down, looping the reins on the hitchrail in front of the saloon. They turned and faced him.

The cork is out of the bottle now, Smoke thought. *They aren't even trying to conceal the reason they came to town. Clint must have upped the ante.*

The quartet of gunhands spread out.

Smoke backed up and entered the cafe. "They don't care that innocent people might be hit by a bullet," he said to Doc Garrett. "I won't have it this way." He paused by the hat rack and took two of the guns belonging to the young men. "I'll return these in a few minutes," he said to the pair.

"Keep them," Evans said. "We won't be needing them no more."

Smoke walked through the kitchen, a borrowed pistol in each hand. The cook, who was the owner, said, "I've got a rifle here, Smoke."

"Stay out of this. I'm going to pull them away from your cafe and try to get them off the main street. People are all over the place opening up for business."

He went out the back door and ran two blocks down to the livery stable. He cut right and stepped out into the street. He was a good two hundred yards from the gunmen, who were standing in the middle of the street in front of the cafe.

"Hey!" Smoke called, stepping closer to the other side of the street where there were two abandoned buildings at the edge of town. "You jerks looking for me?"

Earl Cobb cussed at the distance between them. "Come on," he said to the others. "Jensen's tryin' to get us away from the main drag so's no citizen will take lead."

"Ain't he sweet?" another said.

"He's liable to take up preachin' 'fore long," another added.

Smoke was standing by the corner of what had once been a general store.

"Split up," Earl said. "Luddy, you come with me. Dick, Patton, you cut through that alley and come up behind him."

When he looked up again, Smoke had vanished.

Many of the townspeople had armed themselves. But since Smoke had pulled the action to the edge of town, where no businesses or houses stood, they could not leave their families unprotected. Most knew Smoke had done that deliberately.

"Jensen, you damn yellow cur," Dick called. "Step out here and fight."

"All right," Smoke said as he stepped out of a doorway behind the two men. "Here I am."

The men were lifting their guns as they turned to meet what their fates had long ago planned for them. The borrowed .45s in Smoke Jensen's hands roared and spat fire and lead and gunsmoke. Patton and Dick were down in the litter behind the old building.

"Nice action on these pistols," Smoke muttered, as he kicked the guns of the fallen men away from them and stepped back into the building. He had checked the pistols in the cafe and knew they had been loaded up full. He had fired four times and had put two slugs apiece in Patton and Dick.

Smoke had no illusions about fair fighting. The old mountain man Preacher had grilled that out of him. He never gave a damn for fair; he fought to win. "You always do your best to do right by the good folks of this world, boy," Preacher had told him repeatedly. "To hell with the bad folks. Man comes after you with intent to do you harm, you fight him any damn way you can . . . just win."

Luddy rounded a corner of the building and Smoke fired through a windowless frame. The slug hit the hired gun in the shoulder and knocked him down, the big shoulder joint smashed. Luddy lay on the ground and flopped and hollered in pain, his gun hand useless.

Smoke stepped out of the building just as Earl began pouring lead through the thin walls. He worked his way up the alley and stepped out to the edge of the street just as Earl was jerking out a spare gun he'd tucked behind his belt.

"You do like to waste ammo, don't you, Earl," Smoke called.

Earl cussed, spun around, and fired, the slug slammed into the building behind Smoke. Smoke drilled him clean and dropped him to his knees.

"Give it up, Earl," Smoke told him. "The party's over."

Earl tried to lift his .44. "You dirty son of . . ." He never finished it. The hired gun fell forward in the dirt.

Smoke walked around the building just as the boardwalks began filling with citizens. He stepped up and kicked the pistol out of Luddy's left hand.

"Damn fool," Smoke told him. "Give it up and live, man."

"You ruint me!" Luddy gasped through his pain.

"Maybe now you'll get a decent job and quit trying to kill people," Smoke replied, just as Doc Garrett rounded the corner.

"Go to hell!" Luddy said. "I don't need no damn sermon from the likes of you."

"Whatever," Smoke said, and turned his back to the man. He walked around to the rear of the building. Dick and Patton were still alive and moaning. They lay on the ground and glared hate up at Smoke. But they were smart enough not to try to reach their guns. They could still run their mouths, however, and they did, expelling a lot of wind cussing Smoke.

Smoke turned to the smithy. "Go get those two young men who wanted to brace me."

"They're gone, Smoke. Both of them left out pale as ghosts. I think they got the message. Their gun belts are still hangin' on the pegs."

"Somebody help me with these men," Doc Garrett said. "Pick them up and take them to my office."

"Hell with them," a man said. "They can get there under their own steam. I ain't helpin' nobody who works for Clint Black."

156

"Sorry bastard!" Luddy cussed the man.

"Look who is calling who sorry," the citizen said, then turned around and walked away. "My breakfast is gettin' cold."

Smoke waited around until Harris returned and told him what had happened, including the incident with the young men in the cafe.

"How many still alive?"

"Some gunslick called Luddy. The other three are dead."

"Luddy Chambers," Harris said. "He's a bad one. You going to press charges?"

"I didn't know you had any laws in this territory about calling a man out."

Harris sighed. "Well, we do, sort of."

"Doc Garrett said the bullet smashed his shoulder joint. He'll only have limited used of that arm for the rest of his life. And when word gets around that Luddy Chambers has a crippled gun arm, he'll either hunt him a hole and change his name, or get dead."

"You're right about that. There was no attempted stagecoach holdup, by the way."

"I figured Clint had one of his men tie into the line and send that message to get you out of town. But if he did, why not send Bronco or Austin or Yukon in after me? These ol' boys today were not the best he has on the payroll."

"What could he be up to?"

"You tell me. He's your brother."

"A fact I wish I could undo," Harris said with a grimace.

"I'm going back to the Double D. I'll see you in a couple of days."

"Smoke? Thanks for pulling those gunnies to the

157

edge of town. I find myself respecting you more and more each day. And if the day comes when my brother braces you . . . put him down. He's stepped way over the line."

"Maybe it won't come to that."

"You know it will," Harris said, and then walked across to Doc Garrett's office.

"I'm afraid you're right," Smoke muttered.

The attack came that evening, about an hour after supper; a time that no one would expect any raid. Smoke was sitting on the front porch, drinking a cup of coffee and laughing as he sat watching two half-grown hounds play and mock fight with each other, rolling and tumbling on the ground. Suddenly the hounds stopped and tensed, the hair standing up on their backs. They started growling.

"Get to guns!" Smoke yelled, jumping out of the chair and overturning his cup of coffee. The sounds of pounding hooves reached him. "Take cover!"

He turned at his name and Sally tossed him his gun belt and then a Winchester. "Don't you worry about us in here," she calmly told him, then closed the door.

He wouldn't. Sally had been working with the twins and both of them had turned out to be pretty fair hands with a rifle. They weren't very good with short guns, but put a shotgun in their hands and watch out. He didn't have to check the rifle, he'd made it clear that if he found an empty weapon in the house—other than it being cleaned—he'd raise enough hell so it wouldn't happen again.

Raul was back home, staying in the main house, and Smoke could see him on the bed by the window; his aversion to guns was long gone after his beating and dragging. Smoke could see the muzzle of a Winchester sticking out of the bedroom window.

The cook was a frontier woman who wouldn't back

158

up from a grizzly bear. Smoke had seen ol' Denver making calf eyes at her—and she returning them—and knew that Denver would be in the kitchen with her, both of them firing from there—the woman with rifle, pistol, or shotgun.

Then there was no more time for thinking. It was action now, as fifty or more riders came fogging into the front yard, circling the corral, the bunkhouse, and the main house, and bringing with them thick, choking clouds of dust.

Smoke knew then what they planned. They planned an all-out assault on the ground, on foot.

"Be careful in the house!" he yelled over the shooting. "They're going to take us on foot."

"We see them," Sally returned the yell. "You take care of your own business."

Smoke smiled. Hell of a woman, his Sally.

A shotgun roared from the side of the house and a terrible scream followed the blast. "My legs!" a man hollered hoarsely. "My legs are tore up. I think they's blowed plumb off. Help me. Oh, you damn Eastern hussy bitch you!"

The shotgun roared again. There was no more screaming.

Smoke arched an eyebrow as he searched for a target. He had a .44 in each hand. The man shouldn't have called the Duggan woman that. She sure took umbrage at the remark.

A man came running out of the dust and Smoke cut him down. He hit the ground, tried to lift himself up, then collapsed to the dirt. A slug whined off the stone of the house and went whistling wickedly off into the cooling air. Mask-and-duster-wearing riders continued to circle the grounds, dragging broken limbs behind them to keep the dust whirling. Smoke lined one up and shot him out of the saddle. He hit the ground, bounced, and then was still.

The hound pups had scampered under the porch, out of harm's way. They began barking furiously and Smoke turned in time to see a man swing one leg over the porch railing. The man looked up, his eyes wide with horror at the sight of Smoke, standing calmly, a .44 pointed right at the raider's head. That was the last thing he would see on this earth.

Raul's Winchester barked and a man slumped to the ground just outside the bedroom window. Raul called him a lot of very ugly names in the lilting Spanish language.

The boys in the bunkhouse were laying down a withering fire that was taking its toll. Through the dust, Smoke could see half a dozen bodies sprawled on the ground.

"That's it!" a man yelled. "To your horses. It ain't workin'."

"Hold your positions!" Smoke yelled. "Stay put until they're gone."

In half a minute, the sounds of hard-pounding hooves had faded into the waning light.

"Is everybody all right?" Smoke lifted his voice.

"Stony's got a scratch on his head and Joe's got a burn on his arm," Malvern called. "Everybody else is okay."

"In the house?"

"We're all right," Sally called.

Moaning could be clearly heard from all around the grounds. The dust had settled, coating everything and everybody.

"Reload before you step out," Smoke called. "Then we'll see to the wounded. Cletus, you hitch up a wagon. That old one that we were going to junk."

"Right, boss," Cletus said with a chuckle. "And I'll pitch a few forkfuls of hay in it."

160

"You do that. We want them to be comfortable on the ride back. And hitch up those two hammer-headed horses. The ones no one can ride."

Cletus laughed aloud. "They ain't harness-broke, boss."

"Yes," Smoke said. "I know."

He walked around the grounds. Seven dead and that many more wounded, two of them badly. They would not last another hour under the best of care. Smoke looked at each wounded man with cold contempt in his eyes. None of them would meet his gaze for more than a few seconds.

"Throw the dead in the wagon first, then the badly wounded on top of them," Smoke ordered. "The rest of you night-riding sorry sons can either find your horses or walk back."

"Say, now," a wounded Circle 45 rider mouthed. "I . . ."

"Shut up!" Smoke roared at him. He had jerked the masks off each one and every Double D rider had taken a look. "When you do get back to your range, pack your gear and get gone. If I see you again in this part of the country, you're dead on the spot. In a café, saloon, emporium, or church, I'll kill you, and I'll do it without warning. Now get up and get moving before I decide to end it right now."

Even the more seriously wounded moved mighty quick.

Eli tossed the reins to a leg-shot night rider sitting on the seat. "You take care now," he said with a chuckle. "This wagon's old and the road is mighty bumpy."

"You boys is cold," the night rider said. "Mighty cold. Tossin' the wounded in with the dead."

"You think you deserve any better?" he was asked.

The hired gun chose not to reply. He clucked at the

reluctant team and the wagon lurched forward, the horses fighting the unfamiliar harnesses.

When the wagon was out of sight and sound, Smoke said, "Two men on guard tonight and every night. You work out the shifts, Stony. No riding alone. Ride in pairs at all times. Denver, give those hound dog pups something special from the kitchen. They saved our bacon this evening."

He walked back to the porch and righted the overturned chair, then took a rag and wiped the dust off of the porch furniture. The cook brought out a fresh pot of coffee and a tray of cups. Smoke sat down beside Sally. "There wasn't a known gunhand in the bunch. If there had of been we would have knocked at least one of them out of the saddle. Clint sent his hands at us this night, keeping the best—in a manner of speaking—in reserve. Why?"

Denver and the twins had joined them on the darkened porch. A slight breeze had kicked up and it was pleasant. But the odor of blood and sweat still hung about the grounds.

"The only way he'll be able to get any more men in here will be to double the wages," Denver said. "One of them wounded told me that some of the gunfighters is talkin' about this bein' a stacked deck. He also said that Clint's talkin' about attackin' the town."

"That would be a very stupid thing to do," Smoke said.

"That's what the hired guns said."

"I've never met anyone like this Clint Black," Toni said.

"Sure you have," Sally spoke. "The East is full of them. They just operate in a different manner, that's all. There are ruthless industrialists who are like vultures, waiting to rip and tear at smaller businesses who are faltering. Bankers who pounce if a payment is one

162

day late. Men like Clint Black are all over. They just use their powers differently, but the end result is the same. Smaller, less fortunate, less powerful people—businessmen and ordinary people—are still ruined, homeless, and left penniless."

"I'd never thought of it like that," Jeanne said. "But you're right."

"The West is still raw, Missy," Denver said. "And it will be for years to come. Men like Clint Black come in here and tore the land loose from Injuns and outlaws. They fought blizzards and droughts and floods. The only law was their own. They ain't likely to change real swift."

"Only at the muzzle of a gun or at the end of a rope," Smoke said. He stood up and stared out at the night. "This is fine country up here. And it'll be a lot finer once the likes of Clint Black are out of the picture."

"Riders comin', boss," a lookout hollered.

"Here we go again," Smoke said, as the others on the porch scrambled for their guns.

Eighteen

"It's the sheriff and a posse," the lookout called. "Stand easy at the house."

"I'll make some more coffee," the cook said.

"I'll help you, Liz," Denver said. He did not see the smiles of the others.

Harris and a dozen townspeople and regular deputies swung down and crowded the porch. "A farmer came gallopin' into town and told me he saw a large group of men headin' this way. We met what was left of them a couple of miles back," he added, his tone dry. "They weren't in real good shape. Anybody hurt at this end?"

"A couple of scratches and burns," Smoke told him. "We were lucky. I was watching the dogs play. They warned me in time for us to get set."

"You going to press charges?"

"It isn't my property. You'll have to ask Toni and Jeanne."

"Ladies?" the sheriff asked.

The twins exchanged glances and Toni said, "Sheriff Harris, I think you are a good man . . . in your own peculiar way. But what would be the point in pressing charges? All your brother would do is blow up the jail again. That is, if the structure is even repaired at this time. Besides, I doubt seriously that any of those men whom we just sent on their way would testify against your brother. I've seen how Western justice works . . . when it does work. Those hoodlums would just claim they came over to . . . what is the word I'm looking for? Sort of like after a country wedding when the couple is . . . ah, shivareed by friends."

"Hoo-rahed, ma'am?" the sheriff asked.

"Yes. That's it. They would say that they were only having fun and that we opened fire on them. Oh, I'm learning, Sheriff. I'm learning."

"Yes," Harris said. "I can see that. But it might not work out that way. One of my deputies is escorting the men into town. I'll talk to them and see what develops from it. But don't count on much."

"We won't," Sally said.

Liz came out with a huge coffee pot and Sally had made doughnuts that day and the men all dug in. Smoke was conscious of the sheriff's eyes on him.

"You got something stuck in your craw, spit it out," he told the man.

"What is my brother up to? Those weren't top guns he sent over here this evening. Not a one of them has any kind of name. Least none that I saw. He's got something up his sleeve, but I don't know what it could be. Those gunnies who braced you in town—the same thing. It's puzzling to me. Mighty good doughnuts, ma'am. Mighty good."

"I don't know what your brother is up to," Smoke said, after finishing a doughnut. He reached out for another and pulled back his hand at Sally's warning look. He'd already eaten about twenty that day.

The sheriff caught the look in the lighted porch lamps and smiled. Doesn't make any difference if a man is the toughest gunslinger in the West, his wife could still back him up with just a glance. Sheriff Harris Black helped himself to another doughnut, and

Smoke grabbed one when he thought Sally wasn't looking. Quickly.

Liz fixed a sackful of doughnuts for the men to eat on the ride back to town and the sheriff and posse mounted up. "After this raid," Harris said to Smoke, "I don't think there is any turning back for my brother. Personally, I'd rather see him go down in a hail of bullets than for me to have to put the noose around his neck, and I would have to be the one to do it. He's heading for a violent end, and I don't know of any way to stop him. See you folks."

Smoke left the ranch the next morning long before anyone else other than the guards were up. He rode back to the valley where the ambush had taken place. For a long time he sat near the flat where the men and boys were buried. He smoked a couple of cigarettes and thought about the lives that had been snuffed out in that murderous raid. Baylis would have told Clint about the young boys working the remuda . . . and Clint had not cared. Clint had callously ordered the deaths of three women with no more feeling than swatting at a bothersome fly. The law was unable to contain Clint and his raiders. It wasn't that the law wouldn't deal with him, the law *couldn't* deal with him. For whatever reasons, known only to Clint, the wealthy rancher was determined to drive the Duggan twins from their ranch and possess it.

Why?

Gold? Smoke didn't think so, even though there had been gold strikes in this area there was no evidence that any gold was buried in the earth of the Double D. No, it was just stubborn pride and ruthless greed and callousness on the man's part. Clint wanted everything he saw and would stop at nothing to get it.

Smoke walked among the lonely graves, pausing for a time at each rock headstone his men had carefully placed by each grave, the name and date carefully chiseled into the stone. Nate, Little Ben, Shorty, Davy, Duke, Matt, Harris, Eton, Johnson, Forrest. He paused for a longer time at the graves of the boys. Fourteen-year-old Rabbit and the fifteen-year-olds, Willie and Jake. Boys who wanted to earn some money and see some country and have a little fun.

They had found violent and senseless death.

Clint Black had ordered it, and his men had coldly and brutally wiped out half of Smoke's drovers. No Indian attack could have been any more savage.

Smoke knelt down by Rabbit's grave and let the coldness of the tomb wash over him and settle in his mind. When he stood up, he knew he was going to end this war. Clint wanted a fight, so be it. Clint was going to have a fight, but from now on, it would be a fight on Smoke Jensen's terms.

He headed back to the Double D.

Sally was sitting on the porch when Smoke rode back to the ranch compound. She looked for a moment at the way he sat his saddle and then stood up.

"What's wrong?" Jeanne asked.

"I'm going to fix a packet of food for Smoke."

"Is he going somewhere?" Toni asked.

"Yes," Sally replied mysteriously, and walked into the house.

"How strange," Jeanne remarked.

Toni watched as Smoke stepped down from the saddle and walked toward the house. "Maybe not," she said.

"What do you mean?"

"There is something quite different about Smoke.

167

Look at him. He's moving like some great predator cat. See the difference in him?"

Jeanne looked. "I do believe you're right. There is a more, well, determined look about him."

The sisters looked at each other and smiled. Toni said, "I think Mr. Clint Black is about to discover that he has angered the wrong man."

None of the hands said anything to Smoke when he emerged from the house. There was a look about him that warned people away. He had changed clothes. He now wore earth tones that would blend in with his surroundings. He had selected a big rugged horse that was mountain bred, would not stand out, and who was a better sentry at night than a trained dog. Smoke had a packet of food, a small coffee pot, and a bedroll. He had put moccasins in the saddlebags. There was an extra rope on the saddle. He had shoved a Winchester .44-40 into the saddle boot and bandoleers of ammunition crisscrossed his chest with extra boxes in the saddlebags.

He had said his goodbyes to Sally while in the house. She knew her man and was stoic about their temporary parting.

When she had asked where he had been that morning, she knew even more what he was going to do when he replied, "Over in the valley, by the graves."

He held her for a moment, kissed her, and was gone. Sally busied herself baking pies.

"You boys hold it down," Smoke said to the hands that were gathered outside the barn. "I'll be back when you see me."

Smoke headed for Circle 45 range.

As the twins had suggested, Sheriff Harris Black got

nothing out of the wounded raiders. Since no one was filing any charges, he could do nothing except let them go. Two of the raiders had died before reaching town and a third was not expected to live. Dr. Garrett's little clinic was jammed to overflowing, with pallets on the floor.

"They'll be more," one of the deputies warned him. "This situation ain't even built up a good head of steam yet."

"I'm running out of medicines," the Doctor complained.

"You better order some more," the deputy told him. " 'Cause when Smoke Jensen gets a gutful of this mess, he'll come a-foggin' like something out of Hell. Clint Black ain't seen nothin' yet. You mark my words, Doc."

The Circle 45 rider felt the loop settle around him, the rope tighten, and he was jerked out of the saddle before he could holler. Not that yelling would have done any good, since he was miles from the ranch house and riding alone.

The wind was knocked from him as he hit the ground. He managed to roll and shake the loop. He got to his feet spitting mad and cussing and reaching for his gun. Out of the corner of his eyes he caught a blur of motion and turned just in time to receive a big leather-gloved fist right in his mouth. The blow knocked him on his butt and addled him for a few seconds. He crawled to his feet and a combination of lefts and rights flattened him, bloodying his mouth, busting his nose, and watering his eyes. The blows came so fast he still was not sure who was throwing them. But he had him a pretty good idea. The Circle

45 hand tried to make a fight of it, but he never had a chance to get set.

The would-be tough felt himself picked up and hurled into a stand of trees. His head impacted against a tree and his world turned black. When he awakened, he had the world's worst headache, his face felt like someone had worked him over with a two-by-four, and to add insult to injury, he was hanging upside down from a tree limb.

Smoke Jensen was sitting on the ground, his back to a tree. He was chewing on a biscuit and staring at the puncher. The Circle 45 rider quickly decided the best thing he could do was to keep his mouth shut.

Smoke stared at him for several very long moments. He finished his biscuit, walked to his horse and took a drink from his canteen, returned to the tree, and sat down. "You have a home?" Smoke finally asked the upside-down man.

"Utah," the puncher said. "I'd like to see it again someday. Sir," he added.

Smoke reached down and pulled out a long-bladed knife. The bladder of the Circle 45 rider gave it up and a dark stain appeared on his jeans.

"How bad do you want to see Utah?" Smoke asked him.

"Real bad. Like I'd leave right now ifn I was able."

"I ought to just go on and split you wide open and be done with it."

"Oh, man!" the hired gun hollered. "Look . . . you cut me down and I'm gone. You won't never see me again. That's a promise, Mr. Jensen. Look here, I'll level with you. Clint's hirin' more men. He's payin' money can't nobody pass up. I'm tellin' you the truth."

Smoke stood up and walked over to the puncher. He

cut him down and the man landed heavily. He lay on the ground and looked up at Smoke.

"You've got a bit of food in your saddlebags," Smoke told him. "I've taken your pistols and left you your rifle. If you think it's worth your life to ride back and collect what wages are due you, then do so. But I would advise against it. The best thing you can do is put some miles behind you."

"I'm gone, Mr. Jensen. I swear on the Bible, I'm gone like the breeze."

"Get up and get gone!"

Fifteen seconds later, the hand was in the saddle and riding. Montana would not see him again.

Smoke stayed on the fringe of Circle 45 range, whenever possible staying in timber and never skylining himself. The smell of food cooking drifted to him. He picketed his horse, slipped on moccasins, and taking the .44-40 from the boot, began stalking the source of the smells. He quietly walked to within a hundred feet of the camp. Four men sat drinking coffee and frying bacon. A pot of beans hung over the fire. Smoke injuned his way closer and smiled at the laxness of the men. They obviously believed that since they were on Circle 45 range they were in no danger. Rifles were in saddle boots and only one of the men was wearing a gun. The others had tossed their gun belts onto rumpled blankets. Smoke rose as silently as any Apache and stood for a moment, staring at the men. He knew one of them would spot him.

One did, his eyes taking in the rifle pointed right at him. His eyes widened and his mouth dropped open. "Morris," he finally said. "Boys. Don't none of you do nothin' itchy."

"What are you talkin' about, Granville?"

"Smoke Jensen."

"What about him?"

"He's standin' 'bout fifty feet behind you with a rifle in his hands."

"Sit right where you are," Smoke told the group. "Or die right where you are. The choice is yours."

"We're calm," Granville said.

Smoke walked into the camp site and placed the muzzle of the .44-40 against the head of the only one who was armed. He reached down and took the man's pistol. Smoke backed off a dozen feet and sat down. "Turn that bacon and stir those beans," he told the group. "Then dish me up a plate. I'm hungry. We'll talk while we eat and then you boys can saddle up and drift on out of the territory."

"Huh?" Morris said.

Smoke thumbed back the hammer on the .44-40 and the Circle 45 hands tensed. "You ride or you die," he said simply. "It's that easy. I'm tired of this war. I'm tired of the likes of Clint Black. And I'm tired of the likes of men such as you. I don't want to have to look at your ugly faces again."

"You ain't got no call to insult us," one said.

Smoke smiled. "There is nothing I could say about you that should insult you. You're murderers, thieves, and God only knows what else. But your lives are about to take a turn for the better. I think you boys are about to see the light."

"I don't think you'd shoot an unarmed man," one of them said.

"Then you're a fool," Smoke told him. "The only rules I play by are my own. I was raised by mountain men, boys. Preacher and Nighthawk and Cherokee Jack and Dupre and Powder Pete and Lobo, just to name a few. I put my first man in the grave long before I had to shave. I'll shoot every damn one of you

172

then sit amid your bodies while I eat your food and then I'll leave you for the buzzards and the critters. And don't you ever think for one second that I won't. You crap and crud killed my men and killed young boys and tried to kill my wife and me. Put yourself in my boots and think about that."

The four men were beginning to sweat as Smoke's words sank in. The one called Granville was pale, his eyes shining with fear. He said, "I can't talk for the others, but you let me, and I'll drift. You'll never see me again, Jensen."

"I won't," the one called Morris said. He looked at Smoke and his lips moved in an evil smile. "I'll hunt you down and kill you and then have my way with your wife. See how she likes a real man. What do you think about that, Jensen?"

Smoke shot him. The slug took the gunhand in the center of the chest and he was dead before he fell back on the ground.

"Dish up the food," Smoke said. "And then you boys can saddle up and ride out of here."

"You damn shore got that right," Granville said.

Nineteen

"We're short one hand," Jud reported to Clint. "He should have been in a long time ago. And that ain't all. Fatso rode out to the boys' camp this afternoon to see if they needed anything, what with them hidin' out after the jailbreak. The camp was deserted, except for Morris's dead body."

Clint came out of the chair. "What?"

"That's right. He was shot right through the heart." He held out the brass. "Forty-four-forty at close range. Didn't none of those boys carry a forty-four-forty."

"Jensen?"

"Has to be. Camp wasn't churned up with boot prints. Just the prints of the boys and one set of moccasin tracks. And one hell of a big man wearin' 'em."

"He is actually on *my* range, attacking *my* people?" That anyone would be so bold as to openly declare war on Clint Black was astonishing to the man. "Well . . . I won't have that. I will not tolerate it."

"Boss, don't order the boys out at night. That's what Jensen wants."

"What do you mean?"

"He'll attack the house if you pull the men away."

"One man will attack this house? Jud, you're turning into an old woman. Jensen isn't a fool. He's just stupid. He's up in the high country. Miles from here."

Actually, Smoke was standing by the front porch, listening to every word. Since Clint hated dogs, and shot everyone he saw, there were no dogs around to sound the warning. The corral was too far away for the horses to act as sentries. Smoke had been busy around the Circle 45 headquarters, having more fun than a half a dozen schoolboys. And more fun should start at any moment.

A scream came from one of the outhouses behind the bunkhouse. Smoke smiled, thinking: *let the fun begin*.

"What the hell's the matter over there?" Jud hollered.

"They's a goddamn rattlesnake in the shitter!" a hand bellered.

"Well, shoot the damn thing," Jud yelled. "Jesus! Act like a bunch of women sometimes."

Jud stalked off the porch and stepped on a rake that had just been placed on the path, placed in a manner that was tantamount to sabotage.

The handle flew up and smacked the foreman right in the face, almost knocking him down. Clint ran off the porch to see about his friend and foreman. "You all right, Jud? Jesus, your nose is busted. Come on back to the porch. I'll get a wet cloth." He started hollering for the cook.

Smoke ran around to the back of the house where he had placed a jug of kerosene he'd swiped from Clint's storeroom. He poured the kerosene all over the back porch and waited until it soaked into the dry boards.

A Circle 45 hand started hollering for someone to let him out of the outhouse, the door was jammed.

It sure was. Just as soon as the hand had stepped inside and closed the door, Smoke had wedged a stick in tight.

Before leaving the house, Smoke had found a long string of old firecrackers someone had left behind. He had taken them along. He lit a match, started the porch burning from underneath and slipped to the bunkhouse. He lit the fuse to the firecrackers and tossed them through an open window. Then he decided he'd better get the hell gone from that immediate area.

"Let me out of this damn crapper!" the hired gun hollered.

"Fire!" another yelled.

The fuse burned down to the firecrackers and pandemonium took over as what appeared to be an attack on the bunkhouse opened up. The hand trapped in the outhouse was rocking the entire structure back and forth in his frantic attempts to get out. He turned it over. Backwards.

The hands in the bunkhouse began shooting all over the place at imaginary foes.

When the other hands reached the water barrels, they were all empty. Smoke had cut holes in them with his knife. Everybody began using blankets and coats and brooms to beat out the fire which by now was threatening the wooden part of the house.

Smoke was still laughing when he reached his well-chosen and hidden little camp.

"The sorry son actually was *here!*" Clint exclaimed. Come the dawning, he had looked at the few firecrackers that had not exploded in the bunkhouse, and at the bullet holes caused by nervous hired guns.

Stared at the wedge in the door of the outhouse—the hand had finally succeeded in kicking out the bottom of the crapper. Clint had found the jug of kerosene, and looked at the cause of the water barrels being empty. "He violated my property, almost burned down my house, and sabotaged the water barrels. I can't believe it."

"It's almost like he was playin' a joke," Fatso Ross said. "Like he was havin' fun with us." Fatso looked at Jud's swollen face where the rake handle had popped him. "But I don't 'magine it was much of a joke, right, Jud?"

"I get that bastard in gunsights, the joke'll be on him," the foreman said.

For once it was Clint who had the level head. "We don't strike at the Double D. Not yet. We don't cause any trouble in town. Not yet. I want five men around the house at all times, the rest of you fan out, during the daylight hours only, and start searching my spread. Ride in pairs. No lone-wolfing it. The man is too dangerous for that. Take off. The offer still stands: five thousand dollars to the man who kills Smoke Jensen."

Smoke had risen before dawn and rode back to Double D range. He stripped the saddle from his horse and hid it, then wrote a short note to Sally, tying it in the mane. He slapped the horse on the rump, knowing it would head straight for the corral. He took his sack of food and his other gear, including the ropes, and headed back to his little camp, deep in Circle 45 territory.

Longman and Steve Tucker were riding together.

Wyoming could not have produced any sorrier pair than these two. Both were wanted in at least five states and two territories. And both of them were thinking about that five thousand dollar bounty that Clint had placed on the head of Smoke Jensen. And they were not watching their backtrail.

Two seconds after they had passed along the narrow trail, Smoke stepped out and fireballed a fist-sized rock, then ducked back into the brush and slipped up the side of the trail. The stone hit Longman on the back of the head and knocked him slap out of the saddle and unconscious on the rocky ground. If he had not been wearing a hat, the blow might have killed him, which was what Smoke had in mind.

"What the hell . . . ?" Steve said, turning in the saddle at the sound of his buddy hitting the ground. There had been no shot and the rock lay among other stones on the trail. Steve couldn't figure out what had happened. He swung down from the saddle and knelt by his friend. Steve felt a blinding flash of pain and then he was stretched out beside his friend.

Smoke peeled them both down to their long-handles and took their clothing, boots, guns, and horses. They were a good ten miles from the bunkhouse and barefooted. It was going to be a long and painful hike back. Smoke threw the clothing away several miles from the still-unconscious men and unsaddled the horses, turning them loose.

He slipped back into the timber and brush.

The men of the Circle 45 hunted all that day for Smoke. The more fortunate of the hunters could not find a trace of him. Longman and Tucker staggered into the bunkhouse late that afternoon, their feet badly bruised and bleeding. Longman was seeing double and very nearly unable to speak. Bankston, Nelson, and Clements had not shown up by late afternoon.

"You better find them men 'fore dark," Bronco Ford told Clint. The gunman was not afraid of Smoke, but he did have a lot of respect for him. "You send search parties out after dark and none of 'em will come back. Smoke Jensen's like a puma in the woods."

"If I want your opinion," Clint told the man, "I'll ask for it."

Bronco shrugged his shoulders and walked off.

Bankston had become separated from his riding partner and was now tied to a tree, his own rope wound around him from ankles to neck and pulled tight. He was to spend a very uncomfortable night. Nelson and Clements were tied in the saddle, their hands behind their back, their horses wandering in a roundabout way back to the ranch. Smoke had gagged the men before tying them.

"There they are!" Grub Carson shouted, as the horses came ambling into the area. The gunslicks were untied and lowered to the ground. Neither man could feel anything in his hands.

The gags out of their mouths, Nelson croaked, "Man's like a damn ghost. He come out of nowhere. There wasn't no brush where we was. No place for him to hide. He's worser than a damn Apache."

"Nelson's right about that," Clements said. "Jensen was a-layin' right on the ground, right there in full open. And we didn't see him. You boys be careful. We're dealin' with an Injun here."

Clint was outwardly calm. Inside he was seething. He managed to ask, "Either of you men see Bankston?"

179

"No, sir," Nelson said. "But we seen his horse grazin', saddle and bridle was gone."

Clint turned to walk back to his house and his hat was blown off his head by a .44-40 slug. The man hit the ground belly down and got a mouth full of dirt.

Smoke had carried five Winchester .44 rifles to his position on a ridge near the big house—rifles taken from Circle 45 hands. They were loaded up full, giving him awesome firepower before he had to think about reloading. He laid down his .44-40 and picked up one of the .44s and began spraying the area below him with lead. He sent Circle 45 hands and hired gunslicks scrambling in all directions in the fading light of early evening. Smoke put ninety-five rounds of .44s into the house, the bunkhouses, and the outhouses before it was all over.

He put lead so close to sprawled Circle 45 men they could feel the heat of the bullets. He could have killed a dozen men that day, but chose not to kill or really injure anyone. But he made life miserable for those below the ridge.

He knocked out windows in the house and the bunkhouse. He perforated doors and stove pipes and punched holes in the roofs of buildings. His bullets smashed water buckets and the fancy chandelier that hung in the dining room of Clint Black's big house. The lead from his rifles clanged into cook pots, off of the stove, and into the outbuildings of the Circle 45. He poured lead into the gate posts of the corral and knocked the gate loose, stampeding the horses. Several of the panicked horses ran over men sprawled in the dirt, putting them out of action for days.

When darkness covered the land, Smoke left the empty rifles on the ridge and in a distance-covering run, vanished into the night. Clint Black rose wearily from the ground and walked to his house. He sank down to the steps and sat there, looking at the hole in his expensive hat.

A gunfighter called L. J. McBride picked himself up from the floor of the bunkhouse and began gathering his possibles, stuffing them into a bag.

"You leavin'?" another gunny asked.

"You better believe it," L. J. said. "I read Jensen's message loud and clear."

"What message?" Cleon asked.

"Man, he could have killed twelve or fifteen men from up there on that ridge. But he didn't. He tellin' us if we wanna live, we better fly. I'm flyin'."

"You just hold on and I'll ride with you," another hired gun said. "Smoke Jensen is a one-man war party. And this is one party that I'm skippin'."

"You gonna turn your backs on that five thousand dollars?"

"Five thousand won't help you if you're in a grave, partner. I ain't never seen no armored bank wagon followin' a hearse."

Sheriff Harris Black and one of his deputies made the Double D in time for breakfast the next morning . . . just the way they'd planned it.

Over coffee, Harris said, "Talked to three gunnies last night. They stopped in town for a drink before riding on. Seems that some unknown rifleman's been doing all sorts of mischief out at the Circle 45." The sheriff had to smile. Then the smile changed to a chuckle. "Seems this feller burned down the back porch, tossed firecrackers into the bunkhouse, shot up some outhouses, and in general made life pretty mean

181

for my brother and his hired guns. Is your husband around, Mrs. Jensen?"

"Why, no, Sheriff. He isn't. He's off on a business trip."

"Looks like it's a successful one," Harris replied. "Ammunition factories are going to be operating around the clock if this keeps up."

"Supply and demand, Sheriff," Sally said with a smile. "That's what keeps the economy strong."

Just as she was saying that, a horrified Bankston, still tied to the tree, watched as a passing parade of skunks paused a few feet from him, turned their backs to him, and lifted their tails.

"Oh, no!" the hired gun said, just as the skunks fired.

Twenty

"We found Bankston," Jud told Clint. "We drew straws to see who'd cut him loose. Fatso lost."

"What are you talking about?"

Jud explained.

"Where is he now?"

"Down at the crick, washing, for all the good it'll do him. Them skunks scored direct hits, Clint. It was so bad Fatso got sick."

Clint pointed his cigar at his foreman. "Let me tell you something, Jud. I don't like jokes being played on me. Jensen thinks this is funny. But I'm not laughing. The man is not only making a fool out of me, but you and the men as well. You think about that and pass the word to the boys."

Clint watched his foreman's face and saw a scowl form amid the bruises from the rake handle. "I didn't look at it like that, Clint. But you're right. What do you want the boys to do?"

"That's the problem. I don't know. I feel like I'm a prisoner on my own land. Damn Smoke Jensen!"

Stony handed Sally the note from the horse's mane and she read it and smiled. "He's fine. And having fun."

"Fun?" the cowboy said. *"Fun?"*

"Yes. It's only a few lines, but I sense that he doesn't want to kill unless he's forced into it. He's trying to demoralize Clint's hands."

"I, ah, ain't real sure what that means, Miss Sally."

"He's trying to get them to quit."

"Oh. He ought to just plug everyone he sees. That's the best way I know of to get them to quit."

"It might come to that, Stony. But I hope not. There has been far too much bloodshed already."

"Clint ain't gonna quit, ma'am. I know the man. He'll fight to the bitter end."

"Then the man is a fool," Sally said.

"Yes, ma'am," the cowboy replied. "I reckon he is. But a dangerous fool. I hope your man ain't takin' him too lightly."

"Oh, I assure you, Stony. My husband is taking Mr. Black very seriously."

Smoke shifted his camp, moving much closer to the home of Clint. He lay on a ridge in heavy brush and watched the grounds through binoculars. Someone had rigged a tent about two hundred yards from the bunkhouse and Smoke couldn't figure out what in the world it was for. Only one man was staying in the tent and Smoke recognized him as the man he'd tied up in the woods. Every time he tried to leave the tent area, the others would curse and wave and shout him back.

"Strange," Smoke muttered. "Very odd behavior. Maybe the man has measles or something."

Taking a longer look, Smoke could see that few hands had left the ranch grounds. They had rounded up their stampeded horses—most of them anyway—and the corral was full. Clint had called a halt to the search and was making plans. And he'd do it much more carefully than before. Smoke had stung the man and he'd be smarting from the sting. Smoke suddenly had a hunch that he had overstayed his welcome and it just might be time to get gone from Circle 45 range. The more he thought about it, the better that idea sounded to him. He gathered up his gear and headed back to friendlier territory.

He spent that night in a cold camp sleeping under the stars. He woke up just one time. But it was only a bear rooting and grunting around. Smoke stayed awake long enough to hear the bear's sounds fade away, and then he went back to sleep.

He was back at the Double D at noon the next day. He'd have to make a new pair of moccasins, for the ones he had on were nearly worn out.

After a bath and a shave and a change into fresh clothing, he told the others what he'd done.

Everyone got a kick out of it, especially about the hand trapped in the outhouse and about Smoke blowing Clint's hat off his head.

"But," Smoke told the group, "while I did have some fun at Clint's expense, he's not going to let it rest. He'll never forgive me for terrorizing his home and for making a fool of him. I don't know what he'll do next. But you can bet it won't be anything nice."

"We need to go into town for supplies," Sally told him. "We're running low on nearly everything."

"Make a list, get the wagons ready, and we'll go in tomorrow morning," Smoke said. "We'll take four men with us; the rest of you stay here and keep watch. We're not prisoners on the spread. If Clint or his men are in town and want trouble, I'll damn sure oblige them."

They were, and he did.

The Circle 45 hands were in no mood for fun and games; they were still smarting over the antics of Smoke Jensen. Tucker and Longman could not pull boots on over their mangled and swollen feet. A half a dozen Circle 45 riders had just disappeared without a trace. Several others had ridden back to the bunkhouse, collected their gear, and left, a couple without even staying around to get their pay. A man couldn't get within fifty feet of Bankston, he still smelled so bad. So it was a trouble-hunting bunch who waited in Blackstown that morning.

Sheriff Harris Black and all but one of his deputies had been called out of town, helping to chase down two men who had robbed and murdered an elderly farmer and his wife the night before. It was a nervous deputy who watched the Double D people come in from one direction and the knot of Circle 45 hands ride in from the other. Lucas stepped back into the office and took a sawed-off from the rack, breaking it open and loading it up with buckshot—or what passed for buckshot in those days, usually nails and tacks and ball bearings and sometimes small rocks.

"Well now," Tex Mason said. "Would you just look who's ridin' in."

"I see them," Weldon Ball said. He stood by his horse, looking over the saddle. "We play this right and we got Jensen cold."

"Let's let them get all spread out. Some of them boys will stay with the women, guardin' them. John, you and Ballard go with Weldon. Art, you and Fatso stay with me. Austin, you take Cantrell and Miller. If we play this right, we can end it today and ride out with money in our pockets."

"Yeah," Austin said. "If we put Smoke Jensen down, we can name our price from here on out."

"We'll have a drink and let them get started doin' their business," Weldon said. "Then we'll make our move. Stay loose and ready."

"I think it's gonna pop this day," Stony said, swinging down from the saddle in front of Hanlon's Emporium. They all, out of long habit, freed the hammers of their six-shooters. "That bunch of no-counts ain't taken their eyes off us."

"Check your guns," Smoke ordered the men. Stony, Malvern, Waymore, and Eli checked their guns and loaded up the empty chamber. "See how they're standing? There'll be three groups of them. Watch yourselves. Sally, you and the twins get inside the store and take your time shopping. Stay clear of the windows."

Smoke paused for a moment, standing by his horse. "Waymore, you and Malvern pull the wagons around to the rear of the store. Let's get our horses off the street while we're at it." Smoke walked down to the sheriff's office. He pushed open the door and told Lucas, "Pass the word to get the women and kids off the streets, Deputy. I think it's going to explode this day. Where's Harris?"

"Him and the others are out chasing a double murderer. And it's no joke this time."

"All right. Lucas, we're not going to open this ball. But when the music starts, we won't be wallflowers about hitting the dance floor."

"I understand. I'll start spreadin' the word."

Within minutes, the street was cleared of horseflesh and humans. The sun beat down; already it was a hot day. A wind devil spun around in the center of the street, then vanished, whirling like a dervish. Dr.

187

Garrett began laying out bandages and instruments.

Smoke and the Double D hands had fanned out, all up and down the street. They stood in the shadows of buildings and alleyways and watched and waited. Inside the saloon, the Circle 45 hired guns were sipping rye, working up their courage to try to do what so many others had attempted and failed. To kill the legendary Smoke Jensen.

A drifting cowboy rode slowly into town. He stopped at the edge of town and took in the scene. Nothing was moving. Not a horse or man, woman, or kid in sight. Even the dogs had cleared the street. He turned into the livery and swung down.

"What's goin' on here?" he questioned the hostler.

"The Double D hands and the Circle 45 riders are gettin' ready to settle some old scores."

"Who's your money on?"

"Let's put it this way: the Double D is bein' bossed by Smoke Jensen."

"Smoke Jensen!" the cowboy exclaimed. "Here?"

"Durn sure is. In the flesh. You'd be showin' some smarts if you just stood right here 'til this is over."

"I ain't never been known to be real bright," the cowboy said. "I think I'll go find Mr. Jensen and ask for a job."

"Now?"

But the cowboy was gone, walking up the boardwalk. He stopped at an alleyway and grinned at Waymore.

"Git in here, Conny," Waymore said. "You damn fool. I thought you was lookin' at the rear end of cows down in Kansas?"

"I quit 'em after me and the foreman had a slight disagreement."

"You mean, you punched him in the mouth and he fired you."

Conny grinned. "Yeah. After he beat the stuffin's out of me."

"You never did have no sense. What happened?"

"He called me a bad name and I busted him on the nose. Your boss hirin'?"

"Now I know you ain't got no sense. You know who's ramrodin' this outfit?"

"Man down at the stable told me."

"And you still want to sign on?"

"Why not?"

"Now I'm sure you're crazy. Yeah, as a matter of fact, we could use another hand or two. You got a horse?"

"How the hell do you think I got here from Kansas — walk?"

Before he could reply, boots sounded on the boardwalk. "Yonder comes the boss," Waymore said.

Conny whistled softly. "He sure is a big'un, ain't he?"

"And hell on wheels with them guns." He waited until Smoke had calmly strolled up as if on a Sunday walk. "Boss, this here terrible-lookin' saddle bum is Conny. He ain't to be trusted around food nor whiskey, and he likes to fight — even though he don't never win — but he can ride anything with hair on it and he'll give you a good day's work. He needs a job."

Smoke smiled and shook hands with the man. "You're hired. Can you use that gun you're wearing?"

"I ain't no fast gun. But I generally hit what I'm shootin' at."

"You're stepping into the middle of a war. I want you to know that up front."

"If you're fightin' that damn Clint Black, I'd ride

189

for nothin' but bunk and board."

"Don't hire him on them terms, Boss," Waymore said. "He can eat more'n any two men you ever seen."

Smoke chuckled. "You're a pretty good hand at the table yourself, Waymore. All right, Conny. Clint's hired a lot of gunhands. Some of them are pretty good. He's got nine men in town right now. Including Weldon Ball, Tex Mason, and Austin Charles. They're all over at the saloon. We wait for them to start the show."

"It's a good thing I ain't eat in a day," Conny said. "Eatin' makes me sleepy."

"If that was the truth you'd be asleep all the time," Waymore remarked. "You ridin' the line, Conny?"

"I ain't got a dime to my name."

Smoke handed the puncher a twenty dollar gold piece. "That might make you feel better."

"Durn sure does, Boss," Conny said, pocketing the money. "Now if them bad'uns over there will just get this party goin', we can get it over with and I can get me something to eat 'fore I fall over from the hungries."

"You better get you some boots first," Waymore told him. "I can see your dirty socks on both feet."

"Conny," Smoke said, after looking at the cowboy for a moment. "You stay here with me for a moment. Waymore, use the alleys and tell the boys to move this thing to the edge of town. Up next to the bridge. I don't want a stray bullet to kill some innocent person."

"Right, boss."

"Conny. You follow Waymore and stop in at the general store and get you a hunk of cheese and a handful of crackers. You're staggering on your feet, man. How long's it been since you've eaten?"

190

Conny grinned. "Several days, boss. It just ain't in me to beg. And times is hard out here."

"All right. Go get something to eat and meet me behind the store in a few minutes."

Smoke gave Conny enough time to reach the store, then he rolled a cigarette and smoked it down, always keeping his eyes on the saloon batwings. There was no sign of the Circle 45 hands. Smoke ground out the butt with the toe of his boot and walked up the alley. Conny was sitting on the loading dock, wolfing down a huge sandwich and drinking a bottle of sarsaparilla. The puncher grinned at him. He was missing two front teeth, and Smoke suspected they'd been knocked out in a brawl.

"After three of these sandwiches, I could take on a mama bear with cubs," Conny said.

"Three!" Smoke said.

"I eat quick when they's shootin' to be done."

Sally appeared at the back. "I'm laying in extra supplies," she said with a smile. "Your new hand can put away the food."

Smoke shook his head and Conny brushed a few crumbs off his patched shirt and drained the sarsaparilla. He checked his Colt and loaded up the empty chamber. He hopped off the loading dock. "Now let's go see your varmint, boss."

As they walked, Smoke brought Conny up to date.

"I know Clint Black," Conny said. "He's as lowdown as they come. No mercy or feelin's for nobody in him. If you have to shoot a rabid animal, you're scared of it, but you can feel sorry for it. 'Cause he didn't want the disease. But I could shoot Clint Black or Jud Howes and not feel nothin'. I tried to work for them. Man, I can't harm no woman or child. Until farmers just got so many around here there

191

wasn't no stoppin' them, Clint burned out and killed many of them. I worked one week for him and then hauled my ashes. And don't feel sorry for no hand that hires on with the Circle 45. After they've been there a week, they know what's goin' on."

Smoke turned toward the street and the boys fell in with him.

"Are we goin' out in the street and face them gunhandlers, boss?" Malvern asked.

"No. You men aren't gunfighters. We're going to make them come to us and meet them around these shacks here. We'll step out into the street and then at my word, dive for cover and start shooting."

"I like your style!" Conny said, just as one bootheel came off and he started limping along.

Waymore shook his head. "Make your shots count, Conny. With all that crowd up yonder in the saloon, they's got to be one with your size."

Twenty-one

"They're all lined up acrost the street up yonder," Fatso said. "They got a sixth man with 'em."

"Who is it?"

"I can't tell from here. But it looks like one leg's shorter than the other."

Weldon pushed away from the bar. "All right, let's do it." He walked out of the saloon and into the light and heat of the street. He cussed as he realized Jensen and his men had their backs to the sun and were forcing the Circle 45 hands to walk east, into the morning sun.

"Slick," Austin Charles said. "I figured they'd be waitin' for us right outside the saloon."

"Thinkin' never was your strong point," Tex told him.

"They must think we're stupid," Eli said. "They really think we're gonna just stand here and get plugged?"

Stony and Waymore were to Smoke's right. Malvern, Eli and Conny to his left. "Steady now," Smoke cautioned in a very low voice. "If they've got any sense at all, they'll have it in their minds to wait until there's about fifty feet between us before they pull. But that fat one is getting nervous already. See how stiff he's walking?"

"That's Fatso Ross," Stony said. "I want him."

"You can have him," Waymore said. "Bad as you shoot, you need a wide target."

"Art Long's had his eyes on me for a spell," Malvern said. "Me and him's had words more'n once. Even at this distance, I can see that he's got his eyes straight on me."

Behind the windows of stores and homes, the citizens of Blackstown were lined up, watching the slow walk toward death.

"Why, hell," Ballard said. "That's Conny Larsen. No-good saddle bum. He's mine."

"Ballard," Conny said in low tones. "He fancies himself a gunslick. He's in for a surprise. I always could outshoot, outfight, and outdrink that lowlife."

"Couple of more seconds," Smoke said. "Get ready. I've changed my mind. I'm going to open this dance and get it over with."

"Mason!" Smoke called over the ever-shortening distance. "It's a good day to die. Are you ready? Or have you lost your guts?"

Tex Mason's hands lifted and closed around the butts of his guns.

"Now!" Smoke yelled, and the street erupted in muzzle flashes and gunsmoke.

The Double D hands jerked iron, fired, and scrambled for cover. The move took the Circle 45 guns by surprise. They had not been expecting that and were caught flat-footed and in the open. Fatso Ross was down in the street and so were Tex Mason and Art Long. Nick Ballard was trying to hunt cover, dragging a busted leg as he scurried off to the side of the street and dropped down in a shallow ditch.

"Oh, Christ!" Fatso hollered. "It hurts!" His gun was in the dirt and both hands holding his bloody belly. He roared in pain and fell over on his face as the lead started whining and whistling all around him.

Tex Mason was down but not out. Smoke's bullet was true, but the gunhand still had fight left in him. Sitting in the dust, he filled both hands with Colts and eared the hammers back and let them bang. Smoke, down on one knee, leveled a .44 and ended the bloody career of Tex with one shot. Tex fell over dead in the dirt.

Waymore coolly put a slug in John Wood and the hand doubled over, dropping his pistol. Waymore had a bullet burn on his left arm.

George Miller got a slug into the leg of Eli that knocked the puncher down. Cussing, Eli leveled his .45 and drilled George neat, right through the brisket.

Fatso staggered to his boots, cussing, both hands filled with guns. Conny plugged him and Fatso tumbled to the dirt of the wide street.

Art Long panicked and started to limp toward the boardwalk. He got as far as the deserted building that once housed Nadine's Dress Shoppe before six-guns roared. Art was slammed against the old door. The door gave it up and Art died on the dusty and trash-littered floor.

Smoke's hat was blown off his head just as he turned his guns on Austin Charles. The gunfighter was snarling and shooting at Smoke as Smoke's bullets found him and turned him around, spinning like a top. Austin tried to lift his guns, but they were too heavy. The fancy engraved Colts fell from his numbed fingers and Austin collapsed to the street. The last words from his mouth were curses, directed at Smoke Jensen.

Ballard had dragged himself off behind Nadine's and was slowly staggering toward the saloon, hoping to get to his horse and get the hell gone.

He lurched past the rear of the leather shop just as the owner stepped out and conked him on the head with the butt of a shotgun. Ballard slumped to the ground, a swelling knot on his noggin.

Weldon Ball and Roy Cantrell made a dash for safety and jumped into the saddles of the first horses they reached. They fogged it out of town on stolen horses.

Smoke and the Double D hands slowly stood up. Stony had a cut on his face, Waymore's arm was bleeding, Eli's leg was throbbing with pain and he was supported by the strong arm of Conny. No one else was hurt.

Smoke quickly reloaded and stepped over to view the carnage. Fatso was dead in the dirt. Tex Mason was dead. George Miller was alive, but not for long. Eli's bullet had punched right through him, high up, nicking a lung. Austin Charles was dead. John Wood was badly wounded.

"He'll probably make it," Dr. Garrett said, panting from his run up the street.

"I got one over here," the shop owner hollered. "Wounded in the leg. I busted his head for him."

"I want a posse formed up right now," Lucas said. "Weldon Ball and Roy Cantrell stole them horses in plain sight of everybody. You stay in town," he said to Smoke.

"I'll be right here," Smoke replied. He looked at his bullet-torn hat. "Shopping for a hat."

The dead were hauled off to be measured for a box, and the wounded escorted to Doc Garrett's office. The doctor worked on the Double D men first, while the Circle 45 hands hollered and complained about it.

Smoke went to the store for a new Stetson. He picked out one with a lower crown. "Presents less of a target," he told Sally and the Duggan twins. "Maybe this one will last me longer." He looked around as his men came in. Doc Garrett wanted to keep Eli for a day just for insurance.

"You boys get the supplies loaded up and escort the ladies back to the ranch. I'll wait around for the sheriff and give a statement. Get a few more boxes of ammo. After this, there is no telling what Clint Black might do. Stay close to the ranch and no riding alone with the herd."

Clint Black was furious when the deputy and the posse thundered into his front yard, but he had sense enough to know that to fight would be stupid.

"Get Weldon Ball and Roy Cantrell out here right now," Lucas told him. "They're under arrest for horse-stealin'."

"Deputy . . ." Clint started to bluster.

Lucas lifted the muzzle of the Winchester. The posse members had fanned out and circled so they could cover in all directions. Twenty rifles were lifted. The sound of hammers being eared back was very loud in the stillness of the morning.

"I said right now, Clint," Lucas told the rancher.

"Or you'll do what?" Clint said, anger taking over his mind.

"I'll place you under arrest for interfering with a peace officer and then kill you right where you stand."

"Lucas!" Jud called from the bunkhouse. "I'm bringin' the men out. Just calm down. Everybody calm down."

"Tell one of your men to saddle horses for them,

197

Clint," Lucas said. "And bring out those horses they stole from town."

"Do it, Tom," Clint said, his voice heavy with rage and his big hands clenched into fists.

Jud walked up, Weldon Ball and Roy Cantrell with him, shuffling along behind. Lucas stepped down and handcuffed the two men then waited until Tom brought up two horses. "Up," he ordered the Circle 45 men. Back in the saddle, he looked at Clint Black. "You won't break these two out. There's been some cell changes at the jail . . . while we were repairing the other damage. Be seein' you, *Mr.* Black."

The posse left in a cloud of dust. Weldon and Roy did not look happy at all.

"You boys get busy doin' something," Jud ordered the hands. "You might get together the gear of the men who ain't gonna be comin' back and see if they got clean clothes to get buried in." He turned to Clint. "We got to talk, boss. Right now."

"In the house," Clint said. Seated, whiskey poured, Clint said, "Speak your piece, Jud. You know you can shoot straight with me."

"It's got to stop, Clint," the foreman implored. "This just can't go on. We gonna be buryin' six men tomorrow. Six more men. We . . ."

". . . Have had this talk before. I thought we settled it then." Clint drained his whiskey glass and slopped more booze in.

"We settled nothing, Clint. Clint? Did you see the looks on the faces of the men in that posse? Did you *really* see them? They're not going to ever bow and scrape for you. Not ever again. You've got to understand that. You've been the big bull in the woods for years and you're gonna have to settle for it being over. Cleon's got a newspaper from Helena; got it from the stage driver. This war is front-page news. Smoke Jensen's name is like bees to honey. There'll be reporters in here 'fore long, and they'll dig and pry to see what started all the ruckus and find out about the ambush and the kids gettin' killed and all of it. Then what kind of a light will you be under? I'll tell you what kind: a real bad light. We got to stop this and stop it right now!"

Clint had paused in the lifting of glass to his lips. He frowned and set the glass down on the table. "Go on, Jud. You're not through."

"Just like I said to you before, the last time we talked. We fire all these gunhands and get back to the raisin' of beef. We live and let live, and mind our own business."

"And live with the knowledge that a damn gunfighter and a bunch of weak-livered, two-bit ranchers and saloon keepers and storekeepers beat us? Not me, Jud. Not me."

Jud left his whiskey untouched. He stood up and plopped his hat on his head. "All right, Clint. If that's the way you want it." He turned and headed for the door. Clint's voice stopped him and turned him around.

"Is this it, Jud? It is over for you?"

"Yeah, Clint. For me, it's over. I won't stay in the game with a stacked deck. See you, Clint." He walked out.

Clint sat for a long time in his study. He did not drink. He'd been drinking far too much of late, and for him to come up with any sort of plan, he needed to be clear-headed. He heard the sounds of a horse trotting away and knew it was Jud. Jud! He and the man had been together for years. And now his foreman and best friend had lost his guts. He rose and walked to the front porch and waved to a hand.

"Yeah, boss?"

"Was that Jud riding out?"

"Yes, sir. He packed his duds, got him a packhorse, and was gone in fifteen minutes. I never thought Jud would turn his back to you."

"Neither did I," Clint said with a sigh. "Tell Bronco Ford I want to see him."

"Right away, boss."

Clint sat down on the porch. Bronco walked over and Clint waved him to a seat. "How many men do we have still around, Bronco?"

"Eighteen, last count. And that includes you and me and the cook."

Clint's laugh was short and bitter. "God, a month ago I had *fifty!*"

"Some just rode off and didn't look back, boss. I reckon Smoke Jensen read some scriptures to them that we busted out of the jail. They sure cut out. We got some with busted legs and busted arms and knotty heads. You want I should send out some wires and see what I can drag up?"

"Yes. Today. I don't care where you get them or what they've done in their past. The meaner, the better. You're now foreman of this ranch, Bronco. Move your gear into the foreman's house. You get rid of Smoke Jensen for me, and you'll have a job for the rest of your life. That's a personal promise—from *me.*"

"Might be best if I flag down the stage and send them wires out of Helena."

"Good idea. Do that. Get packed to go. I'll have money for you when you're ready."

"Buckskin Deevers is around. He busted out of Yuma some months back. I know where he's hidin'."

"Get him. Get all you can find. I'll turn this coun-

200

try red with the blood of any who dare stand up to me."

"Sounds like my kind of war, boss. I'll be ready to go in fifteen minutes."

"I'll be here," Clint said grimly. "Right here. And I'll be here when all those who oppose me are buried!"

Twenty-two

Jud Howes rode into Blackstown and stabled his horses. He planned to spend one night and then be on the trail come first light. He knew where he was going and when he got there he was going to stay. He conducted his business at the bank, closing out his sizeable account. Then he walked over to the sheriff's office. Harris had just ridden in and was talking over the morning's events with Smoke when Jud opened the door.

"I'm peaceful," the ex-foreman of the Circle 45 said quickly. "And I intend to stay that way. From now on. I want to talk to both of you."

"Fine," Harris said. "Have a cup of coffee and sit."

Jud poured his coffee and took a seat. He startled both men when he said, "I just quit the Circle 45."

When he found his voice, Harris said, "That's probably very good for you, and very bad for us."

"Yeah, that's the way I see it. That's why I come over to talk. Now if you think I'm here to confess to anything, you're wrong. Clint and me been friends for years and years, and I'll admit we both done some terrible things. But for me, that's past. This is now. I ain't here to talk against him. I got me a pretty good hunch he'll make that no-count Bronco Ford foreman. Which will be fine as long as Clint don't plan on runnin' no cattle, cause Bronco is a gunhandler and that's all he's been since he growed up.

"Now then, Bronco will be callin' in some salty ol' boys that he knows. And he knows plenty of them. Clint ain't gonna give up. Put that out of your heads. He's goin' to fight until he's either top man on the hill again, or he's dead. That's the way it's goin' to be." He looked at Smoke. "I don't like you, Jensen. But I ain't goin' to fight you. I seen men like you before. Not many, but a few. You really ain't no better than the men you fight . . . not when it comes down to the nut-cuttin'. 'Cause you still kill. You got bodies planted all over the West. But you kill for some sort of highfalutin notion that otherwise decent folk find acceptable. That's always puzzled me. But I realize something else, too: men like you nearly always win. I don't know why that is, but it's true.

"You're goin' to have to kill Clint Black, Jensen." He cut his eyes. "Or you will, Harris. There ain't no other way. And I just don't want to be around to see that." He stood up. "I can't bring myself to wish you boys luck. I just can't do that. 'Cause I don't know whether I'd mean it or not. Men like Clint built this country. Oh, they're hard men, and they've done terrible things to others who come out later, when it was a lot easier and them others come in to squat on land that was settled by Clint and men like him." He waved his hand in a curt gesture. "Well, that's neither here nor there."

"You want to speak to Weldon or Cantrell?" Harris asked.

Jud shook his head. "I got nothin' to say to them two. You'll never seen me again, Harris. Nor will you ever hear of me. Jud Howes is not my real name. When I get to where I'm goin', I'll have a new name and paper to prove it. I'll ranch, and not do no harm to any man who don't come pushin' and shovin' and lookin' for it." He walked to the door and paused, looking around. "I was goin' to spend the night, but I think I'll just ride on and get clear of this place." He looked at Harris. "You're a good man, Harris. I mean that. And when all this is over, you'll do well at the Circle 45. 'Cause it'll be yours. I just hope you change the brand." He cut his eyes to Smoke and stared at him for a moment. "You, now, I ain't got no use for. I just don't like you one goddamned bit." He stepped out and closed the door behind him.

"Strange man," Harris said, after a quiet moment had passed. "There goes a man who is just as vicious as my brother, who probably had a hand in planning the ambush against you and the Duggan twins, and who now says he's had enough. I never thought he'd leave my brother."

Smoke stood up and reached for his new hat. "We'll probably have about a week of peace around here, Harris. Until your brother can import a fresh crew of gunhands. Then I expect we'll face the problem and wrap it up."

"You act like it's just a job of work for you," Harris said, the words spoken much more sourly than he intended.

Smoke put his hat on his head. "How do you want me to behave, Harris?"

The sheriff shook his head. "Oh, hell, I didn't mean that the way it came out, Smoke. I'm certainly not defending my brother. This mess can be laid right at Clint's feet and I know it. But if you'll forgive me for saying it, I really wish you and my brother and all his hired guns would just go away and settle this somewhere else."

"I'll face your brother anywhere he picks. Guns or fists; doesn't make any difference to me."

"Yeah," Harris said, a weariness in his tone. "I know that, too. But he's not going to do that. Not yet. But

Jud was right when he said that one of us will have to kill him."

"Could you?" Smoke asked softly.

Harris met his eyes. "If he braces me and pulls? You and me, Smoke, we're gunfighters. You know that reflex would take over. I wouldn't hesitate. I'd be sick afterward, but I wouldn't stand there and let him kill me."

"You through with me?"

"I wish," Harris said, softening that with a smile. "Oh, yeah. Someday there'll be laws out here against men settling arguments with guns. But that day is a long way off. Watch your back ridin' home, Smoke."

"I always do, Harris."

"Joe Owens seen Bronco Ford flaggin' down the stage this afternoon," Stony reported to Smoke after supper. "Headin' for Helena."

"He's gone to get more men. I expected it. Jud said that's what Clint would do."

"Jud's really gone?"

"He talked to the sheriff and me and then I watched him ride out, leading a packhorse. Said he didn't like me at all. But yes, he's gone for good."

Stony slowly shook his head. "I reckon stranger things has happened."

Conny asked, "So what do we do now?"

"Look after the herd, mend fences, and stay out of trouble. In about a week, we'll have all the trouble we can handle. I want one man in town at all times, starting tomorrow. By this time, Bronco has sent his wires and men will be coming in, some of them by stage. The last stage runs at three, so that'll give the men time to get back here for supper. I want to know who comes in and how many. The men Bronco will hire will be known gunfighters, easy to spot, and he'll probably hire at least one long-distance shooter, too."

"A lousy damn back-shooter," Conny said contemptuously. "Yeah, you're right. I'm surprised Clint hasn't done that already."

"He just hasn't thought of it. But Bronco will. For sure, he'll pick up two or three or maybe more in Helena. And there'll be some hanging around Butte. It won't take long for them to get here. Tell the men who ride in not to brace any of these ol' boys. Bronco will be hiring professionals. And they'll be quick on the shoot."

"That back-shooter will be coming in for you, boss," Stony said.

"It's been tried before," Smoke told him. "I'm still around. You boys relax while you can. In a few days, it's going to get real tense around here."

The first of the hired guns arrived three days after Bronco sent the wires. Waymore described them to Smoke. "The first one is a bad hombre called Tall Mosley. He comes high. The redhead is a Irishman named Danny O'Brian. Danny came from a real nice family down in Southern Colorado. He went bad early. Killed his brother and left the country. He's left a lot of dead men behind him. I can't place the other one you described."

"I heard him called Ned in the saloon."

"Ned Burr. He'd make Sam Bass look like a Baptist preacher."

The following day, Conny reported back. He looked shaken. "Man, some bad ones come in this day. I seen Luke Jennings, Little John Perkins and Tom Wiley. Half a dozen more I didn't know, but they looked right capable."

"You catch any names?" Smoke asked, marveling at the man's ability with a knife and fork. His elbows never stopped working.

"Yeah. There was a Dan, a fellow called Rod, and one other name that sounded familiar: Morton."

"Might be Dan Hutton. Rod is short for Rodman; I don't know his first name. Morton is probably Henry Morton. They're all bad ones. Clint is hiring the best, or the worst, depending upon how you look at it."

The next day, Stony reported back shaking his head. "Boss, we got to hire some hands. Gunhands. You ain't never seen the like of what rode in this day. I heard 'em talkin'. Clint wired 'em money to ride the trains in and money to buy fine horses when they got to the gittin' off point. And they was all dressed up fancy." He began ticking them off on his fingers. "James Otis. Paul Stark. Ed Burke. Tom Lessing. Hal Bruner. Big Dan Barrington. Half a dozen more that I didn't know."

"Rider comin', boss," Jeff called.

Smoke stood on the porch and shielded his eyes. Then he smiled. "Well, I'll be double-damned."

"You know that feller, boss?" Tim asked.

"Huggie Charles."

"Huggie Charles!" Malvern almost shouted the name. "The Arizona gunfighter?"

"That's him."

Smoke stepped off the porch as Huggie swung down from the saddle and beat the dust from his clothing. The two men grinned and shook hands.

"You ol' warhoss, you!" Huggie said. "Damn, but you're lookin' fine, boy."

"You're looking fit and fine yourself, Huggie. Sally!" he called. "We've got company."

Sally came out on the porch and began smiling. She skipped down the steps and Huggie grabbed her. "Sally, girl. How you doin', Missy?"

"Now you boys see why he's called Huggie," Smoke said with a smile. "He never misses a chance to hug a woman. Slim or fat, tall or short, beautiful or so bad looking she'd stop an eagle in a dive, Huggie grabs them."

"It's been too many years since you stopped by the Sugarloaf, Huggie," Sally admonished the man. "Just too many years."

"Well, I got me a spread down on the Verde. I was up in Denver lookin' for stock to improve my herd—Herefords are the way to go now—and I heard about all the trouble up here. Why I just saddled up and took to ridin'. Here I am."

"In time for supper, too."

"If you cooked it, honey, that in itself is worth the ride."

"Huggie!" Denver bellered from the porch. "You ol' biscuit-stealin' outlaw!"

"My God, Smoke," Huggie said with a grin. "What ever possessed you to hire something as dis-reputable as that ol' coot? Me and him go back more years than either of us care to think about."

"Huggie's got to be sixty years old," Conny said to the hands gathered on the porch. "Or better. But I bet you he's still quick with them guns. Look at them Peacemakers. If he carved notches there wouldn't be no handles left."

Over supper, Huggie said, "Del Rovare is a day behind me. I told him what was happenin' up here and he quick started windin' up his business and he'll be along."

"I haven't laid eyes on Del since . . . why, it's got to be before Nicole was murdered."

Those around the table fell silent as everybody remembered how Smoke Jensen went after the men who had molested and murdered his wife and son.

"I come through that part of the country some years back, Smoke," Huggie said. "That land is bein' farmed by a real nice couple and they're doin' well. I told them the story of the graves. They musta come in right after you left. They been takin' care of Nicole and the baby's restin' place. Flowers all the time around the graves."

Smoke nodded his head. "Good," he said softly, then excused himself and walked out onto the porch.

Conny started to rise to join him and Sally touched his arm. "No. Let him alone. Nicole and Smoke had a special relationship. Part of him will always belong to her memory. And that's the way it should be. It was a terrible thing what those men did to her and a tiny baby."

"Did Smoke really stake one of them out over a big anthill and pour honey on him?" Ted asked.

"Yes, he did. He also gelded another and cauterized the wound with a hot running iron."

Several of the cowboys suppressed a shudder at just the thought of that.

"He must have been some riled up," Conny said.

"When my husband gets riled up, Conny," Sally said, "believe me, you'll know it."

By the end of the week, Smoke figured that all the new-hired gunslicks that was coming in, were in. And the names were impressive. One-eyed Shaw, Curly Bob Kennedy, Stew Lee, Purdy Wilson, Phil Dickinson. There were other lesser-known gunhands, but all were good at their trade.

Del Rovare had ridden in, looking about as old as God, but still rawhide tough, nimble, and very, very fast on the shoot. He owned a ranch down in Wyoming, the D/R brand. But when a friend was in trouble, Del buckled on his guns and saddled up for the ride.

And it was rumored that Buckskin Deevers was on Clint's payroll. If that was true, Clint had sunk to new lows, for Buckskin was just about as sorry as any man who ever lived. There was nothing he wouldn't do.

Smoke personally knew some of the gunhands that Clint had hired, and felt that if he could talk to them, a few might just pull out. With that thought in mind, Smoke rode into Blackstown one week after Jud Howes had pulled out and Bronco Ford had been named foreman at the Circle 45. The hitchrails in front of the saloon were lined with horses, some with brands Smoke had never seen, many wearing the Circle 45 brand. He paid a visit to Harris Black before heading for the saloon.

"I was hoping my eyes were deceiving me," the sheriff said. "But I might have known you couldn't stay away from a fight."

Smoke smiled at the man and took a seat. "Actually, Harris, I came to town to talk to some of those men over there. I know a few of them."

"So you convince two or three of them to ride out. My brother will just hire more. What will you have accomplished?"

"Why do I get the feeling that you are not in a real good mood?"

"I got fifteen hired guns belly up to the bar over at the saloon. The word I get is that they're under orders to shoot any Double D rider they see. I can't prove that, but that's the word I get from several sources, including the bartender, who is so scared of my brother he'd walk on fire before he'd testify to that in any court of law. Now you ride in just as bold as brass and tell me that you're going over to that saloon to *talk* to some of those tanked-up hired guns. You're right, Smoke. I'm not in a real good mood."

"Who's over there, Harris?"

"I don't know all of them. But I did see Tall Mosley, Little John Perkins, and Paul Stark. I spent half the morning sendin' out wires to sheriff's offices all over the west. There isn't a warrant out for any of them. Except for Buckskin Deevers and he isn't about to show his face in town."

"Sheriff, I don't want a lot of bullets flying around the main street of town. If you tell me to haul it out of here, I'll leave without a word."

Harris shook his head. "I can't do that. Hell, I *won't* do that. But I tell you what I will do. I'll walk over there with you. It's right at noon and a cold beer would taste good before I grab something to eat."

"Let's do it."

Harris stood up, checked another pistol for loads, and shoved it behind his belt. He checked his other Colt and then smiled thinly at Smoke. "I believe in insurance. You loaded up six and six?"

"I'm full."

"I think both of you are crazy!" Deputy Simpson said, moving to the gun rack. "Sheriff, you want any of us to come with you totin' shotguns?"

"No. Just stay handy in case the lead starts flyin'."

The men stepped out to the boardwalk and stood for a moment. "What does it say in the Bible about Daniel in the lion's den?" Harris said.

"I don't know. But he made it out."

"Let's hope we'll be so lucky."

"I think God had something to do with Daniel getting out."

"I had a feeling a month ago I should start goin' to church more often."

Smoke chuckled and stepped off the boardwalk, the sheriff right beside him. Citizens and shoppers started ducking inside buildings. The wide main street suddenly became deserted.

Twenty-three

The two men pushed open the batwings and stepped inside the saloon, walking shoulder to shoulder. Once inside, from long habit, they moved apart. The place was filled to overflowing with gawkers, ne'er-do-wells, gamblers, and hired guns. The hum of conversation died as the two men were noticed.

Smoke leaned against the wall and surveyed the situation through cool eyes, his gaze stopping at Tall Mosley. "Been a while, Tall."

"Several years, Smoke," the long lanky gunfighter said. "Down around Boulder Creek, I think it was."

"That's right." He shifted his eyes to Little John Perkins. "John."

"Jensen," the little gunslick said. "You finally stuck your nose into something that you can't handle, didn't you?"

"Oh, I wouldn't say that, John. I'm still here."

Paul Stark turned and put his back to the bar. He stood smiling at Smoke. "Ain't seen you in two-three years, Jensen. You lookin' prosperous."

"I'm well."

"Your family?"

"They're fine."

"I heard your wife is here."

"Out at the Double D."

Paul's smile was not pretty. He straightened and

dropped his hands to the butts of his guns. "I been lookin' forward to this. Ever since I first laid eyes on that wife of yours. When you're cold in the ground, Jensen, I'll lift the skirts of that pretty woman of yourn. I'll strip her nekked and see how she likes it rough."

Smoke shot him. He did not change expression nor blink an eye. He just pulled, cocked, and fired before anyone could move a muscle. The bullet took the gunfighter in the center of the chest and Paul Stark was dead before his butt hit the floor. No one saw when he pulled his second gun.

"He had no right to say that about your wife," a Circle 45 hired gun said. "I might be shootin' at you 'fore long, Jensen. But I'll not say a word about a good woman."

"Paul raped a woman down in New Mexico a couple of years ago," another man said. "I never did have no use for him."

Smoke eased the hammers down on his .44s and a sigh could be heard from the crowd. A few of those who had witnessed the blinding speed and deadly accuracy of Smoke Jensen would finish their drinks and ride on. No amount of money was worth dying for.

Tall and Little John and the others now knew how fast Jensen was. And several of the smarter ones knew he had come to town to show them. If it hadn't of been Paul Stark, it would have been one of them. The eyes of the hired guns widened as the batwings were pushed open and Huggie Charles and Del Rovare stepped in. These men were living legends in the West. Right up there with the old mountain man, Preacher. These two old gunhandlers rated up there with Smoke Jensen and Louis Longmont and Johnny North and Earl Sutcliffe and the Mexican gunfighters, Al Martine and Carbone. What the hell was this pair of ol' rattlesnakes doing here?

"We always miss out on the fun," Rovare said, his eyes on the stretched out Paul Stark.

"Well, maybe it's for the best," Huggie said, stepping around Smoke and the Sheriff. "Man gets to our advanced age, too much excitement ain't good for him." A Circle 45 hand stood in his way. Huggie gave him a shove that nearly put him to the floor. "Get the hell out of the way, boy. Ain't you got no respect for your elders?"

"Who you think you're shovin' around, you old son of a bitch!" the punk popped off.

Huggie slapped him. Huggie was not a young man, but he had worked hard all his life, and his arms and shoulders still were packed with muscle from spending years wrestling cattle. His hands were hard and callused and the blow rocked the young tough back on his bootheels and brought blood to his mouth. He reached for his guns.

"No, Will!" Tall shouted. "That's Huggie Charles."

"Who the hell is Huggie Charles?" the punk said, and dragged iron.

Huggie shot him twice before the would-be tough could clear leather. The kid rose up on the tips of his boots and gasped, then fell forward, landing on his face. He moaned and rolled over, staring up at Huggie.

"I'm Huggie Charles, boy," the old gunfighter told him. "A man ought to know who killed him."

"But I can't die," the young man said, both hands holding his shot-up belly.

"That's what you all think," Del said, looking around the room. "But me and Huggie know different. Like Jensen here. A month from now, not a soul in this town will remember this boy's name. Six months from now, the wooden cross will have begun to rot. A year from now, his grave site will be known only to God—or the devil."

214

"That's a hell of a thing to say to a dyin' man!" the punk said.

Del looked down at him. "What'd you want me to say, congratulations?" He walked to the bar, Huggie beside him. "Rye, with beer chasers, for me and my friend."

The barkeep was so scared he could hardly pour and pull.

Doc Garrett pushed in and knelt down beside the dying gunhand. He looked up at the sheriff. "Not a chance."

"But I can't die!" the man hollered. "They said I was fast."

"They lied," Smoke told him, then walked to the bar, stopped by Tall. "Get out of this one, Tall." He spoke quietly, his elbows on the bar. "Go on back to where you came from."

"You got a couple of old gunslicks, ten or so punchers, and you're tellin' me to pull out? You ain't got that many friends, Jensen."

The batwings were shoved open and heavy boots thudded against the floor, accompanied by jingling spurs.

"Aw, hell!" a Circle 45 hand said.

Al Martine and Carbone, the Chihuahua gunfighters, walked to the bar. Smoke smiled at the expression on Tall's face. "You think Bronco Ford is the only one who can send a telegram, Tall?"

Martine dropped a hand on Tall's shoulder and spun him around. "You and I, amigo, we have differences to settle between us, no?"

Tall stiffened. He didn't want to pull on Al Martine, even though he knew he was just as fast. But 'just as fast,' won't get it. Both men would have lead in them. And standing one foot apart, the wounds would be hideous.

The batwings pushed open and two of the most disreputable-looking men anyone had seen in a long time walked in. They both looked older than dirt. They were dressed in buckskins, except for hat and boots. Both wore bright red sashes around their lean waists. Pistols tucked behind the sashes. They carried Winchester rifles, the '73 model.

"What the hell is *that?*" a Circle 45 hand asked.

"Puma Buck and Lee Staples," Smoke said. "You boys have heard of them, I suppose."

"Heard of them?" another gunny said from his chair, staring up at the old mountain men. "Hell, they been *dead* for years."

With no wasted motion, Puma laid the butt of his Winchester into the hand's face, busting his nose and knocking him out of the chair. "I'm a long way from dead, lad," Puma told him. "And you put a hand on that short gun and I'll kill you."

The hand cursed and came up with his fist wrapped around the butt of a .45. Puma pulled the trigger of the Winchester and punched the gunfighter's ticket for a long dark ride straight to hell.

"Whiskey!" Lee Staples hollered. "And plenty of it. It's been a dusty ride. Smoke, my boy!" He stepped up and pounded Smoke on the arms and shoulders. "It's been a long time."

Puma stepped over the man Huggie had left on the floor and walked to the bar, shaking hands with Smoke. He smiled at Tall, but there was no mirth in his eyes. "This one I helped raise. Me and a whole passel of other mountain men. Get out of my gawddamned way."

Tall's eyes widened in shock. No one talked to him like that. But he moved away, stepping lightly, his back still to the bar. This crazy wild-eyed old man scared him. Tall knew to leave old folks alone. For they had very little to lose and would kill you in a heartbeat.

"Another time, Tall," Martine said. He turned his back to the gunfighter and extended his hand to Puma. "I have heard of you for years, and I am honored to finally make your acquaintance. I am Al Martine, Mr. Buck, and this is my compadre, Carbone."

"Pleased, boys. I've heared of you. You come up to hep my boy, here?"

"Your . . . son?" Carbone was startled.

Puma cackled. "No. Not no blood kin. But a bunch of us mountain men sort of adopted him when he was a tadpole. Any man who is an enemy of Smoke's is an enemy of mine." He turned to face the crowded room. "And I'll kill any man who lifts a hand agin him. I'll shoot you in the back, I'll shoot you in the front. But I will kill you."

"Now just wait a minute," Harris said. "I'm the sheriff here, and I . . ."

"We don't give a damn who you are," Lee Staples said. "We don't believe in waitin' till a rabid skunk bites us 'fore we kill it. And don't even think about givin' me no lectures, I don't take kindly to them. Me and Puma there, we're somewheres around eighty years old. You think we really give a damn what you or anyone else says? Fifty years ago, I probably peed right here where this buildin' is standin'. Probably leanin' up agin a tree 'fore folks come in and cut 'em all down. Now you go run along and tend to lost dogs and treed cats. We'll handle this."

Harris stood speechless.

Puma looked at a young rider standing at the bar. "You work for the Circle 45, boy?"

"A . . . I, uh, yes, sir. I do. I hired on a couple of days ago."

Puma hit him a vicious blow in the belly with the butt of the Winchester, knocking the wind out of him. He doubled over, gagging, and fell to the floor. "Now you hear me, boy," Puma said. "Playtime is over. I talked with some Injuns over on the Divide a few days ago. They tole me that this here Clint Black who owns the Circle 45 had hired men to kill Smoke Jensen. Is that what you hired on to do, boy?"

"I reckon so," the young man gasped.

"Well . . . you a young man, you entitled to make a mistake. I did, a time or two. So I tell you what I'm gonna do. I'm not gonna kill you."

Lee Staples had turned around, facing the men in the saloon, his Winchester level, hammer back. Carbone and Martine stood with him, hands over their guns. Huggie and Del faced the crowded room, smiles on their faces. Not a Circle 45 hand moved a muscle. Most tried to not even breathe.

"Git up!" Puma snapped, and the young man rose painfully. "Walk out of here, get on your horse, and ride. Don't never let me see you within a hundred miles of this place whilst this little war is wagin'. 'Cause ifn I do, I'll kill you on the spot. You understand all that?"

"Yes, sir."

"Git!"

The young man got.

Puma turned around, facing the men in the room. "Anybody else here work for the Circle 45? If you do, make your peace with the Almighty, 'cause you're dyin' today."

"That son of a bitch is *crazy!*" a man whispered.

"Shut up," his buddy whispered.

Puma smiled. "Lee? You step on outside and get ready to shoot anyone who tries to mount a horse wearin' a Circle 45 brand."

Sheriff Black smiled grudgingly. These old boys were putting on the pressure and screwing it down tight. The pot might take the steam a while longer, but everything

218

was coming to a head and it had to blow the lid off soon.

He cut his eyes to Jensen. The man was leaning up against the bar, a slight smile on his lips. In a strange way, he's enjoying this, Harris thought. Then he thought: well, why shouldn't he? He was halfway raised by the likes of these randy, uncurried, wild ol' mountain men. Their philosophy is his own.

None of the Circle 45 hands made any attempt to move toward the door. They did not doubt to a person that Lee Staples would shoot them down like a rabid animal if they went near any horse wearing Clint Black's brand.

Smoke cut his eyes to Tall Mosley. "See you around, Tall."

"Yeah," Tall said. "Bet on it."

Smoke walked out of the barroom, followed by Al Martine, Carbone, then Huggie and Del. Puma was the last one to leave, cautiously backing out, a wicked grin on his face.

Harris came out to the boardwalk a moment later.

"Think I won't shoot you if you interfere?" Puma asked the sheriff.

Harris slowly shook his head. "No, Puma. I don't doubt it for a second."

"That's good, Sheriff," the old mountain man said. " 'Cause me and Lee is gonna bring this here little pimple to a head." His grin turned into a smile. "And we got a few more surprises to spring on you."

"I can hardly wait," Harris said drily.

Puma cackled out laughter. "Course your no-count brother ain't gonna like it a bit."

"You gun my brother down, without it being a fair shooting, or any other man in my jurisdiction for that matter, and you'll face murder charges."

"Hee, hee, hee," Puma cackled. "And you think you

219

be so keen with the high country you think you could find me out yonder in the lonesome?"

"No," Harris said honestly. "I imagine you could lose yourself back there and I'd never find you. I'm just telling you what the charges will be, that's all."

"I think you a good man, Sheriff," Puma told him. "Took you awhile to come to that, from all that I hear about you and your no-count brother, but you made a clean break. Now you ponder this bit of advice: don't confuse bravery and duty with foolhardiness. You just sit back and concentrate on catchin' chicken thieves and footpadders. Stay out of our way. And if you're thinkin' 'bout tryin' to 'rrest any of us, from Smoke Jensen to me, think agin. 'Cause it ain't gonna happen."

"I'll do my job," Harris said stiffly. "This is not eighteen-thirty, Puma. It's halfway civilized out here now."

Puma spat his contempt for that remark. "If it was civilized, men like your brother would be rottin' in the grave instead of hay-rassin' decent folk."

"You break the law, and I'll arrest you, Puma."

"You'll never do such of a thing."

Harris turned, stepped off the boardwalk, and walked to his office.

"What other surprises do you have in store, Puma?" Smoke asked.

"Hee, hee, hee," Puma cackled mysteriously.

Twenty-four

Those few hired guns who had ridden their own horses into town rode back to the ranch to get any horse that didn't have a Circle 45 brand on it. They had taken Puma at his word, which was wise, for the old mountain man had meant what he said, Sheriff Black or no Sheriff Black.

"He *what?*" Bronco and Clint both screamed at the news.

Tall repeated what Puma had threatened, and added, "He meant it, Boss. That old man wasn't kiddin'. I got to get some horses for the boys back in town."

"Oh, go on, get them," Clint said, shaking his head. "I should have guessed something like this would happen. I'll be glad when those old coots are all dead. But Al Martine and Carbone? I can't figure that. They were *after* Jensen not that long ago."

"They switched sides," Tall said. "I know the story. Martine and Carbone stopped hirin' their guns and went to ranchin' down in Mexico. Got them a right nice spread, so I hear. Call it the M/C. And believe me, they don't have no trouble with rustlers or bandits."

"Get the horses for the men," Bronco said. When Tall had left the room, he said to Clint, "You really think that crazy old coot will shoot anyone ridin' a Circle 45 horse?"

"Oh, yes," Clint said without hesitation. "But I've got horses with every kind of brand you can imagine. And I have bills of sale for them. That's no worry. Let's walk outside to the porch. Stuffy in here."

The rancher and foreman stepped out on the porch and a rifle barked, the slug howling off the stone of the house. Clint and Bronco hit the floor. Another slug, fired from a different direction, came screaming over their heads. A coyote yipped and a wolf replied in a howl.

"Those damned old coots brought friends with them," Bronco said. "That's no coyote or wolf."

Tall Mosley and a few others, caught in the corral, could do nothing except stay low in the dirt, crouched behind whatever cover they could find. Which was precious little.

"Crawl back toward the door," Clint said. "We can make the house."

A hand came galloping in from the range and he went galloping back out as long-barreled Springfield rifles, with a range of over three thousand yards, began barking. One knocked his saddle horn off—and another blew his hat off his head. He laid down on the horse's neck and got the hell gone from there.

The old mountain men on the ridges began making life miserable for those in the house and the hands in the bunkhouses. Stove pipes were knocked loose and windows were shattered. Doors were soon rendered useless as the lead knocked out great chunks of wood. Outhouses were riddled with heavy caliber lead and the horses in the corral screamed and reared and panicked and knocked down the gate. They went thundering out to open range, away from the frightening gunfire and the howling bullets.

Clint Black and Bronco Ford could do nothing except seek cover behind the stone of the house and cuss.

Back in town, the Circle 45 hands sat in the saloon and wondered when in the hell Tall and the others would get back with horses they could ride out on? Not a one of them even remotely considered attempting to mount up on a horse wearing the Circle 45 brand.

Smoke, Martine, Carbone, Huggie, Del, Puma, and Lee waited across the street from the saloon. Waited and watched and smiled at the plight of the hired guns. Harris Black and his deputies sat on the edge of the high boardwalk in front of the sheriff's office.

And the citizens of the town, men, women, and kids, passed by the saloon in a never-ending stream, pointing and laughing at the grounded gunnies, while the hired guns drank whiskey and got madder by the minute.

"It's comin' to a head, Sheriff," a deputy said. "We ought to stop them people over there. They're gonna make them gunnies mad and they'll be a killin'."

"Not this day, there won't," Harris said, rolling a cigarette. "Those boys over there in the saloon aren't fools. They know that if they opened up on civilians, they'd be slaughtered in two minutes. Smoke and those mountain men and Mex gunslingers would shoot that place to splinters and pick their teeth with what's left."

Farmers and riders for other small spreads came into town, saw what was going on, and immediately turned around and beat it back to their places, telling others of the events taking place in Blackstown. By early afternoon, the town was filled up with onlookers.

Out on the Circle 45 range, old mountain men were rounding up the horses and driving them out of the country while others of their kind were having fun riddling the house and bunkhouses with rifle fire.

Up to now, no one had been hurt on either side. Then Clint gave the orders—by shouting—to start making a fight of it.

"Is he out of his mind?" Jim Otis questioned. "Those

223

sharpshooters are a good half mile off and on the ridges. Hell, we can't even see them."

"And I seen at least three riders makin' a gatherin' of the horses in the south range," another said. "There's something goin' on that I ain't too sure about."

Bullets slammed through broken windows and through the now doorless frame. One clanged into a potbellied stove and whined off, spending itself against a wall.

"I'm gettin' awful tired of this," Curly Bob Kennedy said. "There's a wash out back that I think we could make if we stay in the trees. How about it?"

"Let's go," another said. "Anything beats this."

Then the firing abruptly stopped. The hired guns looked at each other for a moment, then slowly began getting to their feet. Most of them veterans of dozens of range wars and shootings, they sensed the sniping was over, at least for this day. A Circle 45 hand walked his horse into the corral. One arm was hanging useless and his shirt was bloody. He was helped from the saddle just as Clint and Bronco walked up.

"Old men," he said. "Looked like they was all older than God. They rounded up the horses and drove them off. I tried to jerk iron on one of them and he shot me just as cold as could be. Told me to give you a message, Mr. Black. Told me to tell you that you wanted this war, you got it. Now what the hell are you goin' to do about it?"

Clint's face hardened. "Who were they, Tim?"

"Boss, I don't know. I never seen none of them before. They was all dressed in buckskins. And they was *old!* All of 'em old men. They looked like them drawin's of mountain men."

"That's what they are," Tall said. "They've come out of the caves and hidden cabins up in the high lonesome to help Jensen."

Clint Black did some fancy cussing. Scoundrel and

murderer that he was, he was still a man of the West, and he knew what this development meant. There had never been a breed quite like the mountain man. They were, for the most part, solitary men who could go for months without seeing or speaking to anything other than their horses. They would brook no nonsense from any man, and if they were your friend, you had a friend for life. But if you were their enemy, they would shoot you on sight and do it without hesitation. Clint became aware that his hired guns had fallen silent and were all staring at him.

"They didn't get all the horses," Clint said. "Saddle them up and go into the east range and round up those over there. They haven't been ridden in awhile so they'll take some topping off. Cleon, you and Donovan hitch up a couple of wagons and go into town and get those men trapped in there."

"In a wagon, boss?"

Clint's hard eyes withered him silent. "You got a better idea, Cleon?"

"Ah . . . no, boss, I reckon not."

"Then get moving. The rest of you start picking up and repairing the damage. I've got to think."

"I think I'll ride in with the wagons," a newly hired gunhand said. "Get me a room at the hotel and take the mornin' stage out. That is, if you ain't got no objections. If you do, I'll walk in." He dug in his pocket and came up with greenbacks. "Here's your advance pay, Mr. Black. I ain't done nothin' to earn it."

Clint waved away the money. "You got shot at. That's enough. Ride in with the wagons and be damned." He turned and walked back to his shot-up house, Bronco walking beside him.

Hal Bruner looked at the gunny. "You think it's that bad, Teddy?"

"I think it's that bad. Man, Clint Black ain't got a

225

friend in this world. The whole countryside is against him. Now these wild men done come out of their holes and is gunnin' for him and anyone who rides for him. I'm gone." He walked back to his bunkhouse to gather up his belongings.

"I think I'll tag along with Teddy," another newly hired gunslinger said. "I'm out of this party."

"Then git," Grub Carson said. "I don't want no man stayin' that I can't count on."

"Let's go get them horses," Yukon said. "Damned if I feel like walkin' into town."

"Who says we're goin' into town?" Slim King asked.

"We're goin'," Yukon maintained. "Clint ain't gonna stand for this. Beginnin' right now, boys, we start earnin' our money."

It was an embarrassed bunch of gunslingers who climbed into the bed of the wagons for the bumpy ride back to Circle 45 range. None of them made any effort to retrieve whatever possessions they might have had in the saddlebags or to get their rifles in the boot. A townsperson talked briefly with Cleon and Donovan, and after the wagons had left he walked over to the sheriff.

"Somebody attacked the Circle 45 headquarters and run off all their horses. They really shot the place up bad. No one was killed, but a hand took a round in the shoulder."

Smoke, who was standing nearby, said, "Don't look at me, Sheriff. I don't know a thing about it and I'd swear on a Bible I had no knowledge of it."

"I believe you," Harris said. "But this little stunt just might be the final straw for my brother. You best brace yourself." He looked around. Puma and Lee had vanished. "Now where did those two old rowdies go?"

226

"I have no idea," Smoke told him. "I didn't send for them. They don't work for me or the Double D. They've lived a long, rich, full life, Harris. They'd rather go out in a blaze of glory. And they damn sure don't take orders from any man."

"Yeah," the sheriff said. "I noticed."

"You think Preacher sent them, Smoke?" Sally asked as they sat alone in a swing in the side yard that evening.

"I'm not even sure that Preacher is still alive, Sally. I think he is, and living in that home for old mountain men and gunfighters. No, I think these ol' boys just heard the news and couldn't wait to jump right in the middle of a good fight."

Sally looked around her in the dim light of gathering gloom. Mountains loomed all around them. "I wonder where they are right now?"

"The old mountain men? Oh, they're gathered around a little hat-sized fire, boiling coffee and searing fresh-killed deer or maybe one of the Double D's steers. They're laughing about what took place this day and figuring on how best to stir up some more trouble tomorrow. Don't worry about them. They've been taking care of themselves since long before you and I were born."

"But they're old men, honey. They're in their seventies and eighties."

Smoke chuckled. "And they're still tough as rawhide and mean as a just-woke grizzly. Sally, those ol' boys are having the time of their lives. They're giggling and cackling like a bunch of schoolboys right now. Oh, they've got aches and pains from rheumatism and the years of badly-set broken bones and the like. But this is fun to them. They've got something to do now. They feel a purpose to their lives. I hope none of them get hurt or killed. But if they do, they went into this with their eyes wide open. I lived with mountain men, Sally. I know the type of men they are; I'm a part of that breed. Don't worry about them."

From miles away, they both caught the very faint howl of a wolf echoing around the mountains. Another joined in, then another. Smoke chuckled. "That's them, isn't it?" Sally asked.

"Yes, that's Puma and Lee and their friends. But they're not doing that for my ears. That's over on the Circle 45 range. They're letting Clint and his gunhands know they're still around. I'd like to be a fly on the wall of the bunkhouses right now.

"Old bastards!" Tall said, as he sat on his bunk, cleaning his guns.

Yukon Golden smiled. "I hear you had your chance at some of them this day. And Al Martine, too. What's the matter, Tall, you have a change of heart?"

Tall stared at the man. "It ain't over yet, Yukon. And was I you, I'd watch my mouth."

"Shut up!" Bronco called from the open door. It would be open for some time, since the mountain men had shot it off. "The both of you. We're riding tonight. We're gonna hit the town and burn it to the ground!"

Twenty-five

"This is a dumb play," Yukon said. "Nobody ain't never treed no Western town and we're gonna get the crap shot out of us attemptin' it."

"We're not gonna treed it," Grub said. "Just burn it to the ground."

"How?"

"With fire!" Ed Burke said with a laugh. "Clint's got all that worked out. Stop worryin' so much."

"Yeah?" Yukon looked at the man. "So you tell me this: we burn the town to the ground, where are we gonna get supplies and food and whiskey? Huh?"

That got everybody's attention. Slim King finally said, "I don't understand why we're burnin' the damn town noways."

" 'Cause the boss says to do it," another summed it all up.

"That's right," Bronco said from the doorway. "These folks are gettin' too uppity for Clint's tastes. We burn them out and then when they move on, we rebuild the town and fill it with folks who'll show some respect for Circle 45 hands. Get your dusters and your masks. Let's ride."

But Clint's plan wasn't a very good one. Had he halted the thunderous drum of hooves a mile from town and sent men in in small teams, they could have easily burned down the town. Instead, the paid gunhands galloped up to the bridge, stopped, lit their torches, and then roared into town. By that time, the townspeople had armed themselves and were waiting. The Circle 45 men got the crap shot out of them.

They made only one pass through town and Bronco hollered at them to head for home range, taking the long way around to get there. There were six men dead in the dirt and four more wounded, their torches burning brightly on the ground beside them. Several buildings were set on fire, and that delayed the forming of a posse while the fires were extinguished.

"No point in going after them, Sheriff," Harris was told. "We all know who ordered it. They'll just alibi for each other like they've always done. Tomorrow we'll put signs up at both ends of town. No Circle 45 riders allowed in town. We're not going to sell your brother any more supplies."

"Do whatever you want to do, Felker. It's fine with me."

"And from now on, we all go armed, at all times. Swede over to the blacksmith's is gonna start sawing the barrels off of shotguns starting at first light. We've had all we're going to take, Harris. Any trouble starts, we're shooting."

The sheriff met the feed store owner's steady gaze. "All right, Felker. I guess it's way past time." *Past time for a lot of things,* Harris thought as he walked away. He turned up a darkened street toward his small house. Guns blossomed flame in the night and Harris Black fell forward on his face.

"Is he still alive?" Smoke asked Doc Garrett the next morning. A deputy had ridden out before dawn to tell them the news and Smoke had ridden back into town with him.

"He's hanging on," Garrett said. "I've done all that I can do. He took two slugs in the chest. Forty-fives, I think. One passed right through and the other lodged. I dug it out. He has not regained consciousness."

"He's a good man, Doc. The community would feel his loss."

"Yes. It took Harris a time to see his brother for what he really is, but he came around and then tried to do his best. They shot him down in the dark, from hiding. I doubt that he'll be able to add anything to that. If he ever regains consciousness."

"You're not from the West, are you, Doc?"

"No."

"I've seen men soak up half a dozen .45 slugs and stay on their feet and kill the man who put them there, and then go on to live to be old men. It's a tough breed out here, Doc."

"Well, Harris' breathing has evened out. He's got a chance. That's about all I can say."

"Tall Mosley hasn't."

"What on earth are you talking about? Has there been another shooting?"

"One is about a minute or so away. Al Martine rode in with me. And there's Tall stepping down at the saloon."

"What is it between those two?"

"They just don't like each other." Smoke walked out to the street and leaned up against an awning support post. He rolled a cigarette and waited.

Tall turned and faced Martine, who was standing on the boardwalk across the street. "What do you want, greaser?" Tall tossed the question out.

"Satisfacción, you son of a puta."

Doc Garrett stepped out. "I know what that means," the doctor said.

"Yeah. Very uncomplimentary," Smoke said, striking a

231

match and touching the flame to his cigarette.

"I'll kill you for that," Tall said.

"Then try."

Tall grabbed and Al put two holes in him. Tall stumbled backward, dropping one gun into the dirt.

"I told him a long time ago that jerking both guns was gonna get him killed someday," Smoke said. "Cuts your speed down just a tad."

Tall lifted his right hand and tried to cock his pistol. Martine waited. Tall painfully eared the hammer back and pulled the trigger, blowing a hole in the dirt. He fell to his knees and dropped that Colt. Then he toppled over into the hoof-churned earth.

"One less," Smoke commented, as Al turned and went into the general store to buy some candy for his sweettooth.

The two deputies who were in town had watched it all and they walked across the street to stand over the dying Tall Mosley.

"Sweet Baby Jesus!" Lucas said, looking up the street. "Look at that!"

Ten riders were walking their horses slowly into town. Smoke had already recognized Danny O'Brian and Yukon Golden. As they drew nearer, he could make out Slim King and Grub Carson. He was not familiar with the others.

"What do they want?" Doc Garrett asked.

"Me," Smoke told him.

"And you're going to do what about it?"

"Meet them."

"All *ten* of them?"

Smoke smiled. "Well . . . in a manner of speaking, yes."

Smoke looked across the street toward the general store. Al Martine had just stepped out and was standing in front of the store, sucking on a piece of peppermint candy. He pointed up the street and Smoke cut his eyes. Carbone was riding in and Smoke could tell by the tenseness of the man's body he was quickly sizing things up. Smoke nodded.

"Get up to those deputies, Doc. And tell them to clear the street. Quick, now. Those gunslingers are hunting blood and they're liable to start shooting at any moment." He stepped back inside the doctor's office, and exited out the back way just as Martine was angling for a better position.

Smoke trotted down to the saloon and slipped in through the back door. He wanted as much of the shooting as possible off the street, for the town was unusually crowded this morning, and a lot of kids were in town with their parents.

The bartender saw him and nearly had a heart attack. This barkeep was about the most timid Smoke had ever seen. He put a finger to his lips, shushing the man, and moved to a corner of the room, near a table that was shrouded in shadows. He loosened his guns.

Donovan and a hired gun from over Kansas way named Lessing entered the bar. They failed to see Smoke standing in the shadows. Tom Clark, George Miller, and Ed Burke faced Al Martine. Carbone was walking up the center of the street toward Danny O'Brian and Yukon Golden. Slim King and Grub Carson had slipped down an alleyway, looking for Smoke.

"You, ah, boys want a drink?" the nervous barkeep asked.

"Shut up," Lessing told him. "If we want a drink we'll ask for one." He looked around him, his eyes finally picking out the shape of a man standing in the gloom. "Who the hell are you?"

"The grim reaper," Smoke told him.

"The what?" Donovan asked.

"The pale rider."

"Don't give me no lip, boy," Donovan said. "I want a straight answer." He stepped away from the bar and walked slowly toward Smoke. "Damn!" the word left his mouth as he finally recognized the man in the shadows. He jerked iron.

Smoke's .44 roared and spat flame and lead. Donovan doubled over and slumped to his knees, his belly on fire and his lips spewing painful screams. His six-gun slipped from his fingers. Lessing's guns roared just as Smoke dropped to one knee. The slugs went over his head and slammed into the wall. Smoke leveled his .44 and drilled Lessing clean, the lead taking him in the center of the chest.

Out on the street, guns were roaring and men were dying. Lessing cussed Smoke once and then fell forward, no longer able to stay on his feet. Donovan was out of it, stretched out full length on the floor, screaming in pain. Smoke picked up Donovan's gun and shoved it behind his belt. He walked toward Lessing as the man was fumbling to lift his six-shooter. Smoke took it away from him and tossed it on the bar. He loaded up his own .44 and then loaded up the gun he'd taken from Donovan. He sensed more than heard movement in the storage room. Smoke stepped back and waited. The barkeep was nowhere in sight. He had laid down on the floor behind the long bar.

Out on the street, Burke was down and dead with a bullet in his brain and Tom Clark was on his knees, both hands holding his bloody belly. George Miller had dashed down an alleyway.

Danny O'Brian was sprawled in the street and Yukon and Carbone had taken cover behind watering troughs and were exchanging shots.

Slim King pulled open the storage room door and cautiously stepped into the salon, both hands filled with guns. Grub was right behind him, holding a sawed-off shotgun. Both of them saw the bloody body of Lessing and looked around until their eyes found the source of the screaming. Donovan was jerking on the floor, just moments from death. Smoke gave no warning. He just lifted both .44s and started firing as fast as he could cock the hammer and pull the trigger.

One slug hit the shotgun just as Grub was turned and lifting the weapon. Both barrels fired, the full charge taking Slim in the back at a distance of no more than two feet. The man was blown apart and dead instantly. Horror in his eyes at what he had done, and his fingers numbed from the unexpected discharge, Grub dropped the shotgun and clawed for his pistols.

Smoke let him clear leather and then shot the man twice, both .44 slugs striking him in the chest. Grub would no longer have to worry about his next meal. Reloading, Smoke carefully avoided the mess by the storage room door and walked out the rear of the saloon.

A slug knocked out chips of wood by Smoke's head. He flattened against the wall, then edged back the direction he'd come and slipped under the saloon, hoping he would not disturb any rattler who might be seeking shelter from the hot sun. He worked his way toward the front of the building and after carefully checking the rear of the alley, he slipped out near the mouth and stood for a few seconds, watching the action in the street. Yukon's back was to him.

"Hey, Yukon!" he called.

The gunfighter spun around and stood up. Smoke and Carbone fired as one. Yukon Golden lifted himself to his full height. He wore a very curious expression on his face. His guns clattered to the boardwalk and he pitched forward.

"How many left?" Martine called.

"Two, I think," Carbone returned the shout.

"Clark and Miller," someone shouted from behind

235

walls. "They're down near the smithy's shop."

The sound of galloping horses thundering out of town followed the shout.

"The bastards stole my horses!" a man yelled.

"That's it then," Smoke said, walking up to where Tom Clark lay in the street. Ed Burke lay dead a few feet away. Tom was still alive, but not by much. Smoke knelt down behind the mortally wounded gunhand.

"If you have anything to say, you'd better say it quick," Smoke told him.

"Go to hell," Tom gasped.

"I am thinking you will be there before us," Carbone said, punching out empties and reloading.

"You the one that shot me?" Tom asked.

"I did," Martine said. "I think."

"You go to hell, too!"

The Mexican gunfighter shrugged his shoulders philosophically. "All in due time, pistolero. But I have friends down there you might look up and say hello."

Tom cussed them all and then closed his eyes. His fingers clawed at the dirt for a moment, then he relaxed.

The undertaker and his assistant ran up, both of them smiling. Business had never been this good. People began crowding the streets, eyeballing all the dead and congratulating the Double D men. But Smoke, Carbone, and Martine all knew the congratulations were hollow. They were welcome now, but whenever the shooting finally stopped and Clint Black was either dead, gone, or in jail, the welcoming would cease and the citizens would begin to drop hints that perhaps it was time for the gunfighters to leave. They had all been through it many times in the past.

"Somebody come in here and help me clean up all this mess!" the barkeep squalled. "I'm gettin' sick to my stomick. I never seen such a terrible sight."

The two deputies walked up, Dr. Garrett with them.

"Harris just opened his eyes," the doctor told them. "When all the shooting started," he said, 'Smoke Jensen must be in town.' "

Twenty-six

Three of Clint Black's hands disappeared while out rounding up the last of the horses. Horse and rider just vanished. No trace of them was ever found.

"Them ol' men got them," Bronco opined. "They're camped all around the edge of the range. Brazen about it, too. They don't make no effort to hide their cookfires. They're darin' us to come get them."

"Hell with them," Clint said. "They're not our main problem." He was still shaken by the news that eight of his best gunhands had gone face down in town. Now it looked like his brother was going to live, and that irritated him. Everything was going sour. He'd lost two more of his hired guns. They had just saddled up and ridden out. Didn't even ask for any pay. They just left.

What made matters even worse was not a single reply had been received on his latest bid to hire more men. No one wanted to tangle with a dozen or more living legends. Including the cook, he had twenty-six men. At one time, Clint had boasted he could field seventy-five of the toughest hands in the territory. Now he didn't have a single working cowboy left. Not that it mattered, for he personally had ridden his range and found that he didn't have a steer left. They had all been rustled, probably by the mountain men. His house and all the outbuildings were in a shambles from hundreds of

238

rounds being pumped into them; the roofs all leaked. He could not find any workmen to repair the damage. No one would work for him. And he had even put ads in the Helena paper.

Clint sat in his den, his thoughts dark. The Double D was now in good shape, with a large herd and at least fifteen tough, seasoned hands to maintain it. Clint and his men had been banned from ever setting foot in Blackstown—the name of which had now been changed to Canyon City. His town no longer.

Clint was under no illusions about facing Smoke Jensen—the one person he blamed for all his misfortune. He wasn't as fast with guns as the man and he didn't think he could take him in any type of stand up fist-fight.

Any reasonable man would have called it quits and tried to make peace. But Clint Black was not a reasonable man.

He rose from his chair and looked out a bullet-shattered window. He could almost smell the odor of defeat. It was not a smell he liked.

"God, I hate you, Jensen," Clint whispered. "I despise you."

He walked slowly back to his chair and sat down heavily. He did not know what to do next. But he did know this: he was going to kill Smoke Jensen. He just didn't know how he was going to accomplish that.

"I think you ladies are reasonably safe now," Smoke told the twins. "Unless I completely missed the mark, I believe Clint has shifted his hatred to me. Sending those ten gunhands into town this morning tipped his hand."

"Then you feel we could safely ride our own range, Smoke?" Toni asked.

"As long as you have a couple of hands with you. I

239

know some of those old mountain men are watching your range. I've seen their smoke."

"Their . . . smoke?" Jeanne said.

"Indian talk. They're out there. And remember this: you've got twelve pretty salty ol' boys on the payroll now, and that's plenty for a spread this size. And they're good men. Clint, on the other hand, has been losing men steadily. He can't have more than twenty-five men on his payroll right now. And none of them can tell the difference between a steer and a buffalo. I know gunhands. When they start sensing defeat, they'll pull out. And I'll bet that right now, it's pretty darn glum over on the Circle 45 spread."

"What do you think Clint will do next?" Toni asked.

Smoke shook his head. "I wish I knew."

Nelson, Clements, and Bankston (who was now free of the skunk odor) rode into town, their gunbelts hanging from the saddle horns. They stopped in front of the general store and were immediately met by a shotgun-toting deputy.

"Whoa!" Bankston said. "We don't work for the Forty-five no more. These are our horses. Look at the brands. All we want to do is provision up, have a hot meal at the café, and we're history, deputy."

"All right. Suits me, boys. I'll pass the word to leave you be."

" 'Preciate it, Deputy," Nelson said.

The word quickly spread up and down the street, and the former Circle 45 riders were shocked when the townspeople actually spoke to them and were friendly. They certainly were not used to that from the citizens of the newly named town of Canyon City.

And true to their word, they bought supplies, had a drink and a meal, and were gone within the hour. Harris

Black lay in the bed at the doctor's office and watched them leave.

"My brother's little empire is falling apart," he said to the doctor. "It couldn't happen to a more deserving person. He fooled me for a long time, Doctor. He lied to me and I believed him. Then when I finally began to suspect him, I still believed him. I just couldn't, no, *wouldn't* believe that my own brother would lie to me. I was a fool."

"What do you think Clint will do next?"

"I don't know, Doc. But he'll go out with a bang. You can bet on that."

Clint had strapped on his guns and gathered his men on the grounds around the front porch. "From this day on, I'm paying triple wages for the men who stay with me to the end. And the five thousand dollar bounty still stands on Jensen's head. If you're going to leave me, do it now."

The gunslicks looked at one another and shuffled their feet and whispered among themselves. One-eyed Shaw finally spoke. "I reckon we'll stay, Boss. But we want a month's wages in advance. You might get killed and then we'd be stuck."

"That's fine with me. Line up and draw your advances."

As the men were being paid, Buckskin Deevers asked, "What's the plan, boss?"

"I don't have one," Clint replied truthfully. "And I'm sure open to suggestions."

Buckskin stepped to one side of the porch, allowing the other hired guns to be paid. When the last had drawn their pay and only Bronco remained, Buckskin said, "Whatever we do, we've got to leave the ranch on the quiet. Those old mountain men have ringed us."

"I still think we could take those old farts out," Bronco said.

Buckskin looked at him. "Ellis and Jones and Harden had that some idea. You seen them since they rode out?"

Bronco shook his head irritably. "Only their horses."

"That's right. Only their horses. Boss, I'm gonna say something that you ain't gonna like. But here it is. Those old men out yonder in the hills don't have no job of work they got to return to. They can stay here forever, and if Smoke wants them to, they will. Sooner or later, probably sooner, one of them will get a clean shot at you and it'll be over."

Clint slowly nodded his head and looked up at the murderer. "Go on," he said softly.

"We got twenty-three men able to sit a saddle and that includes you. We're not going to win this war, so you might as well put that out of your mind."

"I had already reached that conclusion," Clint said. There was no anger in his voice, just resignation.

"So you want . . . ?" He trailed that off, already knowing the answer.

"To kill my enemy."

"Smoke Jensen."

"Yes."

"The twin sisters?"

"Once Smoke is dead, they can be dealt with."

Buckskin suppressed a sigh. Clint just couldn't get it through his head that if harm came to Smoke Jensen, those old mountain men would wait until Hell froze over to get a shot at him. Buckskin was a murderer, thief, rapist, and thoroughly worthless, but he wasn't stupid. Every fiber in his body told him to get clear of this fight. It was clearly over. There was no way that Clint could win and to hang around was suicide. But Buckskin had taken the man's money and would stay.

And he knew that the others would do the same.

"Thank you, Buckskin," Clint said, standing up. "I'll come up with a plan."

"Okay, Boss. Me and the boys will do whatever you say." Back in the bunkhouse, he said, "He has no plan. If we had any sense we'd give the money back, tie a white handkerchief to our rifles, and ride out of this damn country."

A gunhand known only as Burt stood up and walked to the open doorway. "I want to see Smoke Jensen dead on the ground. That's what I want to see."

"I'm afraid Jensen will be walkin' around long after someone buries you, Burt," One-eyed Shaw said.

"Bull!" Burt said. He stepped outside, and a heavy rifle cracked from more than a half-mile away. The big slug took the hired gun in the center of his chest and slammed him back against the outside wall. Burt slid down to the ground, dead on his butt.

After walking to the front door and seeing what had happened, Clint sat in his now heavily fortified study and cussed. All the windows had been boarded over and bookcases shoved against them. He was a prisoner in his own damn house. He cursed the old mountain men who had surrounded his home and he cursed Smoke Jensen. He cursed his brother and he cursed the Duggan twins. He cursed the citizens of Canyon City and when he couldn't think of anyone else to curse, he just sat and cussed. He was still cussing when Tom Clark and George Miller tied white pieces of cloth to the barrel of their rifles and rode away.

Puma Buck and Lee Staples stopped by the Double D late that afternoon and swung down from the saddles. They declined the invitation to come inside the house. Neither of them much liked houses. They sat on the porch and accepted coffee and doughnuts.

"Clint Black lost three more men this day," Lee said. "They buried one and two rode out with white handkerchiefs tied to their rifles. We let them go."

"It's gettin' plumb borin' on them ridges," Puma said. "The boys want to attack the house and get done with it, Smoke."

"No," Toni said. "As much as I hate Clint Black, I want all the men who will to just go away and leave us alone."

"Let's ride over there and try to make peace with the man," Jeanne suggested.

"Bad move, Missy," Puma said. "No tellin' what Clint might do. Situation like it is, he ain't predictable no more. He just might shoot you both on sight. Me and the boys will stay just as long as it takes. We got no place to go and nothin' to do when we get there. We're living off Circle 45 beef. We rounded them up and moved them over into that valley where you-all was ambushed. He ain't got nary a steer left. All he's got is some mangy hired guns and a heart full of hate for Smoke. He can't get no supplies. We got the road watched all the time."

"I don't think he can hold out too much longer," Smoke said. "You boys keep up the sharpshooting, Puma. It's taking a toll on those guns of his. He's losing one or two every day. He's got to crack soon and then it'll be over." He smiled. "And I think I'll just heat up the fire a little bit."

Sally looked over at him. "Every time you get that look in your eyes, I start to worrying."

He reached over and patted her hand. "Don't worry. This isn't gun-talk, honey." He stood up. "Excuse me, folks. I have a letter to write."

Everyone looked at Sally. She shrugged her shoulders. "Don't ask me. I'm just his wife."

Smoke returned in ten minutes with a sheet of paper. He handed it to Sally. "Sally, how long would it take you and Toni and Jeanne to write out about fifty or sixty copies of this?"

She read the short letter and started laughing. "Not long. Come on, girls. Let's get busy."

Cleon Marsh came fogging back to the ranch early the next morning. He had found the note tacked to the gate, read it, and for a moment was stunned. Then he was in the saddle and riding hard.

Clint's face turned beet red when he read the letter. "It says here he's posted this . . . thing all over the country. I'll be the laughing stock of the territory! The son of a bitch!" He threw the paper to the ground.

Bronco picked it up, read it, and said, "You sure will be if you ignore this. Did you read down at the bottom?"

"No!" Clint shouted.

"If you don't meet him, he's going to mail this to every paper in the territory."

Buckskin Deevers read the note. "He's callin' you out, Boss. You ain't got no choice in the matter. If you don't meet him and slug it out, you might as well ride on out of the country. You know as well as me how Western folks are."

Clint knew. Only too well. He took the letter and re-read it.

THIS IS AN OPEN CHALLENGE FROM SMOKE JENSEN TO THE MURDERING, RAPING, AMBUSHING, NIGHT-RIDING, YELLOW-BELLIED CLINT BLACK. I SAY YOU ARE AFRAID TO MEET ME IN A STAND-UP FIST-FIGHT. YOU HIDE BEHIND HIRED GUNS

AND DO NOT HAVE THE COURAGE TO MEET ME AND FIGHT IT OUT MAN TO MAN. I WILL BE WAITING IN THE MAIN STREET OF CANYON CITY AT NOON ON SATURDAY. IF YOU FAIL TO SHOW, THEN EVERYONE IN THE TERRITORY WILL KNOW EXACTLY WHAT KIND OF CRAVEN COWARD YOU REALLY ARE.

It was signed Smoke Jensen.

Clint lifted his eyes. All his men had gathered around the front porch. And he knew then that if he didn't meet Smoke Jensen, he would not have a hand left. They would ride out, showing their contempt for him. The rules were few in the West, but they were enforced rigidly. And if a man was called out by another man of approximately the same size and age, you went, or you got on your horse and rode out. No one in the rugged, wide-shouldered west would tolerate a coward.

Clint was between a rock and a hard place and he knew it. He slowly folded the paper and stuck it in his pocket. "Well, boys, looks like we take a ride come this Saturday morning."

Twenty-seven

Of course Clint had far darker plans than just the fight on his mind. But those were quickly dashed when One-eyed Shaw told him the mountain men had left the Circle 45 range and had taken up positions all around the Double D ranch and grounds. His plans of burning the Duggan twins out while all the Double D hands were in town watching the fight were tossed out the window with that news. Then he thought he might have a sniper shoot Jensen during the fight. But on this Saturday, all guns were to be banned in Canyon City. Every man would leave his guns at check points at both ends of town. And Harris had ordered all able-bodied townsmen to be sworn in as special deputies and they would be heavily armed.

"Jensen don't fight by no rules," Bronco Ford told his boss. "He fights to win. And he'll offer no mercy nor give no quarter."

Clint nodded his head in agreement. Since he had made up his mind to fight, he had not taken a drink of anything stronger than coffee. He knew he was in excellent physical shape, for he had always been vain about that. He was strong as a bull and had knocked men unconscious with just one punch. But could he whip Smoke Jensen? He didn't know. He would have to rely on good footwork and lots of bobbing and weaving and ducking and try to wear the man down.

But he had to win. He had to. Everything was at stake. If he lost, he would be a humiliated and broken man in the eyes of all the people. He could not allow that to happen. One way or the other, by hook or by crook, he had to win.

"He's a bull of a man, Smoke," Waymore told him. "Strong and can punch like no man I ever seen. He'll gouge your eyes and use his boots on you if he gets the chance. I saw him cripple a man like that. He likes to hurt people, really likes it. He's a cruel brute."

Smoke nodded his understanding. "Thank you, Waymore." He wasn't particularly worried about Clint Black. He'd fought bigger and better men than Clint . . . and stomped them into the ground. During the time between the challenge and now, Smoke had cut out tanned leather and made himself a pair of gloves. They were almost double the thickness of ordinary gloves, and would enable him to hit harder and also protect his hands.

"Lots of bets on this fight, boss," Conny said, after returning from Canyon City. "Folks comin' in from seventy miles away to see it. The papers in Helena have sent reporters in. They wanted an interview with you. I told them I didn't have no authority to speak for you."

"The fight will be an interview that will speak for itself."

"You get a good night's sleep, boss. Tomorrow is a big day."

"I assure you, Conny, I will sleep like a baby."

"Don't nothin' bother you, boss?" Conny asked.

Smoke smiled at him. "No point in worrying about things a man can't change, Conny."

"I reckon not. Good night, boss."

Smoke ate only a light breakfast the morning of the fight. Sally and Toni and Jeanne had prepared baskets of lunches they would eat after the fight. Baked beans and huge sandwiches and fried chicken and jam and jellies.

"Aren't you worried?" Toni asked Sally. "I would be positively beside myself with dread."

"No. I've seen Smoke fight before. Oh, he'll have a busted lip and a black eye and some bruised ribs and various other abrasions and contusions, but he'll win and he'll be alive. Smoke fights coldly, you see. Never loses control. It will be very brutal, ladies. I doubt that you have ever witnessed anything like it before."

Although neither of the twins would admit it, they both were looking forward to the fight.

Canyon City had swelled to ten times its normal population, with people coming in from as far away as a hundred miles. Entire families had shown up, bringing picnic lunches and planning to make a day of it. Enterprising store owners along Main Street had rented out roof space for spectators. Bleachers had been hastily knocked together and Main Street was blocked off. Street vendors were peddling everything from beer to banners.

Boos and catcalls went up as Clint Black and his men rode into town and checked their guns under the watchful eyes of regular deputies and newly appointed special deputies. A special elevated bed frame had been built in the show window of the general store so Harris Black could look over the heads of spectators and watch the fight in comfort. The sheriff kept his pistols handy, for he suspected the fistfight would only be part of this day's events. His brother did not enjoy losing at anything.

Wild cheering erupted when Smoke and his party rode in. They stabled their horses and checked their guns.

"Keep the Double D people on one side of the roped off area and the Circle 45 rowdies on the other side," Lucas told his men.

249

The arena was a simple one. Ropes had been stretched from one side of the street to the other, so the men could have plenty of room to maneuver.

Smoke took off his spurs, handed them to Denver, and pulled on his leather gloves. He walked to his side of the ropes. There were no rules to this fight. It was kick, gouge, and stomp until one of the men was down and could not continue.

Smoke slipped between the pulled-tight ropes and walked to the center of the "ring."

"Come on, Clint," Lucas said, waving at the rancher. "Let's get this going." He stepped back and leaned against a hitchrail as Clint walked into the ring and up to Smoke Jensen.

"This one is for the boys you killed in that valley," Smoke told the rancher. "You child-killin' son of a bitch." Then he hit Clint in the mouth with a powerful and totally unexpected hard right fist that bloodied the man's lips and knocked Clint Black smack on his butt in the dirt.

The crowd roared and the fight was on.

Clint scrambled to his boots, his face dark with anger and his eyes blazing with wild hatred. He hadn't been knocked down since he was a boy. But he maintained a tight control on himself as he lifted his fists.

Clint jabbed and Smoke flicked the blow away from his face and drove a left straight in. The leather-covered fist impacted against Clint's mouth, and the blow snapped the big man's head back. Clint cursed and swung; his fist caught Smoke on the shoulder. Smoke ducked, weaved, and hammered at Clint's kidneys, forcing the man to give ground.

Smoke followed him, relentless in his pursuit. Smoke took a blow to the jaw that rattled his teeth. Clint could punch like a mule's kick, Smoke would give him that.

"I'll kill you," Clint said. "I'll beat you to death, Jensen."

"I doubt it," Smoke told him, then kicked the man on the kneecap.

Clint howled and jumped around, favoring the throbbing leg. Smoke stepped in and busted the man's mouth with a left and a right. Off balance, Clint tumbled to the ground. Smoke made no attempt to use his boots on the fallen man. Unless Clint tried it dirty, Smoke would keep it as clean as brawling could be in those times.

Clint charged in, swinging wide. Smoke saw what the man had in mind and ducked. He grabbed the thick wrist with both hands and turned his body, throwing Clint to the dirt. Clint landed on his face and came up cussing, spitting dirt, and mad as hell.

The crowd was roaring and cheering, but neither man paid them any attention.

Clint bored in, smashing blows to Smoke's face and body. Smoke's mouth was bleeding and his side hurt where Clint had connected. Smoke stuck his fist into Clint's face and pawed. When Clint lifted his arm to brush away the gloved fist, Smoke blasted a right into Clint's belly. The man whooshed out air, dropped his guard, and Smoke hit him hard on the side of the jaw. Clint's knees buckled and he backed up. Smoke didn't let up. He stalked the man relentlessly, hammering at him with fists that seemed to be made of iron.

Clint recovered and connected with a solid left that hurt. Smoke backed up and Clint jumped at him, swinging both big fists. Smoke ducked and dove at the man, catching him in the belly with a shoulder. Smoke wrapped both strong arms around the man's waist and hurled him to the ground, knocking the wind from him.

Smoke grabbed the man by the hair, jerked his head back, and, standing over the fallen rancher, drove his right fist into the man's face half a dozen times. Clint's lips were pulped, his nose was spread all over his face, and one ear was nearly torn off.

Smoke released his hold on the man's hair, grabbed him by one arm and jerked him to his boots. Holding onto his arm, Smoke threw him across the street, with Clint spinning and staggering and flapping his arms, trying to halt the momentum. Clint slammed into a hitchrail and it shattered under his weight.

Clint crawled to his feet and ducked his head into a watering trough. Then he came up roaring like a maddened bull and charged across the street.

"Punch his head off!" Jeanne Duggan yelled, caught up in the excitement.

"Kick him in the parts!" Toni shouted.

Sally looked at them and smiled.

Clint connected with a wild swing and Smoke went down. He rolled and came to his boots. Clint bored in and Smoke stopped him cold with a right to the jaw. Clint backed up and Smoke came on, hitting him with both fists, belly and mouth. Clint went down and Smoke waited, both hands clenched into fists.

The rancher lurched to his feet and Smoke planted both boots and hit the man with everything he had, putting all two hundred-plus pounds into the blow. Those standing by the ropes heard the man's jaw shatter. Clint was poleaxed to the ground and did not move.

Smoke walked to the horse trough, stripping off his gloves and sticking them into a back pocket. He washed his face and dunked his head into the water. The crowd was yelling and hollering and cheering. Harris rose to his knees. He reached into a boot and came up with a knife. With blood pouring from his mouth, his nose, and one ear, he screamed curses at Smoke and ran toward him. Smoke could hear nothing over the roaring of the crowd. A pistol cracked, the slug taking Clint in the center of his forehead, stopping the man and flinging him backward into the churned up dirt of the street. He lay with arms outspread, the blade of the knife twinkling in the midday sun.

Harris Black had fired through the window of the general store.

The crowds fell silent, staring at the dead Clint Black. The rancher had possessed everything any man could ever want. But Clint had wanted more. And all it got him in the end was a bullet in his brain. A ruthless man's reign of terror had ended. It was over.

Twenty-eight

The hired guns—now out of a job—stood and listened to Lucas's words. The words were familiar; they had all heard them before. The gunslingers were surrounded by fifty heavily armed and grim-faced men. "You got one minute to get clear of this town," the deputy said. "And don't you ever show your faces around here again. At one minute plus one second, we all start shooting. And no, you don't get your guns back. Now, *move!*"

Thirty seconds later, the pounding of hooves was fading into memory.

Harris Black motioned for Lucas to come into the general store. He handed him his sheriff's badge. "I'm through. When I get on my feet, I hope I never have to use a gun against another man as long as I live."

Smoke took a long hot bath behind the barber shop and dressed in fresh clothing. Before leaving the Double D that morning, they had packed for the ride back home. Smoke, Sally, and the three Sugarloaf hands stepped up into the saddles and looked at the crowd, watching them. The townspeople filled the street, standing in silence.

"We'll never forget you," Toni spoke for the twins and the town. The sisters had tears in their eyes as they watched the riders fade into the distance.

Harris, listening from his bed in the store front, muttered, "You can damn sure say that again." He lay his head back on the pillow and closed his eyes. He tried to work up some degree of sorrow and pity for his brother. He could not. "Hell with it," he said, and went to sleep.

The townspeople stood in the streets and on the boardwalks and cheered and applauded as the Sugarloaf riders headed south, back to Colorado.

Swede the blacksmith tossed a shovelful of dirt over the dark bloody spot in the street where Clint Black had lain. He walked back to his shop and picked up his tongs. The undertaker's hammer could be heard, nailing the coffin lid shut on Clint Black. The old mountain men and the famed gunfighters slipped quietly back into history. Felker at the feed store hung a sign in his window: Open For Business.

The last depositor at Clint Black's bank withdrew his money and the manager shut the door, hanging a Closed sign in the window.

Denver and the former cook at the Double D, Liz, hunted up a preacher. They had a new life to begin.

Two traveling salesmen, riding in the stage, passed the five riders heading south. "Say," one of the drummers said. "That was Smoke Jensen!"

"That's balderdash," his companion replied. "Smoke Jensen is just a myth. He doesn't exist."

"Maybe you're right. There's Blackstown up ahead. Say, look at that sign. The name's been changed. Canyon City. Well, I'll be darned. I bet there's a story behind that."

William W. Johnstone
The *Mountain Man* Series